It's. Nice. Outside.

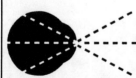

This Large Print Book carries the
Seal of Approval of N.A.V.H.

It's. Nice. Outside.

Jim Kokoris

KENNEBEC LARGE PRINT
A part of Gale, a Cengage Company

Farmington Hills, Mich • San Francisco • New York • Waterville, Maine
Meriden, Conn • Mason, Ohio • Chicago

**LIBRARY OF CONGRESS CIP DATA ON FILE.
CATALOGUING IN PUBLICATION FOR THIS BOOK
IS AVAILABLE FROM THE LIBRARY OF CONGRESS**

ISBN-13: 978-1-4328-4415-8 (softcover)
ISBN-10: 1-4328-4415-6 (softcover)

Published in 2018 by arrangement with Macmillan Publishing Group, LLC/ St. Martin's

Printed in the United States of America
1 2 3 4 5 6 7 22 21 20 19 18

FOR MY SON ANDREW
YOU. ARE. WOW.

PROLOGUE

I arrived at the hospital early and found a space in the garage near the elevator. Ethan was up, alert, and fussing. I heard him crying, a tiny muffled sound. Mary had wrapped him in blankets, and he was now angrily kicking free of them. When I picked him up and put him in the stroller, I dropped his pacifier and, not for the first time that morning, grew angry with Mary for not coming along. *I shouldn't have to do this alone,* I thought. But our babysitter had canceled, and Mary had to stay with the girls. She would wait at home for the results.

I walked slowly through the hospital, my shoes loud against the tile floor, trying not to look at the pictures on the wall: photographs of smiling children, laughing children, children running in fields, children flying kites. Normal children. In an hour I would walk back down this same hallway, knowing whether my nine-month-old son, my youngest child, was normal.

In the admitting room, I filled out forms, and then we were taken to an empty room where Ethan, who had fallen oddly quiet and wide-eyed, was medicated.

After the nurse left, I sat on the edge of the bed and watched my son fall asleep, forcing myself not to think.

The nurse was not particularly friendly. I thought, given the circumstances, she should be solicitous, nunlike, but she wasn't. She was short, squat, and all business as she wheeled Ethan into the room where the MRI was to be taken. I went in with him and sat in a chair against the wall while the nurse and a skinny young male technician picked Ethan up and placed him on another bed. Then there was a loud noise, and the bed slid into the mouth of a cavernous machine where pictures were taken of my son's brain. The whole process took less than ten minutes.

Afterward, the all-business nurse disappeared into an adjoining room marked RADIOLOGY. When she emerged a few minutes later, she was transformed, her face worried, her eyes avoiding mine.

"Why don't we go back to the room and wait for the doctor," she said. She touched

me gently on the shoulder and led us away,
back down the hall.

1

NINETEEN YEARS LATER

The garbage pickers came on Friday evenings in Wilton. At twilight they emerged from shadows, silently trolling the streets in rusting pickups, dented vans, and sagging station wagons, searching for remnants of other people's lives.

The pickers, mostly stoic Mexican men, worked quickly and with purpose. They loaded the backs of their trucks and wagons up high, tying down the things they had chosen with ropes, chains. The chipped barstool, the old mattress, the stained rug — this was all precious cargo to them.

I stood in the driveway and watched a white truck without hubcaps slow then stop in front of our house. A man with a backward baseball cap and a bright orange T-shirt stepped out and sheepishly nodded at me as he circled the large tricycle I had placed by the curb. It was Ethan's old bike.

I watched the man study it. He appeared confused, the knot of his brow tight.

"It's for adults," I called out. "You can take it. There's something wrong with the handlebars, but you can probably fix them."

He seemed hesitant, staring at the bike, his hands in his pockets.

"It's not heavy. You want help?"

He finally glanced up at me, smiled, and then bent down, and in one quick move he lifted the bike into the back of his truck, positioning it next to a green filing cabinet. He nodded in my direction again, climbed back inside the truck, and drove off, his red taillights fading quickly in the growing dark.

I finished packing the van a few minutes later, wedging one last large box with a sleeping bag, the teddy bears, and the photo album into the back. Hoping to maximize every inch, I had started the process with a solid plan, arranging each box and bag like it was a piece of a jigsaw puzzle. But after an hour I abandoned this methodical approach and began randomly cramming things in. It was getting late, and we had to get going.

With the final box in place, I assessed the van, our home for the next two weeks. A 2013 silver Honda Odyssey. Sat seven. Less than twenty thousand miles on it. Brand-new Michelins. Fully loaded, or almost fully loaded, because it didn't have GPS. The van was Mary's, and she didn't think we needed it because she said we never went anywhere. And she was right — we never went anywhere. Until now, of course. I stepped close and rested my hand on the hood and decided to give the van a pep talk. We needed to be on the same page here, work together. I whispered, "We're going to be spending a lot of time together, buddy. A lot of time. We're depending on you. Time to see what you're made of. This is your moment. Make everyone back in Japan proud."

This completed, I turned to Ethan. He had been shooting baskets in the driveway for close to an hour, oblivious to my efforts, the significance of the trip, the moment — of everything.

I took a moment and watched my son: skinny white legs, even skinnier white arms, Illinois cap hiding an explosion of black curly hair, his mouth half open in concentration and wonder as he continued to sink shot after shot. He was good at this, amazing even, a savant. Considering the doctors said he would never walk, might not even sit up, it was more than amazing, really; it was a miracle, a nice-size bone God had

13

decided to toss us after all.

After banking another midrange jumper, I intercepted the ball.

"Shoot!" he said.

"No more shooting."

"Illini!"

"No, we're not playing Illini tonight."

"Illini!"

"We can't."

"Shoot!"

He made a move for the ball, but I held it up high, away from him. Ethan was short, no more than five-six, and I was close to a foot taller. "We have to go now. It's time to leave, dude-man. Long drive."

After a few halfhearted jumps, he gave up on the ball. "Where? Mom. Be?"

"She's with Karen."

"Where? Mindy. Be?"

"Mindy's not here. She's going to be with Karen and Mom. We'll see them all at Karen's wedding in a few days. Now get in, come on. Open the door, and get in. We have a long drive. Chicago to South Carolina. A lot of driving."

"Where? Karen. Be?"

"Come on, buddy. If you don't get in, you'll have to sit in the back."

"Where. Stinky Bear?"

"He's in the van."

14

"Doing?"

"He's sleeping."

"Where? Red Bear?"

"Red Bear is with Stinky Bear. They're together in a box. They're very comfortable. It's a nice box."

"Where? Grandpa Bear?"

"All in the box. The same box. They're all waiting for us. All of them. They want to get going. They want to get to South Carolina. They can't wait."

"Where? Mom?"

I took a deep breath and gently took him by the hand and led him over to the van. "Do not pinch me, do you hear me, do not pinch me! Hands. To. Self. Get in now. That's it. Okay, now buckle up. Good, okay, good." I leaned down and kissed him on the top of his head. Then I shut the door and walked slowly over to the driver's side, taking my time, soaking in the last few seconds of sweet, sweet silence. It wasn't until I was already behind the wheel, had already buckled my seat belt, had already adjusted the rearview mirror, had already turned the key, that I thought to ask him, way, way, way too late, if he had gone to the bathroom.

"Went."

I looked at him. He looked away. "Are you sure?"

"Pee-pee."

"You're not sure."

"Pee-pee."

"You have to go now?"

"Yes! No! Yes! Pee-pee. Pee-pee. *Bad.*"

I closed my eyes and turned the van off.

Though he was quite capable of going pee-pee on his own, I was on a schedule, so I led him back inside the house and to the bathroom, pulled down his pants, and pointed at the middle of the toilet bowl.

"Okay, go."

"Where? Stinky Bear?"

"Just go, Ethan, just go."

"Where? Stinky Bear?"

"We're not doing this now, no Stinky Bear. Go."

"Where?"

"I told you, he's in the van, okay?"

"What. Doing?"

"He's waiting for us. Everyone is waiting for us in Charleston, South Carolina. That's a long way. We're going to drive there. Isn't that fun? Isn't that crazy? Mom thinks I'm crazy for doing this. I'm starting to think I'm crazy for doing this, and we haven't even pulled out of the driveway. Isn't that crazy? Yes, sir, it sure is. Yes, sir."

Ethan looked at me, penis in hand. Then, after an eternity, after I silently counted to thirty backward, after I heard the clock on the kitchen wall tick, after I heard a distant honk of a car on the street, after I started to feel terribly sorry for myself, he forced out a few casual drops of pee-pee.

When he was done, he looked at me without apology.

"All. Done," he said.

"What do you mean, all done? That's all you got? That's it?"

"Yes. Ma'am!"

"You have no more pee-pee in you. None?"

"Yes. Ma'am!"

"So, you didn't really have to go after all, did you? This whole thing was a waste of time after all." Every so often, for reasons I no longer understood, I would try to make a point with Ethan.

"Yes. Ma'am!"

We looked at each other. "Pull your pants up," I said.

"Why? Mad?"

"I'm not mad. Just pull your pants up."

Back outside, I paused in the driveway and glanced up at the moon, now rising full behind the Bakers' house, across the street.

Ethan stopped to admire it too, his mouth once again open in wonder. I took his hand, and we stood together. For years I had dreamed about taking a trip like this, a long, open-ended journey, and here I was.

"A. Lot. Of. Moon."

I didn't say anything. I just held on to my son's hand and kept looking up at the moon, blurry in the purple-and-pink summer sky, and wondered if I would remember this moment forever and fearing I would.

I was a man with an Overall Plan and the first step in this Plan, Phase I, was to drive to Champaign, Illinois, about two hours south, and spend the night. The next day, we would kill time at my alma mater, the University of Illinois, doing God knows what, before moving on to other, slightly vaguer, phases. Though I would quickly abandon this night-driving strategy, I originally thought traveling with Ethan while he slept would be easier.

It would make more sense, of course, to fly, but planes were not an option. Our few attempts with Ethan in the friendly skies had been so traumatic, so disruptive, that I was sure the FAA had us on the No-Fly list. We were driving or we weren't going to Karen's wedding.

I backed out of the driveway and drove slowly with the windows down so Ethan could see Wilton, Illinois, his home, our home, one last time. Wilton was a fine Chicago suburb, delicately torn from the pages of some glossy *House Beautiful, Architectural Digest, Big Homes for Rich People* publication: aspirational, affluent, it had lots of long brick driveways filled with lots of German-engineered cars. I had married into Wilton some thirty years prior and had had, thanks in part to my high-school teacher's salary and South Side of Chicago upbringing, a somewhat uneasy and self-conscious relationship with it from the start. But I had lived there a long time and so had Ethan. It was home.

I turned the corner. "Say good-bye, Ethan."

"Bye! Idiot!"

"You need to stop saying that."

"Okay. Idiot!"

I raised the window, uttered my first official sigh of the trip, and wondered if I should stop for coffee. I was very tired.

The last few days had been an exhausting and emotional blur. I should have been focusing on my daughter's wedding in Charleston, should have been thinking about Karen, my oldest, but as always, my every move, my every thought was dominated by Ethan. The good-byes, the trips to his favorite places — Mariano's, Panera, Rafferty's Pub, Aurelio's Pizza, Denning Park. One more swing ride, one more Sprite from Chuck at the bar, one more piece of cheese from Denetha at the deli, one more bike ride around Wilton. One last day in Ethan's World.

There were details to confirm, phone calls to make — to the Jefferson Davis Inn, Ocean View, to all the hotels we would be staying at along the way. And then there was the packing. What to take, what to ship, what to toss, what to store? A thousand things to do, a million imagined and anticipated scenarios.

The constant activity did serve one positive purpose, however: it had kept me from thinking.

But all that was over. Alone now, without the shield of my to-do list, the Doubt and Guilt returned. In an effort to cope, I reverted to survival mode: keep driving; get to Champaign; get to the hotel. In other words, do what I've always done when it comes to Ethan: just take the next step, just get through the day.

The Doubt and Guilt pressed their advantage, though, pummeling me. Desperate, I tried to cover up, play rope-a-dope, let the Doubt and Guilt have their way until they punched themselves out. To be sure, I could have counterpunched, defended myself, argued my case ("This is the best option"), but instead I just drove on. The moon was in front of me now, silvery and pale, and as we headed south, I envied its solitude.

During a distant, optimistic phase of my life, when I still had hope that things would turn out okay or at least close to okay, when I still believed that I would lead a semblance of a normal life, travel, go interesting places, see interesting things, I signed up for a credit card that rewarded me with Marriott points. The more I spent, the more free nights I would get at a Marriott hotel. A simple and common promotion but one that ultimately proved to have little value for me since we, specifically I, never went anywhere. Consequently, for years, the card served as a cruel and ironic reminder of my landlocked status. Every time I pulled it out at an uninteresting place (Target, Walmart, Hot 'n' Fast Pizza) and saw the Marriott logo, my heart broke a little. Rather than exchange all my points for TVs or computers or a treadmill, I continued to hoard them with the obstinate hope that one day I

21

would cash in. Apparently, that day had come.

Our very first Marriott was a Courtyard just outside of Champaign. Getting Ethan into a room late at night was, as with most everything involving him, a tricky proposition. I had called earlier and in a hushed voice explained that before checking in, I needed to go straight to the room because I had a sleeping infant with me. I had decided to use the word *infant* instead of *child* or even *baby*, believing it had more impact. I had given this considerable thought.

Sure enough, a clerk was patiently waiting for us in front of room 117 at ten thirty, the appointed time. She was a tall blonde and still sorority-perky despite the hour. I was fully anticipating her confused and concerned look when she saw me in the hallway with nineteen-year-old Ethan and not the swaddling newborn she had been expecting.

I offered no explanation. "Hello."

"Oh. Hi." She took a few steps back.

"Dark. Outside," Ethan mumbled. He was essentially sleepwalking.

The girl rebounded, her Delta Gamma instincts kicking in. "Sure is!" she said. Her eyes were resolutely big and bright, and it was apparent that she was trying to act normal, something people felt compelled to do when first confronted with Ethan.

"It sure is," I said.

She stared at us, her big smile growing.

"The key," I finally said.

"Oh. Right, I'm so sorry." She handed it to me. "We only had a room with a king left. I'm sorry."

"That's fine." I gave her my credit card and said I would pick it up in the morning.

"Have a good night!" she said.

"You have a great one."

I opened the door and led Ethan to the bed where I took off his shoes and clothes and asked him if he had to go pee-pee.

"Went."

I thought he might be interested in the hotel room, but his face was already in the pillow.

"You sure?" I asked. "You want to see the bathroom? It's different. Different bathroom, whole new toilet, probably whole new flushing mechanism."

He closed his eyes. "Leave. Now." This was his heartfelt way of saying good night. Like his mother, he could be very direct.

"Okay, I'll leave now." But I didn't leave. I sat on the edge of the bed, smoothed his black, rumpled hair with my hand, and studied him. Despite his age, he still looked like the child he would always be. Upturned nose, smooth skin, large dark eyes that took in a world he didn't always understand. Watching him fall asleep, I saw no hint of the demons — the frustration, the anxiety, the fears — that constantly plagued him. Today had been a good day, a strangely calm day. He did not do well with change and transitions, so I had expected the worst. He had surprised me though. Tomorrow might be entirely different — tomorrow could easily be the worst day of our lives — but with Ethan, today, now, that moment, was all that mattered. I bent down and kissed him on the forehead.

"Thanks for being a good guy today."

"Leave. Now."

"Right."

I stood and stretched my back before unpacking my laptop and ever-present bottle of Jim Beam. I poured myself a small snort, pulled out my brand-new, old-school Rand McNally road atlas, and sat down to review our route.

Rather than proceed straight south through Illinois, I had decided to head due east and spend the next night in Indianapolis before turning south toward Louisville. I was looking forward to that particular stop. Kyle Baker, a neighbor of ours, played college basketball there, and Ethan (and secretly I) worshipped him. Other than possibly the wedding, seeing him and Kyle together again was going to be the highlight of the trip.

I pondered the route awhile longer, worried that Indianapolis wasn't far enough, but decided to proceed anyway. We had time. I next went online to confirm our reservations at the Marriotts in Indianapolis and Louisville, then poured myself a second drink.

My planned late-night driving strategy was certainly going to put a crimp in my two-drinks-a-day bourbon prescription. Life with Ethan had made alcohol a necessity, a medication I carefully rationed. Two drinks, I coped; three drinks, I was drunk. And I didn't want to become a drunk.

I sipped on number two slowly, and found my way to the girls' Facebook pages, stopping at Karen's first. There was not much new there. Just a comment about being seven days away from the Big Day. No new photos, no new comments from her. This wasn't entirely surprising, considering she was getting married in a week and things were no doubt, hectic. I studied a photo of her and Roger taken last year somewhere in Spain or Austria or Greece, someplace that offered the perfect photo op. Both thin, athletic, smiling, confident. Karen, her blond hair pulled back, looked especially happy, her pretty face fully revealed to the camera. Like her mother, she was a quiet and guarded person, but in this photo at least, she seemed to be stepping out from behind something. I had had my doubts about Roger — I feared him a phony — but if she was happy, then I supposed I was happy.

I next checked out Mindy's page, always a source of entertainment. Sure enough, it did not disappoint. There were new photos of her in various costumes, and a link to a video from the last show of the season. She had once again performed a parody commercial for an adult diaper for busy executives who didn't have time to go to the bathroom. The product, Power Pads, would inflate in the middle of a meeting. Though I'd seen this bit before, I never tired of watching it.

The scene opened with Mindy in a dark, conservative, business suit, arguing a case before a packed courtroom. When the judge, guest star Will Ferrell, suggested taking a recess, Mindy waved his request away.

"I don't need a recess, Your Honor! I'm ready to go!" Then she closed her eyes, and her pants inflated to a ridiculous size while a voice-over said, *Time is money, so don't piss it away! Power Pads, for the on-the-go who-have-to-go — but have no time.* The sketch closed with Will Ferrell's pants ballooning as he yelled, "Let's all go!" to the camera.

I watched the sketch one more time, laughed quietly, then clicked on another link: *Extreme Makeover: Home (Crystal Meth Lab) Edition.* This bit featured Mindy as a hyperactive, type-A guru making over a home-based crystal meth lab. "Working from home is always a challenge!" Mindy, hands on hips, explained to a fat trailer trash couple and an ominous-looking Hispanic man with dark sunglasses, "This is more than a meth lab; this is your *home*! And we're going to make it your castle!"

I swallowed another laugh and shook my head. There she was, Mindy, our little pixie, who didn't actually speak until she was almost four years old, who didn't actually have any nonimaginary friends other than Karen until she was six — on the Internet, on TV every Saturday night, in magazines, on websites, closer to famous than almost famous. How this all happened, how she went from math club president to this and how I felt about it, I wasn't sure, but there she was, my little buddy.

I stared at my daughter's face for a moment, remembered how she would make me howl with impersonations of her teachers, her mother, me, even Ethan, then turned off my laptop, and reluctantly returned to the road atlas. I had some more work to do.

Driving two, *maybe* three hours a day seemed about the best we could manage. In addition to Indianapolis and Louisville, our schedule included stops in Knoxville, and then Asheville, North Carolina. Once I reached Asheville, I planned to make a final and frantic Sherman-esque march to the sea and Charleston. Factoring weather delays, traffic, Ethan meltdowns, my increasingly active bladder, and possibly, hopefully, stops at local attractions, I figured on arriving in Charleston by Thursday — Friday, at the absolute latest.

The second half of the trip, the drive up north, wasn't nearly as well planned out. I studied the map, traced a route, and then put the atlas away. I couldn't bring myself to think that far ahead. Just take the next step.

I brushed my teeth and gave myself a long-overdue once-over in the bathroom mirror. Still tall, still thin. My blue eyes, I noted, were now a dull, indiscriminate rainy-day color. Was my nose always this big? And my hair, the gray was spreading like a contagion. I was, at fifty-seven, an old man getting older. A line from some required reading book (*Gatsby?* Fitzgerald?) came to mind: How did you go bankrupt? Two ways: gradually, then suddenly. The same could be said about growing old. I stared at myself, took serious stock: John Nichols, ex-basketball player, ex-author, ex-philanderer, ex-husband, ex-high-school English teacher.

"A. Lot. Of. Exes," I said, and shut the light off.

Returning to the room, I found an appropriate space at the foot of the bed and lined my feet up for my free throws. I did this sometimes. Sometimes this helped. (Note: in my prime, high school, when I could run a five-minute mile, party half the night and still make it through a three-hour practice, then come home and play two hours more in the driveway, I was an excellent free-throw shooter. I couldn't play defense much, couldn't jump, had trouble fighting through picks, but I could shoot, as my teammates used to say, and as my still high-school record of forty-three straight free throws could attest, "like a motherfucker." I attributed this less to form and ability — though both were pretty good —

than to an otherworldly focus that allowed me to shut out the noise, my thoughts, my past, present, and future, the universe, when I stood at that line. My coach at Marist High, Coach Leahy, amazed and confused by my one-trick-pony act, once asked what I thought about when I shot, and I gave him a pure and truthful answer: nothing.)

So I squared my shoulders, aligned my feet, bounced the imaginary ball exactly three times, stared at the imaginary basket hanging over the door of the bathroom, and waited for my mind to empty, the nothingness to come. I then shot, and when I did, I saw the arc of the ball, saw it rotate, saw it sail through the air, saw the bottom of the net sweetly flick as if an angel had just breathed on it.

I made ten straight, and while this helped muffle the drumbeats in my head, I was still too wired for sleep, so I searched for other diversions. Other than my bourbon, I had brought only two with me: a CD — *Exile on Main St.,* by the Rolling Stones — and a book, a dog-eared paperback, *Blue Highways,* by William Least Heat-Moon. I couldn't envision a circumstance that would allow me to play the CD, since Ethan hated all music except for Christmas carols, which we listened to the brink of madness year-round, but the book, I thought, would be a good companion. I pulled it out and slid into bed next to my man.

Blue Highways is a memoir of a middle-aged man's solitary and somewhat desperate trip through the back roads of America. Over the course of his journey, he stops in offbeat towns and meets offbeat people while searching for internal change after a failed marriage. I had read it a number of times, and it fueled a desire in me to do the same thing: to travel, to see, to listen, to write, to rebuild.

For more than nineteen years, my life with Ethan had kept me from taking such a trip, but now here I was, making the most of things and my Marriott points. I opened the book and, for a while, disappeared into faraway back roads.

I had one of my Ethan-is-talking-normal dreams that night. I had had these dreams often when he was younger, but over time they had grown rare. Occasionally, however, they still came upon me during times of inner turbulence, so it was no surprise that I would have one now.

Once again we were back at our home in Wilton, sitting on the deck, having breakfast. As always it was warm and sunny, but off in

31

the distance I heard the first faint peals of thunder. When Ethan heard the thunder, he looked up from his bowl of cereal and spoke in the clear, sweet voice that existed only when I slept: "Where are we going, Dad? Where are we going?"

I woke immediately after hearing his voice, those words, that question, and lay still, pretending I was okay, convincing myself I was fine. But when I heard the sound of the Doubt and Guilt rounding the bend, picking up steam, I got up, made my way over to the foot of the bed, and searched for the free-throw line.

2

I was awake at seven, but still in bed, bloodshot eyes closed, jaw locked, mind doing wind sprints: the trip, the wedding, the relatives, my family, Mary's family, Ocean View. Over the years, I had become quite good at compartmentalizing, at dealing with first-things-first, and I forced myself to do just that now.

Today's lead story: Karen's wedding, ostensibly, the reason for this trip. I was the father of the bride and was paying, per an easily negotiated agreement, only one-third of the costs. This was fair, I thought, considering that Karen made gobs of money at the ripe old age of twenty-nine trading bonds in New York and was marrying Roger Nelson, a rich man from a blue-blooded family. The Nelsons had money, lots of it, along with summer, winter, and *fall* homes, all of which, according to Mindy, looked just like Downton Abbey, "except bigger."

I knew I would have to give a father-of-the-bride speech, something funny, warm, wise; part Atticus Finch; part Steve Martin. I had asked Mindy to help me with this, but the subsequent toast she had produced required that I wear an asbestos suit. Not thinking that practical (note: I look terrible in asbestos suits), I tossed it.

I had been putting the speech off for weeks, so consumed was I with my Overall Plan, but time was running short. Attention must be paid.

I considered starting off with some funny stories about Karen as a little girl, but at that early hour, I couldn't think of any. I suspect I couldn't think of any such stories at any hour because, truth be told, Karen wasn't funny. Mindy got all the funny in our family and then some. I would have no problem telling stories about Mindy, but she wasn't the one getting married, and I suspected my little buddy never would.

I could tease Karen, tell everyone how, at eleven, she had shook my hand and said, "You must be very proud," after I learned my first and, as it would turn out, only novel was being published. But that wouldn't be entirely fair nor true since after a hesitation, she did offer up a quick hug. I didn't think she would appreciate that story. Karen didn't like to be teased.

Karen was Karen. Beautiful, serious, ambitious, an overachiever; a Republican's republican. Great shape. Scores of 5K runs; three marathons completed. A runner's runner. Cool, distant, almost never cried, a hard-nosed head cheerleader, a not-very-benevolent queen bee. Probably, a bitch's bitch. But she was my oldest child, voted most likely to make me a grandfather, and, views on health-care reform notwithstanding, I loved her dearly.

Despite my efforts to compartmentalize, to focus on Karen, my thoughts invariably shifted to Ethan, still asleep next to me. I worried how he would behave at the wedding. He was capable of anything. Visions of a meltdown, complete with screaming and food throwing, appeared. I had to be prepared for a worst-case scenario, make sure contingency plans were in place, hope that the 9-1-1 in Charleston had quick response times. Karen had been lukewarm to the idea of his coming to the reception. I knew I was taking a risk.

I lay there for a moment longer, overwhelmed, my mind spinning, my life pinning me down. I then performed my morning ritual for the past nineteen years: I cursed God, then prayed to Him and pushed myself out of bed.

After Ethan woke up and after I got him ready for the day (bath, brush teeth, deodorant); and after I got him dressed (orange Illini T-shirt, navy-blue sweat pants, white socks, black running shoes); and after we ate at a Waffle House across from the hotel (three pickles, orange juice, four sausage links, and half a pancake for Ethan, several pots of black coffee for me); and after I managed to mention to the waitress that I had played basketball at Illinois ("I was just a walk-on, no biggie, but I played some"); and after we walked around the student quad, and after I realized there was really nothing to see in the student quad; and after an increasingly restless Ethan asked, "Do. Now?" exactly 104,000 times and I questioned the sanity of my late-night driving plan with always-restless Ethan exactly 104,000 times; and after I ignored Mary's phone call, presumably asking where I was, we found ourselves back in the king-size bed at the Courtyard. It was all of ten o' clock.

"Do. Now?" Ethan asked.

"I don't know, maybe go swimming? They have a pool here."

"No! Do. Now?"

"I don't know, maybe watch TV? *Sports-Center?* Top Ten is on in the morning."

"Do. Now?"

"I don't know, maybe tie some sheets together, make a noose, hang myself?"

"Do. Now?"

I knew where this was going. All roads eventually led there. I took a deep breath, considered increasing my daily Beam ration, and said, "I don't know, Ethan. What do you want to do?"

He didn't hesitate. "Stinky Bear."

Stinky Bear was a sassy, horny little teddy bear, full of insightful and often (depending on the size of my Jim Beam ration) outrageous comments about life, love, and the state of civilization. He spoke in a high and mildly irritating falsetto voice, his breathless enthusiasm inspired, in part, by Dick Vitale, the excitable college basketball commentator, and Austin Powers, the excitable international man of mystery. I had created his character years ago to help wile away the hopeless weekend hours when Ethan wasn't in school and respite care was not available. Stinky Bear amused Ethan and me for years and was regarded, along with his mother, Red Bear (a relatively soft-spoken, alcoholic teddy bear with a British accent), and

37

Grandpa Bear (a no-nonsense African American teddy bear who sounded, I was told, or at least liked to believe, like Morgan Freeman) as members of the family.

"What. Do. Stinky Bear?" Ethan asked.

I was lying down on the hotel bed, surrounded by all three bears, Ethan sitting crossed-legged next to me, rocking back and forth. I could tell a tense mood was rapidly coming on, the new surroundings taking a toll. He needed a good dose of the Bears to set him right.

I picked up Stinky and bounced him on my stomach. He was the smallest of the bears and wore a sleeveless red jersey with the number 1 on the front, and matching red shorts. While the other bears all played major roles in the long-running series, Stinky Bear was the unequivocal star of the show.

"A little of this, a little of that!" I answered Ethan in Stinky Bear's trademark high-pitched voice.

This general answer would not do. "What. Do. Today?" Ethan asked again. When it came to Stinky Bear's life, Ethan wanted the nitty-gritty, the who, what, where.

"Well, I got up and brushed my teeth, then I went and had some breakfast. I ate three pancakes and some not-so-crispy bacon at the Waffle House. I saw you eating there with your dad. What a handsome and distinguished gentleman! You're so lucky to have him as a father! So very lucky! Did you know he played basketball here at Illinois? The waitress now knows, and she seemed *very* unimpressed."

"What. Next?"

"Well, after I ate, I passed some pretty big gas!" I made a loud fart noise with my mouth.

Ethan smiled, his teeth slipping over this bottom lip. "What. Say?"

"I say, excuse me! That was really stinky! Oh man! That one was out of the park!"

"Home. Run!" Ethan said, laughing.

I picked up Grandpa Bear. He was the largest and rattiest-looking. One of his eyes was missing, and an ear was crooked. He had been Mindy's, which had to make him close to twenty-seven.

"Passing gas like that! You a disgusting excuse for a human being," Grandpa Bear said in his Morgan Freeman voice.

"Hey, Gramps, I'm not a human being, in case you haven't noticed! I'm a stinky, farty teddy bear. I'm not apologizing. I say what I think. I'm brash. I'm crass. I'm Stinky Bear, baby!"

"What kind of grandson are you? You

39

embarrass me, and embarrass the family."

"Sing!" Ethan demanded.

"No, I don't think I'm in the mood. . . ."

"Sing!"

"I don't think I can muster the strength."

"Sing!"

Ethan, I knew, would not be deterred, so Grandpa Bear dutifully cleared this throat and launched into the politically incorrect "Old Black Joe."

I'm comin'
I'm comin'
For my head is bending low.
I hear the gentle voices callin',
"Old Black Joe."

Before Ethan could demand a second verse, I picked up Red Bear. She had been a gift from one of his speech therapists some ten years before, and he was still wary of her. I suspected it had something to do with the tone of her British accent, which could be intimidating and condescending, even though she was pretty much a tramp.

"Oh please, not that insufferable song." She sighed.

"Oh, what's the matter with you now, another one of your mysterious headaches?" Grandpa Bear asked. He made quote marks

40

with his paws when he said the word *head-aches.*

"A touch of the flu, I believe." Red Bear coughed.

"More like a touch of Sutter Home Chardonnay. More like a *case.* You didn't even come home last night. What kind of mother are you? Out *carousing* all hours of the day? Out *gallivanting.* Leaving your young son with me, an old bear. If your mother could see you now, God rest her soul."

"Oh, please," Red Bear said. "I was hardly *gallivanting.* I just stopped off at Rafferty's Pub for a simple glass of wine. I was parched, what with the heat and all. The next thing I knew, it was morning, and I was waking up in a pool of vomit in the parking lot with my skirt down at my ankles."

"That definitely sounds like the flu!" Stinky Bear said.

Ethan didn't understand much, if any, of the dialogue. It had been developed over the years more to amuse me more than anyone. Regardless, he always seemed to appreciate the effort, the various accents, the voice inflections, and, of course, the farting, something Stinky was quite proficient at.

This morning's bit was an old routine,

41

however. Since I was performing without the aid of my muse, bourbon, I was not particularly inspired, and could tell his interest was quickly flagging. Ethan could be a tough audience; he demanded fresh material, so I redoubled my efforts.

"Hey, Daddy-o, where are we going?" Stinky Bear asked me.

"We're going to Karen's wedding in Charleston, South Carolina." I answered this in my own, John Nichols, voice. "She's marrying Rich Roger. Roger with the big jaw."

"South Carolina. Lord help us!" Grandpa Bear said. "That's the epicenter of racial hatred! The very vortex of bigotry. I remember when they fired on Fort Sumter. Lord, I was just a young little bear, workin' in the cotton field. I looked up and I seen the cannonball like a comet shooting in the air, and I turned to my massa and I say, 'Mr. Massa, sir, you went and got Mr. Abraham Lincoln all mad at you now, and he gonna ride down here and fry your ass. Then I picked up a shovel and hit him right square in his white racist, George Wallace face. . . .' "

I was about to embark on a historical and hopefully educational tale about Grandpa Bear's perilous journey through the Underground Railroad, when my phone rang.

Ethan, who was clearly growing tired of the routine (there wasn't enough farting), leaped over me and snatched it.

"Hello! Hello! Hello!"

I sat up. "Ethan, give me the phone. Give it to me."

He turned away. "Mindy! Mindy! Mindy! Mindy!" He then handed me the phone, and I put it on speaker.

"Dad? It's Mindy."

"I figured that out."

"Where are you?"

"Champaign, Illinois. In a hotel. A Marriott Courtyard, to be exact. I just used up twenty thousand points. Six hundred thousand to go."

"Are you driving with Ethan?"

"Yes."

"Are you alone with him?"

"No. I'm with Stinky, Red, and Grandpa Bear. We're splitting the gas."

"I can't believe you still have those three things."

"Funny, just this morning, Stinky said the same thing about you, Karen, and Ethan."

Mindy didn't hesitate. "Put Stinky on. I want to talk to that bear."

"Yeah, baby!" I said in Stinky Bear's voice. "What's up, Mindy?"

"What's up, Stinky Bear? How's Ethan doing?"

"He's doing good, real good."

"What do today, Stinky Bear?" Mindy asked.

"Well, we got in late to the hotel, and we slept very late, all the way to seven. . . ."

I paused and held the phone out so Ethan could yell, "O'clock!"

"And then we went to breakfast and Ethan was good and the waitress gave us three . . ."

"Pickles!" Ethan said.

"Wow," Mindy said. "Can I have one?"

"Yes! Ma'am!" Ethan said.

"Hey, Mindy," Stinky Bear said, "me and your father watched a brilliant clip of you last night."

"Which one? They're all brilliant."

"The one of you wetting your pants. You should be very, very proud. I'm sure all your fellow Princeton alums are very proud too!"

"My whole purpose in life is to make everyone proud, Stinky Bear. That's the reason I get up in the morning."

"You don't have to make everyone proud, Mindy, just your dad."

"Hey, Stinky, how's Red Bear's drinking going?"

"Wonderful, baby! Thanks for asking!"

"And how's my dad's drinking going?"

I sat up high. "What's that supposed to mean?" I asked this in my John Nichols voice.

"Pretty early for Stinky Bear and Princeton jokes."

"It's not that early. Besides, I do lots of matinees. And I haven't had a drink today."

"I hope not. It's ten thirty."

"I only have two drinks a day."

"I've seen the size of your drinks, Dad. They're like Big Gulps."

Ethan grabbed the phone. "What. Eat. Today?" he asked.

"I had a bagel, Ethan. What did you eat today?"

"Pickle. Poo. Poo."

"Sounds like Dad is feeding you right!"

I grabbed the phone back from Ethan. He reached over and tried to pinch me.

"Don't pinch me," I said firmly. "Don't. Hey, listen," I said to Mindy. "When are you getting there?"

Mindy didn't say anything.

"Mindy? Hello?"

"I don't think I'm going, Dad."

"Me. Talk!" Ethan yelled. He lunged for the phone.

I jumped off the bed and quickly walked over to the window. "Please don't start that again, Mindy. Please. We're a family. She's your sister. You only have one. Please. Come on."

"She doesn't care if I go or not."

"That is not true. She cares, believe me. She cares. Please let me hear you say you're coming. Let me hear you say it."

"You're coming," Mindy said.

"Mindy?"

"I'm coming," she said quietly.

"Thank you. Because I don't need any more problems." Right after I said that, I regretted it. This had been a common refrain in our house, a phrase I had seemingly uttered every day of my life since Ethan was born. "Thank you for being cooperative," I said.

"Cooperative," Mindy muttered.

"Me. Talk!"

"You said you'd be there tomorrow. They're expecting you tomorrow."

"God."

Ethan got out of bed and made another run at the phone. "I gotta go. Say good-bye to him. He's standing right here. Say good-bye. I need to go."

I held the phone close to Ethan's ear and heard Mindy say, "Bye, Ethan."

"Bye! Mindy!" He jumped up and down.

"Wait? Dad?"

"What?"

46

"Why are you driving? You can't spend all day with him alone. No one can."

"I have him all the time at home."

"You have him for maybe two, three hours. Not all day. I said I would come out there and drive with you. Or you should have taken someone. One of the cousins. Or Aunty or Uncle Sal."

"Uncle Sal. Right. I can take less of Uncle Sal than I can of Ethan."

"Uncle Sal is great."

"Right. He's perfect. I keep forgetting that."

Ethan made yet another attempt at the phone, so I moved closer to the window. "Listen, I have to go. He's about to fall apart. We'll talk later."

"Bye, Daddy-o."

I closed the phone and when I did, Ethan pinched me on the arm. Hard.

After Grandpa Bear had a massive heart attack training for *Dancing with the Bears;* and after Stinky Bear successfully revived him by frantically pounding on his chest ("Hang on, Grandpa, you hang on now!"); and after Red Bear attended her very first AA meeting ("Hello, my name is Red Bear, and I'm an alcoholic" — other two bears: "Hello, Red Bear!"); and after we went swimming

47

in the completely empty and kind-of-cold hotel pool where I reenacted several famous catches in sports history with an orange Nerf football (Dwight Clark, Willie Mays, Santonio Holmes); and after we went back to the very same Waffle House for lunch where the very same waitress served us but, for reasons known only to her, failed to acknowledge this fact until I casually brought it to her attention; and after we went for a nostalgic drive through campus, during which I pointed out various places of historical and academic interest ("I kissed a girl there once; I threw up there once"); we drove over to the State Farm Center, which used to be called Assembly Hall when I played there.

"Still there," I said.

The hall is a massive, flying saucer of a building located on the southwest side of the school in what had once been, no doubt, a stark field. Illinois is the Prairie State, and most of it is as flat as a pancake, especially the campus of its flagship university. Consequently, winter winds in Champaign were brutal; they came howling out of the western plains in January and February with malicious intent, and there was nothing to break them, except, maybe Assembly Hall.

"Ethan, see that?" I lowered the windows

and turned off the van. The parking lot was empty, and the afternoon was turning hot. "That's where they play basketball. Illini hoops."

"Hoops! Go Illini!"

"Right, hoops."

"Me. Play."

"Not today."

"Yes. Ma'am."

"No, ma'am."

I pointed at the hall. "Daddy used to play there. I played in twenty games in three years. I scored a total of fifty-eight points, got three rebounds, had four assists, and committed one foul on a guy from Michigan. He made both his free throws because they were in the bonus."

Ethan began to pick at his fingernails.

"In high school I was All-Conference first team, All-State Honorable Mention. I got scholarship offers from the University of Toledo, the University of Wisconsin at Milwaukee, and Loyola of Chicago. But I decided to walk on here. I wanted to play at Illinois. Big Ten, big stage."

"Go. Now."

"I quit my senior year. Coach Hensen persuaded me, said I wasn't going to see the floor anymore. Robby Kleinschmidt was transferring in. He was very nice about it though. He offered me a Coke afterward. 'Hey, John, would you like a Coke?' he said. He was a nice guy."

"I. Starving."

"I should have stayed anyway. Finished what I started."

"Pee-pee."

"Or maybe I should have gone to one of those smaller schools. Probably Loyola. I would have played a lot, really learned the game. Who knows what could have happened? Maybe I could have played in Europe afterward. Basketball, that was my passion. I should have stayed in the sport somehow, found a way to stay involved. Down deep I think I really wanted to be a coach, not a teacher."

"Do. Now?"

"A coach. But they make even less than teachers. I probably could have done both, though. Maybe taught driver's ed. I'm an excellent driver."

I sat and studied the hall, its metallic, silver roof shimmering in the sun. At one time that building was the center of my universe.

"I've been gone for more than thirty years, you believe that? Thirty years."

"Pee-pee."

I sat and continued to stare out the

window, my obligation to feel reflective, to experience an epiphany, strong. It had been years since I had seen Assembly Hall; it might be years before I saw it again, if ever.

"It goes quick, dude-man. It goes quick. I think about everything's that's happened since I left. Everything."

"Eat."

I turned toward Ethan. "Hey, let me ask you something since, you know, we're just talking here: what do you think of me? Man to man. I can handle it. Tell me the truth. Am I a good guy, or am I full of shit?"

Ethan continued to pick at his nails.

"What's that? Didn't hear you."

"Poo-poo," he said softly.

I was a little stunned at the appropriateness of this response. "Wow. Well, you certainly tell it like it is."

I gave the hall one last long look, then started the van. But as I was pulling out of the lot, still immersed in memories and thought, Ethan did something he almost never did — he reached over and briefly put his hand on top of mine.

3

Mary called me at the Marriott Courtyard just outside of Indianapolis, at six the next morning.

"Where are you now?"

Even in the happiest times, the hand-holding in public, sex in the shower, notes-in-lunchbox years, Mary never said, "Good morning, good night, good-bye." Never called just to ask, "How are you, how was your day, how's it hanging?" Never called me "babe" or "honey." (Note: she was maybe the only woman on earth who didn't like foreplay before sex. "In me or off me" was her motto.) This heat-seeking missile approach to life, this ability to get right to the heart of things, was honed at a city law school, then perfected during years working in a windowless office as an assistant state's attorney, dealing, I suspect, with other foreplay-hating, I-don't-have-time-for-bullshit non-bullshitters.

"Good morning," I whispered.

"Where are you?"

"Where are you?" I countered.

"I'm here."

"Charleston?"

"Got here yesterday. Where are you?"

"Indianapolis, Indiana." I tried to mumble that.

"Indianapolis? That's it? That's not far!"

"Oh, it's farther than you think."

"I know where Indianapolis is. This is your daughter's wedding. Her *wedding, John.* We have a rehearsal dinner on Friday. *Friday, John.*"

"We'll be fine. He's doing well. I don't want to push it."

"This isn't right."

"I'm sorry, but what isn't right?"

"My being here while you're out on the road, doing whatever you're doing, joyriding around the country."

"Joyriding. I'm hardly joyriding, Mary."

"You're not fooling me," she said. "I know what you're really doing."

I swallowed hard, glanced over at Ethan in the bed next to me. "What are you talking about?"

"You're finally taking your big whatever, your book trip, your *Blue Road* thing."

"I don't know what you're talking about."

"The one you always talked about. You know, you could have taken that trip anytime, but you decided to take it now, just when everyone needs you. Your daughter is getting married, married, and you're hiding behind Ethan."

"I think I have the hardest job. Being with him is hard. Everything else is easy. You know that."

"For your information, I don't have it easy. There are a million things to do here. Plus, I think something's going on with Karen and Roger."

I paused, sat up. "What's going on? What do you mean? Is there a problem?"

"Just get here."

"What's wrong?"

"I'm not sure yet. I can't talk now."

She hung up.

I put the phone down and was about to begin a solid mulling over of things, when it buzzed again. I reached for it. For the second time that morning, I heard Mary's voice. She started in before I could say a word.

"He's impossible. You can't rely on him. He does whatever he wants whenever he wants. He's just so . . . I need you down here right away. I'm tired of everything." At first I assumed she was referring to Roger

— she was never a fan — or possibly Sal. But when she said, "Mindy, are you there? Mindy? Hello? Are you there?" I realized who the object of her affection was. Ethan was constantly playing with our phones; consequently, our redial numbers were always messed up.

"Good-bye, Mary." I hit end and again looked over at Ethan, who, thankfully, was still asleep. I propped up my pillows; apparently, I was done sleeping, and I started in on an intense staring of the ceiling.

"Mary, Mary, sweet contrary," I whispered.

My phone buzzed yet again, interrupting my musing. I scrambled for it, hoping it was my ex. But it wasn't my ex, at least not the ex I was still in love with. It was, shockingly, lovely Rita. I didn't answer.

If asked, I prefer philanderer to adulterer. Adulterer is very you-are-going-to-hell-old-school, very Ten Commandmentish. Philanderer is more PC. It sounds playful, connotes harmless rolls in the hay. People seem to forgive philanderers, or at least put up with them. Bill Clinton was/is a philanderer, and he's still pretty popular. People idolize JFK. Other than possibly someone on FOX News, no one calls Clinton and Kennedy adulterers. They just fooled around. Hey, some presidents golfed.

(Note: I really wasn't a full-fledged philanderer. In more than thirty years of marriage, I only stepped out with one woman, lovely Rita, and it didn't last long. Then I came to my senses, confessed all, begged forgiveness, had a bar of soap thrown at my head, had a bar of soap hit me in the head, and was told to move out. Nine months later I was a divorced fifty-five-year-old man, living alone, trying to decide whether to have Dominos for lunch, and mac and cheese for dinner, or mac and cheese for lunch, and Dominos for dinner.)

I met Rita at the Mid-City Health Club, a mecca for tennis-playing MILFs and middle-aged men who liked to spend hours in front of locker room mirrors, plucking rogue gray hairs from their eyebrows.

We struck up a conversation by the elliptical machines. Subsequent conversations led to a quasi-friendship, which led to some lunches, which led to some wine, which led to some oral sex in my car, which led to conventional sex, and then, depending on your definition, not-so-conventional sex at a nearby Hampton Inn, which led to the whole Dominos — mac-and-cheese dilemma.

I no longer even try to guess what I was thinking. While very attractive, when she wasn't performing acrobatics at the Hampton, I didn't find her particularly interesting or intelligent. (Note: when she was, I confess, I found her enthralling.)

My mistress had a simple worldview: play tennis, drink Pinot, have sex, finish the Pinot. She was about ten years younger than me, divorced twice; when pressed, she admitted to never "really" having read a book; and when pressed, admitted to never "really" having watched the news. She freely admitted the obvious to me though: she was highly sexually charged.

"My motor is always running," she would say. "Always."

While she wasn't a lot of things, what she really wasn't was Mary, my poor stressed-out, always exhausted, always overwhelmed, and increasingly depressed and bitter wife. The constant demands of Ethan had turned our home into a tense and sad battlefield, and my months with Rita were an escape. When Rita and I bumped elbows at the elliptical station, I was going through my own particularly bitter phase. Ethan was becoming impossible, and my affair, I concluded later, was probably an attempt to even the score with life. Driving to our liaisons, I would rationalize/justify what I was doing: I had not asked for Ethan. This never-ending burden was given to me, so I deserved some pleasure. And I was sticking it out at home, when other men surely would have cut and run. At the very least, I had this coming. In fact, my times with Rita, stolen afternoons when Mary thought I was at the gym, was really for the best since they rejuvenated me, helped me cope.

It was bullshit, but I bought it for a while. It was also very out of character for me. Up until then, I only had eyes for Mary.

I broke things off with Rita one rainy June afternoon. We had just completed the act, when Mary called me. I didn't answer, but seeing her name on my phone with Rita lying naked next to me shook me to my senses. Mary didn't deserve this. Things were bad enough. Neither, for that matter, did Rita, who, at her core, was a decent person.

I dressed quickly, went home, and impulsively confessed all to Mary. A few hours later I was back at the hotel, but this time, alone. I stayed in room 112, right across from the ice machine, for three months until I found an affordable and depressing one-bedroom condo next to the Stone Avenue train station and just a few blocks from home.

It was there that I began my quest to set things right. I actually went to church for a long string of Sundays, actually said confession to a priest (I used the word *adultery* there), and was overly helpful with Ethan, frequently taking him on days that Mary was supposed to have him. On Friday nights, I came by and took out the garbage and the recycling bins; on Saturday mornings, I cut the grass, edged the bushes. I also attended support groups for parents of special-needs children so I could learn coping mechanisms other than cheating on your spouse. In between these acts of contrition, I wrote letter after letter apologizing to Mary, emphasizing, in no particular order, my stupidity and my love. She never acknowledged any of those letters.

Over time, I made progress, baby steps first, then more recently big-boy steps. Mary and I began having breakfast with Ethan, and we took him for walks in the evening after dinner. A few weeks back I sent her flowers on her birthday, and she surprisingly thanked me with a brief voice mail when she knew I was out. But progress was still slow, and time was slipping away; I wanted my wife back.

She was more than worth the effort: Mary was the quiet girl who stood off in the corner at parties taking it all in; the smart girl who graduated second in her class at law school; the hard-to-figure-out girl who secretly read trashy romance novels; the no-frills girl who, other than a pair of "lucky" half-moon earrings, didn't wear or even like jewelry; the dark-eyed, olive-skinned pretty girl who looked wonderful first thing in the morning, and even better late at night.

Smart and a little mysterious, funny and plenty tough, she had been my sweet-sweetie since senior year at the U of I, been my trusted partner in life, and I had torched it all with low-wattage Rita.

Rita. Why she was calling me now, I had no idea. We hadn't spoken in close to two years. But there was her number on my phone, and there was her breathless message, pleading and urgent, on my voice mail: "John, I need to talk to you. Please call."

I replayed the message one more time, put the phone down, considered, then decided to sigh. A moment later I heard a stir and glanced over at the other bed. Ethan was finally awake, studying me with large brown eyes from under a mess of blankets.

"Top of the morning," I said.

My phone buzzed again. Rita again.

"Do. Now?" Ethan asked.

I stared at my buzzing phone. "Funny, I was about to ask you the very same thing."

At the parents support group, we referred to bad days with our children as "survive and advance." Days that you did anything you could just to get by. Days that the anger and frustration and hopelessness over-whelmed you. Days that you felt sorry for no one but yourself, when you contemplated terrible acts, when you just plain flat-out hated the world and went so far as to wish bad things on other people just so they could be as miserable as you. Endless days.

My day in the outskirts of Indianapolis with Ethan was full-fledged survive and advance. He was agitated, the trip finally taking a toll, and I was distracted, worried about Rita, Karen, and our schedule: I was no longer sure we were going to get to Charleston on time.

Things started turning ugly as soon as he got up. Before we even sat down for break-fast at the hotel, he launched into Question Mode, repeatedly and with increasing fre-quency, asking the same question. "Do. Next? Do. Next? Do. Next? Do. Next?" When our food came, he refused to eat anything, even pickles. To make matters worse, we soon heard a rumble of thunder. This was not good, not good at all. When it came to storms, he was absolutely inconsolable. Nothing could calm him. So he moaned and wept and made a not-so-small spectacle of himself until I finally abandoned breakfast and decided to take him swimming.

Wrong move. The pool was in an enclosed glass dome in which we could hear every single drop of rain and see every single flash of lighting. Ethan sat in a chair off to the side, rocking back and forth, crying, while I, slightly freezing, stubbornly stood in the water and tried to coax him in.

"Come on in, dude-man. It's nice inside the water. It's very nice inside."

"Do. Now?"

"We're swimming now."

"No!"

"Yes. It will be fun once you come in."

"No!"

"Come on, buddy. I think I see Stinky Bear over in the corner. Let's go over and find him. I think he's passing gas."

"Shut. Up. Idiot!"

"Come on." I splashed the water. "Don't be afraid of the storm. The storm is an idiot. Idiot storm!"

"No! Do. Now?"

"We're swimming now." I went underwater to prove my point. "See?" I said as I re-emerged. "A lot of fun!"

"Do. Next?"

There was a bang of thunder and, for a moment, I thought the dome shook. Ethan screamed, and I kind of screamed.

"Jesus!" I said. "Wow."

"Home!"

"No, no home. Swimming. The storm is almost over!"

He sunk low in his seat and wept some more. I tried to splash him, but the water fell short.

"Last chance to swim. Come on! Get in. I know you'll like it."

"Home!" He kicked his feet up in the air.

Clearly, this was going nowhere. "Okay, fine." I dog-paddled over to the side and hoisted myself out.

When I approached him, he jumped up from his chair and started to hit me. Fortunately, since it was only eight thirty, the pool was empty. So, the ensuing scene, my grabbing his wrists and dragging him back to the chairs while he continued to kick and scream, was witnessed by no one.

We sat until he had sufficiently calmed down, then made our way back to the room, taking the stairs to the third floor because

Ethan suddenly remembered he was terrified of elevators, even though we had taken one down just minutes before.

As soon as we were back in the room, I lay on the bed in my wet bathing suit, closed my eyes, and attempted to catch my breath.

Ethan immediately tried to sit on top of me. "Do. Now?"

"Ethan, no! Get off. Please. No. Sit next to me, here." I gently pushed him off, but he climbed right back on.

So we stayed like that, father and son, in our bathing suits, his forehead pressed against my cheek. Ten years earlier, I might have gone into a rage, might have broken down and wept, but time and experience had taught me that if I just held on a little longer, things would pass. So we lay there and listened to the wind and thunder, our hearts beating together, waiting for things to pass.

I decided to leave for Kentucky an hour later. Ethan was still agitated, and it continued to rain, so barring a fire, earthquake, or terrorist attack on the Marriott Courtyard, things couldn't get much worse. I gave him a quick bath, ran an electronic razor over his face, and off we went.

Stinky Bear did most of the driving while

sitting on my lap. He kept up a persistent and, I hoped, engaging chatter as we headed south in the rain.

"Hey, Daddy-o, do we really need to listen to this?" Stinky asked in his falsetto voice. I had put on one of Ethan's Christmas carol CDs, and Bing Crosby was singing "Rudolph the Red-Nosed Reindeer." "Christmas carols in the summer is a little weird."

"This is the music we listen to when we drive, you know that," I said in my John Nichols voice.

"You enable him. You need to stretch him."

"We listen to Christmas carols, that's what we do."

We drove for a minute, the music filling the car. "When you think about it, this song, 'Rudolph,' it's really about bullying," Stinky said. "Donner, Blitzen, the other reindeers, they called him names, wouldn't let him play in other reindeer games. And where is Santa in all of this? And they only accept him when they need him? Bunch of pricks. If I were Rudolph, I would have said, 'Screw off, Santa. I'm taking my nose somewhere else.'"

"You know, I never thought about that."

"Well, you got a lot on your mind."

Ethan looked on skeptically from the

65

backseat, where I had made him sit as punishment for his behavior.

"How about this rain?" I asked Stinky.

"Yeah, pretty B-A-D — bad! But my gas is badder. Boy, I got some real stinkers coming soon. Stay tuned! They're coming!"

"Can't wait."

I checked the rearview mirror again. Ethan was intently staring at the back of my head, trying to decide, I'm sure, whether to accept my olive branch of a performance or continue acting up.

"I tell you, Dad, in retrospect, I'm not sure what you were thinking when you decided to make this trip," Stinky said.

"I really don't know what I was thinking either," I admitted.

"You thought you were William Least Heat-Moon, didn't you? You were going to take some kind of interesting, life-changing trip into America. See small towns, meet real characters, see mountains and streams, gain wisdom and insight. Have a real writer's experience, and then maybe write about it, didn't you? Break your twenty-year writer's block by seeing America. A special trip with your special-needs son. Right? A heartbreaking best seller for sure. Real life *Rain Man*."

"It crossed my mind, yes."

"Instead you're on a journey to hell, stuck in a car all day with Ethan and three teddy bears who you're beginning to think are alive and you're about to go crazy."

"I'm not about to go crazy. Everything is okay. The storm will end. We will stop for lunch."

Ethan seized on that word. "Lunch!"

I fell quiet, but it was already too late; the pickles-Sprite launch sequence had been activated.

"I starving. Lunch. *Now.* Eat. *Now.*"

"Ethan, it's too early. Let's drive for a while."

"No! Eat! I starving. Starving!"

"You should have had breakfast. We need to drive now."

"No!"

"Yes!"

"Eat!"

"Listen to your father!" Stinky Bear said. "Listen to him. He's going crazy!"

"Shut. Up. Idiot!" Ethan said.

"You, shut up!" Stinky Bear said.

We drove for a few minutes in a miraculous burst of silence. Then he played his trump card.

"Poo-poo."

I didn't say anything. Though he might have been bluffing, there was a chance he

67

wasn't; he hadn't gone that morning. This could, at least, partially explain his mood.

"Poo-poo."

"Don't start that." I drove faster.

"Poo-poo. Poo-poo *bad*!"

"Jesus, God . . ."

"Poo-poo bad! Now! Now! Now!"

I glanced backward, caught a glimpse of his face, and recognized his poo-poo-is-rounding-third-and-heading-for-home grimace.

"Oh God. Okay! We'll stop!" I flipped on my blinker even though the next exit was a while off.

"Now!" He hit-slapped me on the back of the head.

"Hey! Knock it off!" I was about to retaliate, threaten some kind of pickle or Sprite sanctions, when Karen called.

"Daddy?"

"Thank you, God! Listen, talk to him, will you? Please! He has to go to the bathroom. Just talk to him for a few minutes, calm him down, distract him. We're driving."

"I don't want to talk to him right now."

"You have to talk to him! He might go in his pants. He's done that before." I put the phone on speaker.

"Hi, Karen!" I yelled.

"Hi, Ethan," Karen said. Her voice was

68

soft, dull, resigned.

"Karen!" Ethan stopped stomping his feet. "Where. Are. You?"

"In a hotel. In South Carolina."

"Where. Mom. Be?"

"She's in the room next to me. Daddy?"

"Where. Mindy. Be?"

"I don't know where she is."

"Poo-poo. Bad."

"Hold it, and Dad will stop."

"What. Eat. Today?"

"Nothing, Ethan. I had nothing to eat today," Karen said. She was doing a poor job of hiding her irritation, and this angered me. She only had to deal with him for a few minutes — that was all I was asking, a few minutes.

"Could you make more of an effort?" I said. "This isn't the time to mail it in."

"Can we talk now?"

We finally came to an exit, which I took at fifty miles per hour. "Actually, no. He has to take a crap. I'll call you back."

"Daddy?"

"I'll call you back." I ended the call and threw the phone off to the side.

After a long poo-poo break at a Cracker Barrel; and after I asked the elderly church-lady-looking waitress if they served alcohol;

and after the elderly church-lady-looking waitress reacted like I had just asked her to breastfeed us; and after we ordered and ate fried chicken and fried ham with French fries; and after Ethan put my credit card in his mouth right before giving it to the elderly church-lady-looking waitress who reacted like I had just handed her a severed body part; and after we made a series of unscheduled pee-pee-Sprite-let's-play-catch-with-the-orange-Nerf-football, let's-take-the-pickles-off-of-the-McDonald's cheeseburgers and befriend them ("Hey there, Mr. Pickle, what you knowin'?"); and after Ethan whined and pinched me hundreds if not thousands of times, he fell mercifully asleep in the back seat.

I turned off "Jingle Bells." "I don't know if I can do this," I said aloud.

"Yes, you can, old man," Stinky Bear told me. "Yes, you can. Just hold on."

"This is a big mistake. I don't think I can do this."

"You can do it. Just take the next step. You've been doing this for nineteen years, old man, nineteen years."

Mary suspected that something was wrong with Ethan around nine months. He didn't sit up, and he didn't reach or grab for things. Absorbed in my job, teaching two AP English courses, finishing my book, and contending with two young daughters, initially I paid little attention to her concerns. It wasn't until our pediatrician recommended some tests be taken, including the MRI, that I took notice.

The tests results surpassed our worst fears: global brain damage brought on by a rare chromosome disorder. His primary diagnosis was Trisomy 9 Mosaicism syndrome which meant the ninth chromosome appears three times rather than twice in some cells of the body. (Later he would later also be classified as mildly autistic.) At that time, specifics didn't mean much to me. All I knew was that my only son, my youngest baby, would never be normal.

Instantly, our lives transformed into an exhaustive string of sleepless nights and stressful days, punctuated by an array of neurologists, therapists, and geneticist meetings. Mary was constantly doing research, constantly looking for information on his conditions, hoping for some good news, for some light. I, on the other hand, stumbled through, in denial, overwhelmed and disbelieving. Things like this happened to other people.

The first three years were probably the

worst, since every missed milestone was cause for sadness and stress. He didn't walk, he didn't talk. He didn't play with any toys. He just cried and stared at us with helpless, accusing eyes.

Ethan took his first steps when he was three and a half, a glorious day in the Nichols house. It was Valentine's Day, but more important, an overachieving Illini team was beating a Bobby Knight–led Indiana *at* Indiana, when I glanced away from the TV to see Ethan smiling while he pulled himself up from the couch and then proceeded to let go.

"Daddy," Karen whispered.

We were in the family room, and we all just stared in wonder as he took a few drunken steps. Finally, after he had managed a smooth landing, sitting softly down in the middle of the floor, Mindy broke the silence by saying, "Hey, Ethan, go get me a Coke."

The War Years came next — years when the air raid sirens blared, when you grabbed a helmet and jumped into a trench the second you entered the house, when smiles and laughter were rationed like sugar and bits of chocolate. Really sucky years. This was when he was about five and six. This was when the mood swings began.

There was simply no predicting him. The smallest thing — an unclosed dresser drawer, an errant thread hanging from your sweater, a ringing phone — could send him into a rage. Bedtime became a terror; he never wanted to sleep. Consequently, we took to locking him in his room at night. When he broke the lock, we fixed it; when he broke it a third time, I held the door shut until he grew tired of pulling on it. This could take up to an hour every night.

When he was around six, things took a turn for the better when, after years of speech therapy, and years after we had given up hope, he defied all odds and started speaking. Not well and not often, but he eventually managed two- and occasionally three-word sentences, each utterance an achievement. "Leave. Now." "I. Want. Milk." Once he could articulate some of his needs, his behavior improved, and the tantrums became less frequent, less pronounced. After years as shut-ins, we could finally take him places: out to eat, shopping, to the pool. At restaurants in particular, he was, for the most part, well behaved, polite to the point of debonair. He would say thank you and please, pretend to study the menu, and hold the door open for other customers. Waitresses, waiters, hostesses, and even cooks took a liking to him, and as a result, we spent an inordinate amount of time and money eating out.

Other than a terrifying seizure when he was around eight, physically, he emerged fine. Though he was undersized and had teeth that needed but would never see braces, he was healthy and normal in appearance. His cognitive state, however, was a much different story. Doctors used the term *developmentally delayed*, but we never took to this description, for it conveyed hope, implied a temporary condition. Ethan wasn't delayed. He was going to be three years old forever. Meanwhile, the rest of us kept getting older.

His comprehension, we concluded over the years, was a crapshoot. We were never sure what he was understanding. Some abstract things — death, heaven, where the sun goes when it sets, what the moon was — were simply and permanently beyond him. Others — changing weather, time, anger, the concept of family — he seemed to grasp. Every so often, after listening to a conversation, or observing an action or scene, he would surprise us with an appropriate comment or gesture.

While he had a minimal attention span, adolescence brought some new interests, and additional relief. He began watching basketball on TV, and while he didn't understand most of what he was seeing — the rules, the score — he understood the overall objective of the game, get the ball in the basket, and as a result enjoyed watching others play.

Hoops became his thing. Over time, he began to play with me, developing a skill for shooting. His style was unorthodox, he held the ball down low in front of his chest and shot with both hands, but somehow the ball went in. He could shoot for up to an hour, an astounding length of time for him to do any one thing. Afterward he would summarize the game: "How. Many. Me. Make?" ("You made one hundred baskets, Ethan.") "How. Many. Dad. Make?" ("I made five.") "Go. Illini!"

"Yes, go, Illini!"

Eventually, along with his love of basketball, a basic sense of humor also emerged; he understood and even loved slapstick comedy. Pratfalls and body function references and noises — hence Stinky Bear — were his favorites, so in that one regard, at least, he was a normal male.

He also loved his family. If we were all together, he would bring us into a circle, make us hold hands, and sing, "Family!

Family! Family! U! . . . S! . . . Aaaaa!" I have no idea what the origin was, really no clue, but it became a staple of his, and both a source of embarrassment and amusement, depending on the moment or occasion.

As I drove on, my retrospective inevitably turned into a review of my Overall Plan. Was I doing the right thing? Would he be happy? Exactly how and when was I going to officially fill in Mary? A host of questions, of worries, each one weighing me down.

Being able to think — this was the downside of Ethan being quiet.

Somewhere close to Louisville, my thoughts took a turn for the worse. (Note: I don't know much about depression, I've made no effort to research its clinical definition, never been to a therapist, do not take antidepressants, but I suspect that I suffer from a mild form of it from time to time, an Ethan-induced Black Despair. It didn't stay with me, it was not permanent, but it was there — a hole I occasionally and without warning fell into, impenetrably dark and hopeless. I suddenly felt myself falling into that hole, now falling fast.)

I switched lanes, opened the window a crack, took deep breaths, and tried to settle myself. Nothing was helping, though, so I slowed then stopped on the shoulder; apparently, I had started to cry.

I was at the lowest level, the deepest part of the Black Despair, when I heard my phone go off, a faint buzzing, then louder. The outside world, a thin light down the mine shaft. I groped for it on the seat next to me, answered.

"Hello?"

"Mr. Nichols?"

I opened my eyes, cleared my throat. I didn't recognize the voice. "Yeah?"

"This is Kyle Baker from across the street."

"Who?" I stopped with the crying, sniffled some. "Oh, yeah, right. Kyle."

"I thought you might be coming today, but I wasn't sure."

I sniffled again, wiped my eyes, checked the rearview mirror, tried to get my bearings: Ethan was sleeping, I was in Kentucky, my name was John Nichols, I was on my way to my daughter's wedding and things were going to be okay. "Yeah, right, I am. We are. We're actually about twenty minutes away. I think. We'll be there soon. I'll call you when we get there, and maybe we can meet or get an early dinner or something."

"I was thinking that maybe we can go to a park, shoot around. It's supposed to stop raining. I live right near a park. It has a good court."

"Hoops. Okay, yeah, hoops, that would be good, great. Yeah, I'll call when we get closer. Thanks. Thank you. Looking forward to seeing you. Thank you." I put the phone down, cleared my throat again, and started up the van. Ethan was still sleeping, my name was still John Nichols, and I was on my way to play basketball. Things were going to be okay.

Kyle Baker lived directly across the street from us and used to spend time, quite a bit of time, shooting hoops with Ethan. Their friendship had originally been court mandated. A few years back Kyle had been arrested for plowing into a parked and, fortunately, empty car in downtown Wilton. While drinking was suspected, no official charges were ever filed against him. The local Chicago media had a field day, however; Kyle was Illinois's "Mr. Basketball" — the state's best basketball player. A hailstorm of negative press ensued. Consequently, the Wilton police were forced to come up with some form of punishment to quell the mounting controversy. While I was never privy to all the backroom machinations, the court decided that one of his many penances would be community service, and that one of those many services would be to spend time, four hours a week for six months, teaching a special-needs boy from Wilton, Ethan Nichols, how to play basketball.

After some discussion, Mary and I agreed to this. We were going through our divorce at that time, and both of the girls were out of the house, so any help we could get with Ethan, we took. Besides, we knew Kyle. He had come over a few times before the accident to play with Ethan in the driveway, and we felt he was basically a good kid.

To our delight, the arrangement worked. Ethan lived for his visits with Kyle (which Mary and I were required to dutifully report to the police) and loved playing basketball with him. Long after his probation had ended, Kyle continued to come around and play with Ethan, teaching him how to shoot, how to dribble. During his senior year, Ethan and I went to all of Kyle's games, sitting right behind the bench, staying as long as Ethan lasted.

I hadn't seen much of Kyle since he left for the University of Louisville and, when we met up with him that night at a park somewhere just off campus, I was surprised to see him sporting a buzz cut. His floppy hair had been a trademark.

"Hey, Mr. Nichols. Hey, Ethan!" he yelled as we approached. The park's basketball court was well lit and still glistening from the rain.

I hadn't told Ethan we were meeting Kyle — the anticipation would have been too great — so when he saw his old friend, he went predictably crazy.

"Kyle! Kyle! Kyle!" he screamed. He dropped my hand and ran, stiff-legged, over to him.

The two met in an awkward embrace under the basket, Kyle patting him on the back and smiling, a little embarrassed.

"Hey, buddy. Want to shoot some hoops?"

"How. Many. Me. Make?"

"You're going to make fifty baskets," Kyle said.

"How. Many. You. Make?"

"I'm going to make ten." Kyle looked over at me. "Is it okay?"

"Yes, of course." I remembered to reach out and shake his hand. "What's with the hair?"

He shrugged. "Was getting in the way."

"I never knew you had freckles. When did that start? I guess we could never see your face."

He shrugged again, smiled. He was a

classic-looking all-American kid, right off the streets of Mayberry: blue eyes, blond hair, a major "aw-shucks" dimple-smile thing going. His appearance was deceiving, though; on the court, dude was stone-cold.

"How's school going?"

"Okay."

"How's the team looking?"

"We'll be pretty good. Tyrell is coming back, which kind of surprised everyone, and just about everyone else is too. We lost Tommy, though."

"Herr? The big guy? Did he get drafted? I don't remember."

Kyle shook his head. "He just signed on with a team in Croatia."

"Croatia? I thought he went late second round."

"He'll be okay, he's still making a lot of money."

"Kid could jump. And he was great with those outlet passes. Kevin Love good." I forgot how much I liked talking basketball with Kyle. Made me feel young. "Well, we watch your games when we can. That Kansas game was tough. Ethan and I watched that one at Rafferty's. Remember, Ethan? They let us sit at the bar?"

Ethan had lost interest in our conversation and was picking at his fingernails.

"You played well in that game."

"I missed that free throw."

"You made the second one. Tied it."

Kyle looked off to the side, across the park. I silently cursed myself for having brought that game up: Louisville had lost in overtime. "We'll be okay this year," he said.

"Well, even though you should have gone to Illinois, we're all proud of you. You're the most famous person to come out of Wilton."

"I don't know. I think Mindy is probably the most famous person to come out of Wilton. She's really funny. That diaper thing." He turned to Ethan. "But you're pretty famous too," he said. "Ready to shoot some hoops? Make it rain?"

Ethan looked up from his fingers. "Rain!"

"Do you want to play?" he asked me.

"What? Oh God, no. I'll sit down. You guys go ahead."

"You sure? I remember you being a shooter, Mr. Nichols."

I appreciated the compliment more than I should have, but resisted the opportunity to embarrass myself. "No, thanks. I'm beat."

"Some other guys might come too," Kyle said.

"More reason for me to sit."

I wearily made my over to a nearby bench

and collapsed with a thud, exhausted. I couldn't believe how long the day had been; the pool in Indianapolis was an absolute lifetime ago. I sighed and stretched out my legs. I would have to do it all over again tomorrow.

"Hoops!" Ethan yelled.

"Hoops," I said, but not quite as enthusiastically.

"Illini!"

"No, we're not playing that tonight."

"What's he want to do?" Kyle asked.

"Nothing, this thing we do, this game. He'll be fine. You can just shoot with him."

I watched Ethan take up a position just inside the free-throw line. Once situated, he immediately began making shots: one became two, two became three, three became four, the ball flying in a high, looping arc.

"Man, I forgot how good he was at this," Kyle said, smiling. "He could teach me."

Ethan kept this up for a while, showing off, I suspect, while Kyle and I looked on. Finally, after a few misses, he bounced the ball to Kyle and took a seat on the ground, half-way between my bench and the basket.

"Hoops!" he commanded.

"Okay, buddy," Kyle said. "Guess it's my turn."

Sitting there in the warm Kentucky night

83

while Kyle shot, watching the ball sail smooth and pure against the darkening sky, I felt equilibrium returning. Each time Kyle made a basket and each time Ethan cheered, my head began to clear and my spirits rose. I sat back. I had made it this far.

As Kyle shot, I said a silent prayer of thanks. Like some kind of angel, he had descended, picked me up off the ground, and dusted me off. This was, fortunately, not an uncommon occurrence. Over the years, numerous times, too many times to count, just as I was about to reach my breaking point, just when I thought I couldn't take another minute, another second, out of nowhere — at the grocery store, at the park, at restaurants — angels, Ethan's angels, would appear and save us: strangers in stores would stop to talk to Ethan; neighbors took him for a walks. Once a truck driver in a parking lot, some-one I had never seen before, or ever again, gave Ethan his baseball cap. Another time, while Ethan was in the midst of a meltdown in a parking lot, a policeman distracted him by letting him sit in a squad car. These acts, simple and impulsive, kept me going, re-affirmed my belief in God, in a universe that could, at least at times, mean well. I stretched out my legs farther, exhaled. We had a long way to go; I hoped there were a lot of angels still out there.

About a half hour later three other players arrived, emerging one by one from the shadows that ringed the lighted court. Two of them, giants, wore easy smiles, but the third and shortest, was expressionless. I immediately recognized him as Tyrell Dee. Big. Time. Player. I sat up.

"Ethan, move over here," I said. "Get closer."

"He's okay!" Kyle yelled.

The two Bigs gave Ethan hesitant smiles then nodded hello in my direction before taking their first shots. Tyrell took no interest, however. He stood sullenly near the basket, head down, texting with one hand. All the boys were wearing oversize shorts that hung low, but Tyrell's shorts were outrageous, a comedy, hovering just inches above his ankles. He wasn't as tall as Kyle — I put him at six-two — but in his sleeveless white T-shirt, I could see the coiled power in his arms and chest. The kid was ripped.

I was apprehensive at first and a little embarrassed; I hoped Kyle hadn't asked his teammates to come on our behalf. But after a few minutes I began to relax and enjoy the show. Other than Tyrell Dee, the players clearly didn't mind being there.

Ethan scooted over by me, and we both watched on in silence, bordering on awe as the players shot away.

"Dunk!" Ethan yelled.

"Ethan, shhh!" I said.

Kyle heard Ethan and obliged, dunking the ball with both hands, his mouth wide open with effort. This was followed immediately by another slam, by one of the Bigs. Within seconds a full-fledged dunking contest was under way, the iron backboard shaking as if it were in a hurricane. I sat speechless, not sure, once again, if the players were putting on a show just for Ethan, or if this was some off-season nightly ritual. Regardless, Ethan was more than appreciative, answering each dunk with applause and an exclamation. "Dunk!" he cried.

Soon a small but growing crowd of people, mostly students, began to form on corners of the court: We were in Louisville and this was the UofL basketball team after all. I suspected they drew a crowd wherever they went.

Tyrell Dee remained off to the side, absorbed with his phone, but Kyle and the two Bigs continued to bang away while people took pictures and ooohed and ahhed. After one particularly loud, rim-rattling dunk, Ethan jumped up and screamed at the absolute top of his lungs, "Wow! Wow! Wow!"

This last exclamation caught Tyrell's attention. He finally looked up from his phone and took Ethan in, his face still blank.

"Give me the ball, man," he said to Kyle. He dropped his phone on the grass by the side of the court, hitched up his shorts, and bounced the ball a couple of times, before taking full flight. Whirling a semicircle in the air, he slammed it down spectacularly with one hand. Then he pointed at Ethan.

"Wow!" Ethan quietly said. He was stunned and maybe a little scared by the spectacle.

"Wow," I agreed.

Tyrell Dee walked over to Ethan and slapped him five. "See, that's how it done," he said. "Don't pay no attention to these others, don't be wowing them. They all be playin' in Croatia next year, man. Their mommas gonna have to get some kind of super international dish, see their games two in the morning. They say, 'Oh, look, there's DeMarcus! He just scored for Team Croatia, I so proud!'"

He said this last sentence in a falsetto voice, and even though DeMarcus was a seven-foot-tall, four-hundred-pound beast, I couldn't help but laugh.

"Yeah, where you be playing next year, TD?" Kyle asked

Tyrell sauntered back onto the court. "You know where I be, Sweet LA. Who you think I just be talking to? Kobe, just beggin' my ass to come out there, resurrect the situation."

"You be playin' for DC," DeMarcus said.

"Ain't playing for no DC. I ain't no *Wizard,* man, tell you that right now. LA gonna trade for me. Hey, yo, watch this, man!" He pointed to Ethan, then threw a ball against the backboard, caught the rebound in midair with one hand, and slammed it home. More ooohs and aaahs from the crowd, more phone cameras flashing.

"Wow!" Ethan yelled.

"Wow is right. I *am* wow." Tyrell walked back over to us. He wasn't even breathing hard. "Yo, Baker, what's his name, man?"

"Ethan," Kyle said.

"Ethan, you know talent. What you hangin' out with Baker for? He probably be playin' in Iceland next year. Or be a hockey player. Go play for the Canucks somewhere, man. Be a *Ca-nuck.* " Again he slapped a beaming Ethan five and looked at me.

"All right I give him a ball?"

I was speechless over the offer. "Yes. But

you don't have to."

" 'S all right. Gotta support my fan base. DeMarcus, give me a ball. Over here, man, come on. Give me a good one. That one right there. No, that one, yeah. The one in your hands, man. You *holdin'* it. Come on. Over here."

DeMarcus flipped Tyrell a ball, and he signed it with a marker from his pocket. "You take care of that," he said, handing the ball to Ethan. "Gonna be *worth* when I go next year, man. Just don't let any of these others sign it. They probably write something in Croatian, depreciate the *worth.*"

I laughed again; the guy was funny.

"Shit, TD, he always got a pen on him," DeMarcus said, bouncing a ball and smiling.

"Ain't no point leaving home without one," Tyrell said, slipping the pen away. "Ain't that right?" He slapped Ethan five one more time and asked DeMarcus for another ball. "Yo, Ethan, man," he said. "Watch this close now. You learnin' from the best."

"Wow!"

"You got that right," Tyrell Dee said. "I *am* wow."

After Kyle made me take a few shots to

show the others I once played D1 ball (for the record, not that it matters, I went nine for twelve from downtown); and after I took close to a hundred pictures of Ethan with the players (and one with just Tyrell Dee and me); and after Ethan gave everyone way too many good-bye high fives because he can't do fist bumps; and after I gave Kyle an awkward but very much-deserved bro hug; and after Ethan and I made our way to the Marriott East on the outskirts of town where we had a quick dinner in the bar and watched some *SportsCenter,* we called it an early night.

"Night, dude-man," I said after I brushed his teeth and tucked him in.

"Leave. Now."

"You'll get no argument from me there." I kissed him on the forehead, stripped off my clothes, and fell into my bed. There would be no need for free throws or bourbon or *Blue Highways* tonight. I was exhausted and sensed a night of good sleep on the horizon.

"Good night, Ethan."

I was just drifting off when I heard Karen's voice, and jerked awake. *Daddy.* She had called me Daddy on the phone. Daddy. She hadn't called me that in twenty years.

4

I forced myself to wait until six the next morning before calling Mary. Borrowing a page from her no-foreplay, no-bullshit, in-me-or-off-me playbook, I jumped right in. "What's wrong with Karen?" I whispered.

"Why? Did you talk to her?" Mary asked.

I pulled the sheet over my head in an attempt to muffle my voice. Ethan was still asleep. "No. She tried to call, but I couldn't talk. I was in the van, driving, and things weren't going well."

"When are you going to get here?"

"I'm not sure. We're not moving as quickly as I had hoped."

"Where are you?

"We're getting there."

"Where are you?"

I paused. "Louisville."

It was Mary's turn to pause. "Kentucky?"

"We have a ways to go."

There was a cold silence. Then, "Why are

you doing this? You should be here right now. You should be here. Karen needs you. The family needs you. You're the father, John. The father."

"You know, Mary, just for the record, and if you remember, I always said she should have gotten married at home, in Wilton or Chicago. Not in South Carolina. I said that from the start. This whole thing . . . I mean, no one is from South Carolina. Roger isn't, his family isn't. That might be the one state they don't have a house in."

"That doesn't help her now."

"Why does she need help? What's wrong? What's going on?"

"She and Roger had a fight. A big one. Something happened. I'm not sure what."

I digested this then blurted out, "Let me ask you something. Do you think there's any possibility that maybe —"

"He's not gay! I know that's what you think. You think everyone is gay!"

"I don't think everyone is gay."

"You think your own daughter is gay."

I peeked out from under my sheet. Ethan was still asleep, clutching Red and Grandpa Bear, one in each arm. "I don't think everyone is gay," I said again. "It's just, he made that stink about the centerpieces and how important they are to a wedding. He e-mailed me photos of flowers. Who does that? What guy e-mails flowers?"

"John. Stop it. Just stop it! I don't have time for this."

"Where is she?"

"She's in her room."

"Is Mindy there? Can't she talk to her?"

"Mindy? She's not here yet, not that she would help."

"What do you mean, she's not there? She should be there by now."

"She's not here. She said she's coming Friday."

"Friday? Unbelievable. Friday? God damn her! Well, listen, I'll be there as soon as I can. We'll drive faster and longer. I'll be there in a couple of days."

"Try to call her."

"Mindy?"

"Karen. The one getting married, John. Karen."

"I'll call her now."

"Don't call her now. She's sleeping. She took a pill."

"A pill? Why is she taking pills?"

"Call her later. I have to go."

"Wait!"

She was gone.

Throughout his life, Ethan had gone

through some terrible phases during which he demonstrated uncontrollable, compulsive behavior. Tics, the doctors called them. This was another term we didn't take to. Tics implied something minor, harmless: a twitching of the eye, a slight shaking of the head.

Ethan's tics were nothing like that, and we had endured them all: his Yelping Phase in which he yelled at the top of his lungs unexpectedly in public; his Licking Phase where he tongued anyone and everything in which he came into contact; Question Mode, which featured him repeatedly asking, dozens of times in the same day, the exact same three or four questions in the exact same order: "What Time Is It? Do Now? Where Eat? Where Sit? What Time Is It? Do Now? Where Eat? Where Sit? What Time . . ." His Hand-in-the-Mouth Phase was arguably his worst. It involved him sticking his hand down his throat until he gagged and sometimes threw up; his Fingernail-Picking Phase was fairly benign, since a lot of people fooled with their nails; and finally Ethan had his Squatting Phase, which had him kneeling down in public and feeling the ground with his hands. (This started during the summer when hot sidewalks intrigued him.) Mindy, addicted to old TV shows, referred to this last act as "pulling a Tonto," in honor of the Lone Ranger's sidekick, who frequently felt the earth to determine if horses were approaching. "Dad, he's pulling a Tonto again," she would yell from the driveway. "Hey, Ethan, is Iron Horse coming?"

Over time, the tics, save for the fingernail pickings and occasional licking, all passed, though they could temporarily flair up for a few days here and there.

Unfortunately, while we were walking down the hall to breakfast in the hotel, Tonto reared his head.

"Come on, Ethan, get up, let's go. Come on. Up!" I placed my hands under his shoulders and gently pulled him to a standing position. He was squatting on the ground.

We walked a few more feet, then down he went again, both hands flat on the carpet, his face pensive as a doctor's while listening to a stethoscope. I knelt next to him.

"Ethan, the ground isn't hot. Come on, let's eat. Come on. It's nice inside."

A man in a dark suit, swinging a briefcase, turned the corner and walked toward us. He paused when he got close, and since he was a normal man in the middle of a normal morning, he asked a normal question.

"Lose something?"

Ethan and I were now both on all fours. "Nope," I replied.

"Oh." The man stepped close to the wall and passed.

When he was gone, I tried once again to pull Ethan to his feet. "Okay, let's go, buddy. Up. Now."

We took a few more steps, then once again he sank.

"Please, Ethan!"

We essentially crawled to the coffee shop, where the smell of food, bacon in particular, seemed to overpower his compulsion. When we approached the hostess, he finally stood and allowed her to lead us to a table by a window.

"Thank. You!" he said cheerfully when she left. Then he handed me a menu, said, "It's. Nice. Outside," very conversationally, and politely reached for his water.

I ignored him. Karen, Mary, Tonto. The day was off to a bad start. I checked my phone, scanned the restaurant for our waitress.

"It's. Nice. Outside."

I opened my menu. "Yes," I said petulantly, "I suppose."

"Nice! Outside!"

I closed my menu, glared at him. "Okay,

fine, okay, it's nice outside, whatever. It's perfect. Now, just drink your water and please try to be quiet. I need to think."

"Why. Mad?"

"I'm not mad."

Ethan eyed me suspiciously. Anger always fascinated him. Though he frequently misread it, confused it with other emotions, he liked to explore its root cause, which, more often than not, was him. "Why. Mad?"

I took a deep breath. "I'm not mad. I'm worried. It's not your fault. I'm worried about Karen. And your mom is upset with me. Why, I don't know. Your mom is something else sometimes. She just . . ."

He searched me with his big brown eyes.

"Listen, I'm not mad at you. I love you." I reached out and patted him on the top of his hand.

"Shut. Up. Idiot."

I opened my menu again. "Let's just eat, okay?"

We had just finished ordering when my phone went off.

"Dad, where are you?"

Mindy. Another problem orbiting my cluttered universe. "Oh, it's you."

"Mom says you're only in Kentucky."

"Mom says you're only in New York."

We didn't say anything.

"Why are you only in New York?" I asked.

"Why are you only in Kentucky?"

"I'm closer to South Carolina than you are," I said.

"I don't know about that, Dad. I just checked Google Maps and, *technically,* if I stand at the southernmost point of my apartment and lean —"

"Mindy! Just get down there. Things are hard enough."

There was another silence.

"So how is he?" she asked. "How's he doing?"

I glanced up. The "he" in question was now absorbed by his nails. "Busy."

"What's he doing?"

"He's doing a crossword puzzle. Here, talk to him."

Ethan looked up from his fingers, surprised, and took the phone after I thrust it at him. "Hi!" He listened intently, his eyes narrow in apparent thought. Then he said, "Shut. Up. Idiot," and handed the phone right back to me.

"Always good catching up with him," Mindy said.

I took a swallow of coffee, wished it were stronger. "So, what's going on with your big sister? What's this about some kind of fight?"

"No idea what's going on."

"Nothing?"

"Nothing."

I took another gulp of coffee. "When are you coming down?"

"Soon."

"How soon?

"I'm trying to figure out my travel."

"Mindy, please just book a flight! You're not going to another planet. You're going to South Carolina."

"That's another planet, Dad."

"They picked this date around your schedule. Do you remember that? They waited until you were off for the summer so you could attend."

"I never asked them to do that. Besides, she doesn't even want me there. She'd just be embarrassed if I weren't there."

The waitress placed our orange juice down on the table, and Ethan attacked his glass.

"You're her sister. Her younger sister, and you should be there. And don't come empty-handed. Make sure to bring something. A wedding gift. Buy something."

"I hope she's registered at Newark Airport, because that's where I'm flying out of."

"Mindy." I shook my head and pried

Ethan's juice away from him. It was a huge glass, and he was draining it fast. "You know, I have it hard enough."

Mindy was quiet. "How's he been?"

"Yesterday was bad."

"How bad?" Her voice changed, softened. When it came to Ethan, we usually circled the wagons.

"Bad. He just pulled a Tonto."

"God, Tonto."

"I'm not sure what I was thinking."

"Can't you get on a flight somewhere?"

"I have all our things. And what would I do with the van? Too late for that. I'll make it. We'll be okay. Survive and advance."

Mindy was quiet again. "Where do you think you'll be tonight? How far can you get?"

"I don't know. Knoxville. It's a long drive, but I think I can make it. That's where I'm aiming, at least."

"Knoxville, Tennessee?

"Yes, that's where Knoxville is, yes."

"Knoxville, Tennessee. Okay," she said. "I'll meet you there. We can drive the rest of the way together."

"What? No, don't, don't. I don't need you to come. Your mother needs you more. And your sister. We'll be okay, really. Just get to Charleston."

"Where are you staying in Knoxville?"

I sighed. I had no energy to argue with Mindy. Besides, part of me really wanted some company, some help. I was, in fact, desperate for it. "A Marriott. I don't have the address on me."

"I'll find it. I'll just tell the cab driver to take me to the tall building with electricity. There's probably only one in Knoxville."

"You don't have to do this."

"Tell Red Bear I'll meet her in the hotel bar. Bye, Dad."

I shook my head, then slid Ethan's orange juice glass back to him. "Bye, sweetheart."

After an early but good lunch in a ghost of town called Williamsburg; and after an impromptu, very short, and very disappointing stop at Cumberland Falls (the falls, Ethan and I agreed, weren't all that impressive); and after an impromptu, not very short, and very rewarding poo-poo stop at another Cracker Barrel (his crap, Ethan and I agreed, was very impressive); and after a stop at a McDonald's for Sprites where the bears vocalized their love and respect for me (Red Bear: "I know I speak for all of us when I say there is no finer man or father than you, John Nichols" — me: "Well, thank you, Red Bear, thank you" — Red Bear:

"Now . . . you wouldn't happen to have anything stronger than Sprite, would you?"), we arrived in Knoxville right on schedule. Consequently, I was in good spirits when we pulled into the parking lot of the cavernous Marriott on the banks of the Tennessee River.

"Well, that was a *Blue Highway* kind of morning," I said as we bounded up to the reception desk. "We got a chance to see a waterfall, have lunch. You were good today, buddy, real good. And now we're by a big river. Lots. Of. Water. Don't. Fall. In!"

"Yes. Ma'am!"

The clerk behind the desk, a young guy with thick-framed glasses and too much aftershave, glanced up from behind his computer and gave me the trying-to-act normal-around-Ethan smile. I appreciated the effort.

I smiled back at him. "We'd like a room on the first floor."

He punched some keys, looked up again, and nodded. "Thank you for being a Marriott Gold member, Mr. Nichols."

My chest swelled, and I bowed my head. "You are most welcome," I said humbly.

Since we were early, we had to cool our heels while they readied our room. Ethan was compliant, absorbed in an old batteryless cell phone I had brought from home, a favorite of his. He punched the numbers officiously, mouth open, as we sat in some chairs just off the bar. Blessedly, there had been no trace of Tonto since breakfast.

"You like that phone, huh? Watch the roaming charges though!"

I sat back and watched Ethan work the phone. His face was serious but content as he pressed more numbers and then pretended to listen.

"Who are you calling?"

"Mom."

"What's she up to?"

"Poo-poo."

"Good for her. Give her my best. Tell her I love her and always will."

"Yes."

"Do you think she loves me?"

"Shut. Up. Idiot."

"Did she tell you to tell me that?"

"Yes."

"She's the best. Such a sweetheart." I smiled and continued to watch him. Calm, happy. I never took his quiet moments for granted. I sat back, crossed my legs.

"Who are you calling now?"

"Mindy!"

"Old Mindy. Funny, funny, famous, little Mindy. You don't think she's gay, do you?"

"Yes!"

"Really? Not that it matters. I mean, it doesn't, right? I would like grandkids though. I know that's selfish, but I would. I guess she could still have them somehow though."

"Yes!"

"Adopt or something."

"Yes!"

"You would be Uncle Ethan, and I would be Grandpa. No, I mean, I would be *Super* Grandpa. Hey, here comes Super Grandpa! That has a nice ring to it. Super Grandpa."

Ethan smiled, put the phone down, then said, "Oh!" and picked it right back up.

"Who you calling now?"

"Um, Karen!"

"Karen?" I sat up. "That's right. I should call her too."

Just as I was pulling my own phone out, it went off. The number wasn't immediately familiar, and even though it was a risk — Rita was still at large — I answered.

"Hello?"

"Here's Johnny!"

My heart sank. "Hey, Sal." I stifled the "Oh, shit!" that had started to come out.

"Sal!" Upon hearing his uncle's name, Ethan tried to grab the phone. I pressed the speaker button and gladly gave it up.

104

"Sal!" Ethan cried again.

Sal's Bronx baritone filled the air. "There he is, Mr. Big! Is it nice outside, or what? Ten to one, it's nice outside."

"Nice. Outside. Hot."

"I don't know where the hell you are, but yeah, it's fucking hot here."

"Sal, watch what you say."

"You been a good boy?" Sal asked. "Walking the line?"

"Yes!"

"Yeah? When you get here, we're gonna eat a lot of pickles. Live it up."

"Where. Sally. Be?"

"She's here. I'm in a hotel. Kind of a hotel."

"Where. Karen?'

"She's sleeping, buddy; she's up in her room. Listen, you make sure you're a good boy, okay? We'll play catch or hoops when you get here. And you call me anytime you want, okay?"

"Okay!"

"Now, who's your favorite uncle?"

"Sal!"

"And who loves you, baby?"

"Sal!"

"And who takes you to football games, Bulls games, Cubs games, the track?"

"You took Ethan to the track?"

"Sal!"

"Book 'em, Danno! Now, let me talk to your father. Put the professor on."

Ethan handed me the phone.

"Where the hell are you?" Sal asked. "I'm drinking alone out here."

"I'm in Knoxville."

"Jesus, John, that sounds far."

"It's not that far. So, how's everything there? How's Karen? Is everything okay?"

"She's all right. Some shit going on though. Something."

"You mean between Karen and Roger? What, what is it?"

"They had a blowout, a real knock-me-down. Fifteen rounds."

"What exactly happened?"

"That's all I know. Details are sketchy, you know, the fog of war. Hey, how is he doing on that ride?"

"He's fine. How's Karen?"

"You know, I got to be honest here, I think you're crazy driving with him."

"Where's Karen?"

"In her room. Everything will blow over. The Jaw and her, they gotta work things out. Listen, I gotta warn you about something before you get here though. There's something else you should know about."

More trouble. I braced myself.

"This place, this inn or whatever, the rooms, they don't have no TVs."

Sal paused, waiting, I'm sure, for me to share in his disbelief, raise my voice, scream, "What the hell?" My hulking brother-in-law held very few tenants in life, and one of them, the one he clung to, the one he would take to his deathbed, was that any flat surface required a flat-screen.

"You believe that, John? I mean, what kind of bullshit is that?"

"It's a historic inn."

"What's that supposed to mean? TVs aren't historical? What the hell — I watched, what, the first moonwalk on TV. The Towers go down. *Roots.*"

"*Roots.*"

"So I bought a TV and had them put it in my room."

I digested this before repeating, "You bought a TV and had them put it in your room."

"That's what I just said."

"You bought a TV and had them put it in your room."

"Hello? You hear me okay?"

"Why. Mad?"

"I bought a flat-screen. Small thirty-two-inch, LG. Nothing fancy. And when I'm done, they're gonna ship it back home. I can get one for you, too, if you want. I got a guy down here, in Charleston, this Korean, if you believe."

"I can't believe that."

"They got Koreans everywhere, John."

"The TV, I can't believe that."

"You sound like my wife. What you want me to do all day, huh? How many times I'm gotta stare at the goddamn ocean? I got news for you: that thing never changes. I'm going stir-crazy here. Everyone's walking around crying here."

"Who's crying?"

"No one. Everyone."

"Can you be a little more specific?"

"I don't know details; I just told you. They're keeping me in the dark. Shutting me out. That's why I need a TV. The rooms are already wired for cable, which is very ironic, when you stop to think about it."

I felt the familiar pain of a Sal headache coming on. "I have to go."

"Where you going? What's the rush? What, suddenly you got plans? You're in Knots Landing for Christ's sake."

"I'm in Knox — Listen, tell Karen that I'm thinking about her. Can you do that for me?"

"You want me to wake her with that urgent message? Hold on, I'll run up there

108

and bust down her door. Hey, Karen, wake up, your dad is thinking about you."

"I'm going."

"Put Ethan back on, then. I want to talk to him some more. He's the only one who listens to me. Only one who gives a shit."

"Fine." I passed the phone back to Ethan, who eagerly took it with both hands.

"Hello! Hello! Hello!"

"There he is, Mr. Big!" I heard Sal say as Ethan squealed with delight.

As soon as we got to our room, I started making calls: Karen, Mary, Sally, then Karen again and then again, but got nothing but voice mail. I briefly considered calling the Jaw, but then cooled down and decided to wait for someone to call me back instead.

So we spent the rest of the afternoon killing time, watching baseball at the bar, swimming in the outdoor pool, and briefly touring the Women's Basketball Hall of Fame, which was conveniently located right across the street and featured, much to Ethan's delight, a *huge* basketball at its entrance.

As the day progressed, I grew increasingly agitated about Karen. Why was no one calling? Was this by design? Was I being punished for not being there? Or was I simply not important enough anymore, my place in the family dynamic forever diminished? I didn't know. What I did know was that the silence was worrisome.

I considered, but decided against exploring Knoxville, choosing instead to stay at the hotel for dinner. One of the many Ethan Rules I strictly adhered to was when things are going well, don't press your luck. So it was cheeseburgers and fries and pickles at the bar, then back to our room.

After a final attempt to reach Karen and Mary, I brushed Ethan's teeth and helped him into bed. It was just past eight, but I could tell he was tired.

"You were really a good guy today," I said. "Thank you."

"Leave. Now."

"Really good."

"Leave. Now."

"As you wish." I turned the lights off and waited for the sound of his heavy breathing, which usually commenced soon after his head hit the pillow. Sure enough, a minute or two later, I heard it, soft and sweet.

I relaxed. Even in the most turbulent times, the depths of the War Years, once Ethan was down, he was *down*. So nights were our salvation, a chance to pay the bills, run a few late errands, wash all the surfaces Ethan had licked, and try to fix all the things he had broken that day. As the girls got older, we gradually became nocturnal, staying up later and later. We played board games, ordered pizza, watched movies. Mindy once said that at eight thirty every night we became a normal family. It was a painfully accurate observation.

The nights were also when I used to write, or at least try to. I had published a novel in my thirties: a short, funny, pathos-filled coming-of-age story about a young man in the Reagan eighties working at an accounting firm who steals inside stock information and plays the market. I had written the bulk of it in the evenings right before and after Ethan was born, before the troubles. It had been published by a local university press — then, after some pretty good reviews, later by a larger, New York house. The New York publisher, encouraged by solid, if not exactly spectacular sales, offered me a contract for a second book.

Despite dozens of attempts, false starts, first chapters, titles, outlines, extended deadlines, and more false starts, that book never came. Ethan's issues soon surfaced, and the ensuing chaos made it impossible to find the time, energy, or solitude to work. At least that was what I told myself, as well as my publisher and my newly acquired agent, both of whom eventually left me.

I lay on the bed and wondered about Ethan's irregular ninth chromosome. I wondered, not for the first time, if that chromosome was normal, if it didn't appear more times than it should, if I would have gone on to write other books. I then wondered if that extra cell was a convenient excuse for my literary failings — maybe all my failings.

I got out of bed, booted up my laptop. I was too tired to beat myself up that night.

Nothing much to report on the school front. Football practice began in five weeks. The boys cross-country team would be looking to defend its state championship this season. The first faculty meeting was set for August 19. Time to do *all that* again. I uttered an interior groan and returned to bed. No relief here.

The school year, nine and a-half months of purgatory, was barreling toward me like a runaway freight, and I looked to it with trepidation, if not outright dread.

It wasn't always this way. There was a time when I looked forward to the school year, to standing in front of a roomful of blank-faced kids inspired to inspire. I took pride in what I did, saw every day as a challenge. Occasionally, I wore a bow tie to class, talked in various goofy, foreign accents, did wild, interpretive readings that made my kids laugh. I was into things: I challenged the coach of the boys basketball team to a game of HORSE for charity (I won), and challenged the coach of the girls basketball team to a game of HORSE for charity (I purposely lost). For years I helped publish a funny student newspaper, directed the student comedy show, was the funny emcee at the annual basketball banquet. Three times I was voted most popular faculty member at Wilton Township, an honor that thrilled me.

Over time, however, gradually then suddenly, my desire to be the perfect teacher, cool and funny, faded and, more often than not, I found myself staring at the clock, waiting for the 2:35 dismissal bell. Ethan, obviously, had something to do with this. Irreverent quips about Shakespeare or Steinbeck or Principal Hegenderfer don't fly off the tongue as quickly when your youngest child is trying to gag himself to death. And the girls leaving home, first Karen then Mindy, hastened the transformation. Once they were gone, Mary and I were left with just Ethan. No more Karen cheerleading, no more Mindy onstage. Just Ethan, my man, no distractions, no diversions, just Ethan. It took a toll. Even though I loved him fiercely, things got dimmer when the girls were gone, things got sucked out of me, and Mr. Involved morphed into Mr. Going Through the Motions. Two years ago changes were finally made, and I was dispatched to play right field, otherwise known as "roving substitute teacher," where I bounced from class to class, gazing out windows while I sat at other teachers' desks and waited for my full pension to kick in.

I had started my adult life, my career, with two clear and, I thought, attainable goals: be a writer and be a good teacher. The realization that I was no longer either made for a not-very-good moment in the Marriott in Knoxville on the banks of the Tennessee. So, in the quiet of my dark room, I tried to focus on something positive.

The wedding would be nice. It would be good to see some of my family again. An only child, I looked forward to reconnecting with my handful of cousins. I would work hard on my toast, be the hit of the party, dance with Karen, maybe make more headway with Mary.

But my mind inevitably broke free of my leash and scampered off to sniff out problems, worries. I wasn't sure I liked Roger, the man my oldest baby, my queen bee, Karen, was marrying. I feared him pompous and insincere. Yet here I was, standing by while he took her away. Then, after she and my family disappeared, after all the commotion, the music, the dancing, the distraction was over, I would be left to enact the final phases of my secret and painful Overall Plan.

I pushed out of bed and returned to the computer to check the weather in Camden. Then I went to the Ocean View Web site to see what the main house was having for dinner: chicken, mashed potatoes, and carrots. I grew alarmed. *Ethan hated carrots.* I quickly clicked off and grabbed Stinky Bear, and propped him up on my stomach.

"You think I can go through with this?" I whispered.

Stinky stared back, button eyes blank.

My phone woke me sometime later. I groped around on my hands and knees in the darkness before finding it on Ethan's side of the bed. It was close to eleven o'clock, and I had been asleep for almost two hours.

"Hello?" I whispered.

"Hi, I'm here."

"Where?"

"At the airport. Just landed in Nashville."

"You mean Knoxville, I hope."

"Fuck! Hold on." I heard Mindy saying something to someone, her voice animated, muffled. "Yeah. I mean Knoxville. I'm waiting for a cab or whatever they have down here, a stagecoach. Did you get me a room?"

"No, I guess I thought you'd just stay with us."

"Guess again."

"I'll get you a room."

"Is the restaurant still open? I'm starving."

"I'm sure the bar is. I bet you can get something there."

"I'll be there soon. Can you meet me?"

I glanced over at Ethan. "I can probably sneak out for a few minutes. He never wakes up."

"Okay, I'll see you then."

I checked on Ethan, and then, on a whim, picked up Red Bear and slipped out.

Sitting in a high-back chair, off in the corner of the lobby, I waited for Mindy. And in less than fifteen minutes, there she was, making her entrance, stage left: fast walking, arms pumping, hint of a smirk on her pixie face. When I saw her, I felt a surge of happiness, relief. My little Mindy, my little buddy, my coconspirator, my sidekick, my best audience, was here. When you observed your children from afar, when you saw them making their way in the world without you, even if it was just walking across a hotel lobby floor, that was when you saw them perfectly and that was when, I suspected, you might love them the most.

I watched her. Like her mother, she was small and thin and wore her dark hair pulled back in a permanent ponytail that allowed her large green eyes and turned-up nose plenty of space to be noticed and admired. Mary used to call her Sweet Pixie when she was a girl, which was misleading because Mindy did not meet any definition of the word *sweet*. (Note: As a toddler, one of her first spoken words was *fuck,* a word she picked up from her articulate and emotional Uncle Sal, and one she consistently utilized in all its various permutations throughout life.)

As she approached the bar, I noticed she was wearing her trademark evil elf attire: black hoodie and tight, black jeans, the uniform she had been adopted some years ago upon moving to New York.

I stood when I heard her laugh. "I'll have what's she's having," she said, pointing to Red Bear, who was sitting submerged in a barstool, a glass of wine in front of her. The bartender, a nice young kid who had eagerly played along, smiled.

"She's having a Chardonnay," he said.

"Perfect." She turned as I approached. "Hey, Daddy-o!"

"Hi, sweetie." I hugged her hard and gave her forehead a peck. "How was your trip?"

"Great. Hey, my first trip to Knoxville." She glanced around the bar, which was standard glass, brass, and fern trees. It was empty, with the exception of two overweight men in the corner, one of whom had his head on a table. "And I have to tell you," she said in a stage whisper, "so far, I'm *impressed.*"

"Where's your things?"

"I left them at the front desk." She pulled off her sweatshirt to reveal a black T-shirt, and we both sat down. "He asleep?"

"Yes."

"Is it all right leaving him?"

"He's fine."

When the bartender brought Mindy her drink, I reached over and took Red Bear's glass.

"So, have you talked to anyone, your mom? Karen?"

Mindy drained her wine in three gulps, then motioned to the bartender for another.

"Slow down," I said.

118

"The wedding's off," she said, wiping the corners of her mouth.

There was no way I'd heard her right. "I'm sorry, what?"

"Just don't flip out on me. I can't have anyone else flip out on me. I'm just the messenger. I know nothing."

"What are you talking about?"

"The wedding is off, Dad. It's off. They broke it off. I just got off the phone with Mom. She told me. Then Aunt Sally told me. Then Uncle Sal told me. Then all of the cousins called me. At the airport and in the cab, everyone kept calling."

"What?"

"It's off."

I squeezed my eyes closed. "Okay, all right, I need you to slow down. Let me understand this: there's no wedding? They're not getting married?"

"There's no wedding, and they're not getting married. That's the sum total of what I know. Don't flip out."

"I'm not flipping . . . I'm just . . . Good God! Poor Karen! Who called it off? Did he call it off? Did he?"

"No. She did."

"What happened? Why?"

"He was screwing around. They caught him."

"What? What do you mean?"

"They caught him having sex."

"What? You mean he was having sex with someone?"

"No, Dad, they caught him masturbating."

"I can't believe this. Where? In Charleston? Who was he screwing? How did they catch him?"

"I don't know the details. It's a very fluid situation. There's something about a pool, though, speaking of fluid. They caught him doing it in the pool."

"A pool? What do you mean, he was screwing in a pool? They caught him screwing in a pool four days before the wedding?"

"In his defense, it was five days before the wedding."

I was a lot of things at that exact moment: stunned, confused, angry, and yes, maybe a little, just a little, relieved. "How's she doing, Karen, how's she doing?"

"I don't know. She's the only one who didn't call me."

"A pool. I can't believe this." I felt around in my pockets for my phone. "I have to call her."

Mindy picked up her glass. "Call tomorrow. Mom said they were going to meet with Roger's family. Have a Karen–Roger summit. You know, just for the record, I never liked that guy."

I patted myself down. "I need your phone. I left mine in the room."

Mindy opened her purse and handed me hers. "Here, but she'll see my number and won't answer."

"She'll answer. What's her number?"

"I don't know her number."

"You don't know your sister's number?"

"You don't know your daughter's number?"

"I have it on speed dial." I was having trouble processing this news; the wedding had been planned for months. The inn, the caterer, the guests: who was calling them? What and how were we going to tell them? My cousins had booked flights months ago. I had rented a tuxedo, and it was being delivered to my room. Then I thought of Karen again. What must she be going through? How was she handling this?

"What are we going to do now?"

"I know exactly what to do," Mindy said.

"What?"

"Eat," she said. "I. Starving."

I called Mary while Mindy finished her barbeque chicken quesadillas.

"Hi," I said.

"I can't talk."

"What's going on?"

"I can't talk."

"Tell me what's going on."

"I can't talk."

"Is Karen there?"

"I can't talk."

When I heard silence on the other end, I handed Mindy back her phone.

"What she say?"

"I don't think she could talk." I stared straight ahead at the necks of bourbon and scotch bottles lined up on the back of the bar. "Poor Karen."

"She'll survive."

"That's all you have to say? She's your sister."

"I think we've talked, like, twice in the past year."

"That's ridiculous. You live ten minutes from each other. You know, she scheduled this wedding around your schedule, she planned it this way. She waited until the show was off."

"I know that, Dad. I know that because everyone keeps reminding me of that fact. I'm surprised the invitation didn't mention that: *Planned around Mindy's schedule.*" She pushed her plate away. "God, I'm a pig. I can't believe I just ate that."

The bartender walked over and cleared her things. He was tall and lanky and like every male under thirty, sporting a bit of stubble. He stared hard at Mindy for a moment, smiled, and asked, "Excuse me, but are you Mindy Nichols?"

Surprisingly, she blushed and looked down at the bar. "Thanks, but no. But I mean, I wish. She's amazing," she mumbled.

The man stood there for another second, trying to sift through her response, then smiled again and drifted away.

"That, like, never happens to me," she said.

"He knows who you are."

"Well, that makes two of us." She wiped her mouth with a napkin. "Anyway, I don't want to have the 'how do they get your ass to inflate like that?' conversation right now."

"You didn't have to be rude. He's a nice guy."

"Nice guy." Mindy rolled her eyes. "Just stop it."

"Stop what?"

"Stop trying to fix me up with some guy, okay? It drives me nuts." She grabbed her purse, rummaged through it, then slapped a black American Express card down on the bar.

"I wasn't trying to do anything, but okay,

123

I'll shut up." I picked up the card and handed it back to her and placed my own pedestrian green American Express card down.

"Do you have my key?"

"I've got it here somewhere." I began emptying my pockets. "I know I have it."

"Oh, fuck!" Mindy jumped off her barstool. "Ethan! Stay over there. I'm coming! Stay right there!"

"What?" I looked up just as Ethan, in bare feet and boxers, darted across the lobby toward the bar. With his knees locked and his long skinny arms flapping about, he looked like an electrocuted stick figure.

"Mindy! Here! Mindy! Here! Hello! Hello! Hello!"

"Oh, Jesus!" I bolted from my chair, but Mindy reached him first, covering him with a hug.

"Hi, buddy! Let's get back to your room, okay?"

"Where. Mom. Be?"

"She's not here. Come on. Let's go. Dad, give me the key."

"Cold. Out."

"That's because you're almost naked."

"Yes. Ma'am!" He laughed and kept hugging her hard, his face beaming. He loved Mindy.

I stroked his hair and squeezed his shoulder. I was trembling. I had no idea how he had gotten out. "The door mustn't have closed all the way, or he figured out how to open it or something. He's never done this before. Never!"

"He's fine," Mindy said.

Ethan, one arm still around Mindy, reached out and pulled me close. The three of us were now in a small, tight circle. I suddenly feared where things were heading.

"Oh God," I said.

"What?"

In an off-key voice, Ethan began, "Family. Family! Family! *U!* . . ."

Mindy's eyes grew wide. "Not the family fight song, please. I'm tired."

"Sing!" Ethan yelled.

"Fuck!"

"Just do it," I said. "He won't stop until we do."

"Dad, I can't, come on! Not here."

"You're an actress, act," I whispered between gritted teeth. "No one's here anyway."

"Dad!"

"Sing!"

"Do it," I said. "Please."

So we held hands and sang, "Family! Family! Family! U.S.A!" Over Mindy's shoulder, I saw the bartender, frozen in the act of wiping a glass, his mouth agape.

"There's still only one verse, right?" Mindy asked when we were finished.

"Yes."

"Good, let's beat it."

I handed Mindy her key. "I shouldn't have left him," I said again.

"Everything's fine." She lead Ethan away. "Just get Red Bear. She's probably going to hit on that bartender."

After I put Ethan back to bed, I went into the bathroom, and hit speed dial. Mary surprised me by answering.

"Oh God," she said.

"What happened? Is it true? What is going on?"

"It's off. She's not going through with it. She caught him. He was cheating. Apparently, she's suspected for a while, and then she caught him."

"Unbelievable!"

"She caught him in the pool with Penny."

"Jesus, not Penny!" I said even though, at that exact moment, I hadn't a clue who Penny was. Then, "The pool?"

"The pool."

My mind began to reel. "Indoor or outdoor?"

"What *difference* does it make, John? My God!"

"You're right. I'm sorry, I'm sorry. I can't think straight. Just calm down."

"Don't tell me to calm down! Do you know what I've been through, any idea?"

"How is she? Can I talk to her? Is she there?"

"She's in her room. She doesn't want to talk to anyone."

"I can't believe this. What do we do now?"

"Nothing."

"We have to do something. Start calling people."

"Sally and Sal are taking care of everything. Calling everyone. The caterer, the band. We have to pay for some rooms, most of the rooms, probably."

"God, I cannot believe this."

"We were lucky that this happened now, not two days from now. No one's really here but us. But we're going to have to pay for the rooms."

I was silent, overwhelmed.

"Hello? John? Am I keeping you from something?"

"I don't know what to say." I paused. "Okay, I know I must know her, but who is this Penny person again?"

"A bridesmaid. A sorority sister."

"I don't know her."

"You know her."

"Well, I don't remember her," I said.

"I never liked him. From the start. Never trusted him, that jaw of his. His family, they all have that same damn jaw."

"Let's try to focus on Karen."

"If you cared so much about Karen, you'd be here by now. You would have taken a plane out here, instead of . . . of . . . walking."

"Planes don't work with him, you know that." I stood and tried to pace, but the bathroom was too small, so I had to sit back down on top of the toilet. "Well, Mindy's here. With me. She just got here."

"I know that."

"We'll be there either tomorrow or the day after. You're going to stay and wait for us, right?"

"I guess. We paid for the rooms. We took over the whole inn. It's empty, the whole thing."

"Did Roger and his family go home?"

"I don't know and I don't care. Beth was very unapologetic. She implied that Karen was overreacting."

"What did Everett say?"

"Everett? Not a word. He just sat there like some beaten-down old dog. That whole

128

family is so dysfunctional."

I paused. I had found myself in the middle of an infidelity mine field, and thought it would be best to slow down. "This has got to be tough on them too."

"Please. Do *not* defend them."

"I'm not defending them. But it's not Everett's fault. He didn't screw anyone in the pool. His son did."

"You should have been here for this," Mary said. "She's your daughter too."

"I'm sorry this happened this way. I'm sorry."

She was quiet. I searched for something positive to say.

"At least Ethan had a good day," I said.

"For once, I don't want to talk about Ethan Nichols. We have other children."

"You're right, I know, you're right." I paused, helpless. "Is there anything I can do?"

"No. I'll see you when you get here."

"Are you sure you're going to stay?"

"Yes."

"Well, good night then," I said.

And as expected, she hung up.

5

The next morning, invigorated by a full eighteen minutes of teeth-grinding sleep, I immediately launched into a litany of worries about Karen as soon as we were inside the van. I hadn't gotten far before Mindy cut me short.

"Can we not talk about this?" She was slumped down in the passenger seat, juggling a massive cup of Starbucks and a copy of *USA Today,* compliments of the Knoxville Marriott.

"Why, what's wrong? Why don't you want to talk about it?"

"Because I'm sick of talking about it."

"Sick of talking about it? It just happened."

"There's nothing to talk about."

"Really? I think there's a lot to talk about."

"There's nothing we can do about it. Besides, they'll probably kiss and make up, screw in the pool themselves." She took a deep slug of her coffee. "I'm not sure why I'm even going anymore."

"You have to go. Karen needs you."

"She doesn't need me, trust me. She doesn't need anyone. You know what she said to me, she said, 'You don't have to stay long. Just come to the service and then leave. We don't really need you there.' "

"She didn't say that."

"Yes, she did."

"That doesn't sound like Karen." I shook my head. Unfortunately, that sounded *exactly* like Karen. "Well, then your mother needs you. We all need you. We need to be together."

"Right, right. Family. Family . . ."

"U! . . . S! . . ." Ethan cried from the back.

Mindy and I both reflexively yelled, "A!"

Mindy opened her paper. "Okay, I'll go, but I don't want to spend the whole trip talking about Karen and Roger, okay? I've been hearing about this wedding for six months. It's off, so I don't need to hear about it anymore. If you want me to come along now, then that's the one condition, okay? Is that a deal?"

"She's your sister. You should show some compassion."

"Deal?"

I was disappointed in her offer. But since

we had a long drive ahead of us and since I was confident that the conversation would inevitably head back toward Karen, I agreed. "All right, fine, deal. But you need to change your attitude when it comes to your sister. She loves you." I glanced in the mirror, checked to see if Ethan was buckled, pulled out of the parking lot, and passed by the huge ball in front of the Women's Basketball Hall of Fame.

"Hoops!"

Mindy looked up at the ball. "What the fuck?"

"Okay, now it's my turn to make a deal. Stop saying that word, okay? I don't want Ethan picking it up. That's the last thing I need, him walking around saying that. He'll say it hundred times a day. No more f-bomb. Deal?"

"I don't know what the big deal about that word is."

"Deal?"

"Okay, fine," she mumbled.

I merged onto the interstate, and we drove in silence. Traffic was predictably light; it was midmorning, and no one was heading east toward the mountains. I stepped on the gas, determined to make time.

"So," I said after a while.

"So."

"How'd you sleep?"

Mindy, head in the paper, shrugged, so I shrugged back.

"Where. Mom. Be?"

"She's with Karen," I said. "Your poor, oldest sister, Karen."

Mindy took another large slug of coffee, said nothing.

I made tracks, hanging in the left lane, passing anything that moved, and waited for Mindy's morphine, the coffee, to kick in. After a few minutes, and after a few more slugs, I deemed her properly medicated and made another run at conversation.

"What are you reading?"

Mindy's eyes remained on the paper. "What?"

"The paper. You're engrossed. What's so interesting?"

"Nothing. This study."

"What study?"

"About fat people. It says that four percent of Americans are morbidly obese."

"Oh, well, that's interesting."

"Morbidly obese," Mindy said. "That's a really weird description, morbidly obese. I mean, what's with the morbidly? Do we really need to distinguish between obese and morbidly obese?"

I didn't say anything.

"Do you think obese people make fun of morbidly obese people, go around saying, 'Hey, at least I'm not *morbidly* obese.' Or do you think *morbidly* obese people walk around saying, 'God, if I could just become obese, I could fit into those jeans!' "

I laughed a little. "Good point."

Mindy finally looked up from her paper, and I noticed that in the very top of her left ear, she was sporting a tiny gold stud. More evidence of her growing celebrity stature. My heart sank. Earlier in the year, a prominent entertainment Web site had done a "rising star" feature on her, and she had also recently been on a late-night talk show. I had been detecting signs of a swollen head ever since. I didn't want to lose my little buddy to stardom, gossip magazines, tattoos, heavy drug use. I decided that her bright red high-tops also were a bit showy. I changed lanes and made a silent vow to somehow keep her grounded, remind her that she was the president of the math club in high school, used to have hamsters as pets.

"So this is Tennessee," she said.

"Yep. The South."

"Looks like the North to me."

"It's not. People are different."

"What, you've made a lot of friends?"

134

"Nice. Outside," Ethan said.

"Very nice," Mindy said. She returned to her paper.

"Hot. Out."

"Not too bad," I said.

I passed a semi with Georgia plates, hauling a load of lumber, then flicked on the radio and found a country music station, which I thought appropriate.

"Off!" Ethan yelled after he realized it wasn't Merle Haggard singing "Silent Night."

"So, is Will Ferrell a nice guy?"

"What?"

"Will Ferrell, the actor."

"Why are you asking about him?"

"Just trying to keep the conversation going. I've been alone a long time."

"You've been with Ethan."

"He's not exactly Larry King, okay?"

She folded her paper and tucked it between the armrest and her seat. "Yeah, he's okay. Has kind of a big head."

I glanced at her. "Staying grounded must be hard when you're a big star. But's it's important."

"No, I mean, literally. He has a big head. Like, physically. When you're working close to him, it kind of throws you off; it's like this big thing, staring down at you. But he's

135

okay. Pretty funny."

"Oh." I drove another minute. "Is he married?"

Mindy didn't say anything.

I shrugged. "You two did a lot of skits together. I noticed that."

Mindy pulled out her phone then immediately put it away.

"No service in the Deep South?"

She slid down in her seat. "I'm not gay, Dad."

I jumped. "What?"

"Mom told me you think I'm gay."

"I never said that."

"Yes, you did."

"I'm not sure what she told you." *You can't tell that woman anything,* I thought.

"I'm not gay. I would tell you if I were. It's not like some big deal, okay? I don't like meeting guys, the whole dating thing, that's all. I don't have time."

"Okay . . . I'm not exactly sure how you can get married if you don't like meeting guys and the whole dating thing, but okay."

"Who says I want to get married? Why would I ever want to do that? You and Mom weren't exactly a commercial for it."

"You know, you're right; this is none of my business."

"It's not."

136

"Fine."

"Fine."

I turned the radio back on.

"Off!" Ethan yelled.

I turned it off, drove awhile, then glanced back. Ethan was studying the distant mountains with his mouth open, a sure indication that he was thinking, absorbing, pondering. I wondered what he thought of the mountains, how he was processing them. He had spent his entire life in Illinois, and had never seen anything like them before. I regretted not having time to pull over and explain them to him.

"Mountains," I said. "Big hills."

"I know what mountains are."

"I'm talking to Ethan."

A few minutes later we plunged into a short tunnel, which utterly amazed and frightened him.

"Wow! Dark! Dark! Where. Sun. Be?" He leaned forward and took hold of my shoulder.

"Yes, dark." I reached up and patted his hand. "But we're just about out. See, all done. Sit back now. Go on. All done."

He sat back. "All. Done!"

"So, are you and Mom going to get back together?"

My heat skipped a beat. "Sit back, Ethan.

All the way!" I swallowed and took my time before answering. "What? Why would you ask that?"

"You're probing me about my love life. Why can't I probe you about yours?"

I swallowed again. "Not that I'm aware of." I waited a moment, then, "What brought that on?"

"I don't know. You're not with what's-her-name. . . ."

"That's been over for a long, long time. And I was only with her."

"And Mom isn't with anyone. She's never been with anyone, as far as I know."

I pretended to fiddle with the air conditioner. "Did she say something?"

"No. I'm just asking. You seem to spend a lot of time together. I mean, you live one block from each other. Not many divorced people live one block from each other."

"We actually live three blocks from each other. And it's because of Ethan. It's just easier."

"She misses you," Mindy said. "She talks about you a lot. Do you miss her?"

"You know, let's not talk for a while. I want to concentrate on the road. Get there."

"Whatever you say, Daddy-o, whatever you say." She smirked and moved her seat back some. "So, are we driving straight

138

through or what?"

"We won't make it."

"How far are we?"

"Normal distance or Ethan distance? Normal distance, we're only about five, six hours away. Double or maybe triple that with him, though."

"I bet we can make it. He's quiet now."

"We can't make it."

"Yes, we can."

"No, we can't."

"You have to push him sometimes, Dad. You give in to him too much. He manipulates you. He tangles you up in knots."

I looked over at her. "Tangled up in knots" was an old expression/accusation from the War Years. *Dad, he's tangling you up in knots! Just let him yell.*

"It's been a while since you've spent quality time with your baby brother. I have a reservation in Asheville, North Carolina. I'll be happy if we make that."

"We can make it to Charleston," she said. "I'm here now. There's two of us. Let's just drive through and get there and get this over with. Everything's going to be okay. Isn't that right, Ethan?" She turned and slapped Ethan five. The Starbucks must have been really strong.

"Nice. Outside!" Ethan yelled, smiling.

■ ■ ■ ■

Twenty-five minutes later, after Mindy sang increasingly loud and frantic renditions of "The First Noel," "Hark: The Herald Angels Sing," and "White Christmas"; and after Ethan tried to throw Grandpa Bear and then Red Bear and then Stinky Bear out the window; and after he yelled, "Shut. Up. Idiot," a near-record twenty-eight straight times (note: thirty is the record); and after Ethan pinched Mindy hard; and after Mindy cried, "Fuck," with so much pain and emotion that she made me think of Pavarotti; and after Ethan repeatedly asked Mindy, "Why. Mad? Why. Mad? Why. Mad?" while she closed her eyes and tried to ignore him; and after Mindy finally opened her eyes and pounded her seat while screaming, "I'm not fucking mad! I'm not fucking mad! I'm not fucking mad!" we pulled off at the small, hilly town of Homer's Den and went to a park.

"Why. Mad?" I asked.

Mindy shook her head as she trudged alongside me. "God, that was nuts, just nuts."

We made our way across a deserted base-ball diamond toward the equally deserted playground, taking in the town along the way. The main street, which ran hard against the base of the hills, was made up of brightly colored, one-story businesses: drugstore, diner, bakery, post office. The buildings seemed to have been carved out of the bottom of the hills. I had never been in a place like this, a small town, a village crowded by rock.

"What are you looking at? What's wrong?" Mindy asked me. Ethan started pulling on her hand.

"The town, the hills, it's strange. But it's beautiful," I said.

Mindy had no time to respond, because Ethan had yanked her ahead. I slowly followed.

"You're not having a stroke or anything, are you?" Mindy asked.

"Why would you ask that?"

"Your face, it went, like, slack."

"We're in an interesting place. I was absorbing it. Sponging it up."

Mindy scanned the park, then the town. "Not much to sponge."

"It's different."

"You don't get out much, do you?"

"You know I don't."

Mindy considered me through a squint.

"Okay, why don't you sit down. I'll push him."

"He can swing by himself now."

"He can?"

"Yes, he finally learned. Only took fifteen years."

Mindy looked at Ethan, her pixie smirk replaced by genuine pixie surprise. "Wow. Ethan, you can really swing by yourself?"

He pulled hard on her hand. "Swing!"

"You have to get him started, though," I said. "But he can do the rest."

"Okay, let's go then," Mindy said.

"All right. I'll call Karen."

I sat on a bench and watched Mindy push Ethan. One of the things I always admired about my middle child was how she acted around Ethan in public. Never embarrassed. Even when she was young, she hugged him, laughed with him, teased him. Her natural-ness and, of course, her humor, were infec-tious, disarming, and put other people at ease around Ethan. It was one of her best attributes, maybe what I loved about her the most.

Karen, the cheerleading, sorority girl, was much more self-conscious, checking to see who was looking at us at restaurants, walk-ing ahead or behind us in stores. Her behavior was understandable, particularly during the teen years, when everyone in your family is a source of embarrassment. Mindy never went through that phase, though. I suspected that Ethan fit her worldview: wild, unexpected. At once hilarious and tragic.

"More!" Ethan yelled.

Mindy pushed harder, and Ethan, delight breaking out over his face, kicked his legs up as he soared into the air.

I fished my phone out of my pocket and tried to call Karen, but there was no service. So I sat back and allowed myself to relax. The park was a vibrant field, dark green grass ringed by tall fir trees, the weather somewhere between nice and beautiful. Overhead, the sun inched up to the tip of the hills.

Mindy came over and sat next to me. "You okay?"

"You can stop asking me that."

"You're in, like, a trance."

"It's called relaxing."

She leaned over and made point of sniffing me. "I think it's called Jim Beam."

"I haven't had a drink all day. I've been driving, remember?"

We sat in silence and watched Ethan swing, his feet pointing up to the sky. A few minutes later, a young boy in an oversize

143

T-shirt and short pants crossed the road and cautiously approached the swings. When he got close, Ethan began shouting "Poo-poo, pee-pee, poo-poo, pee-pee," so the boy stopped, perplexed.

"How old are you?" the boy shouted to Ethan.

"He's only three!" Mindy yelled. "He's *really* big, isn't he?"

The boy glanced at Mindy, then studied Ethan one more time before turning back to town.

"I hope you and Karen patch things up," I said.

"She's the one who doesn't talk to me anymore."

"What caused this latest round? I can't keep track."

"I don't know."

"You used to be so close."

"That was a long time ago. We were girls. Things are different now."

"What changed?"

She shrugged and mumbled.

"What?"

"I said, 'I don't know.' I think she's jealous or something. I think she can't deal with, you know, what's going on with me."

"Jealous?"

"Yeah."

"No, she's not. She's proud of you. We all are."

Mindy smirked. "Not everyone is. Trust me. It kind of started when I got into Princeton, but it's gotten really bad since I've been on the show."

I shook my head, sighed. I had suspected this for some time. Karen was used to being the center of attention, the star of the show. Mindy's ascent had upset the natural order of things. "Some sibling rivalry is normal. But you're still sisters. And I hope you get along with her tomorrow. She needs her family."

"She'll be okay. She's always okay. She's the amazing, unsinkable Captain McBrag."

"Could you do me a favor? Could you please stop calling her Captain McBrag? She doesn't brag anymore, okay? You know she was devastated by that skit. That upset your mother and me too. You shouldn't have done that. Making fun of your family on TV — that's not right."

"It was loosely based. Inspired by."

"You called it 'Captain McBrag.' "

"That's not her legal name or anything. No one knew who it was about."

"The character was named Captain Karen McBrag."

"Just drop it, okay? It was a stupid bit; we

only did it once. It's over." She pulled out her phone. "So, how long are we going to stay there anyway? I'd like to get back."

"She was always nice to you. She always looked out for you. Always."

"Right. She's a bitch, and you know it."

"Don't say that."

"Just drop it. I don't want to talk about Her Highness."

"Fine."

"Fine."

We were quiet, then Mindy blurted, "For the record, just so you know, when that writer called her and was looking for some quotes about me, she could have said something more insightful, more supportive, more *something,* than 'no comment.' Do you know how that looked? That's my career she's fucking with. My own sister, my only sister, saying, 'No comment.' What the fuck was that all about? People think I'm a bitch now. On the show, all I heard was 'no comment,' from everyone for, like, six months. It was, like, the big fucking joke!"

"Okay, calm down. Just relax." I, of course, had read the article in question and had been mortified by Karen's 'no comment' comment. "I'm sorry I brought this whole thing up. I'm sorry. I just want everyone to get along, that's all. Let's drop it."

"You always want everyone to get along."

"That's my job. I'm the dad."

We were quiet again. Ethan yelled something indecipherable to the sky and grinned madly.

"Anyway, switching gears here — we have the rooms until Monday."

"God. Monday."

"It's just a few days."

"I need to get back home," she said.

"Home? For the record, Wilton is your home."

"I've lived in New York for almost five years now."

"Yes, but I'm just saying, technically speaking, Wilton will always be your home."

"Don't worry, Dad, if New York City ever declares war on Wilton, I'll come home to fight."

"Good. Because we're counting on you."

Mindy kicked the ground with her celebrity-red sneakers. "So, what's the point in staying in Charleston? Do we have to help clean out the pool or something?"

"I don't know, family time. The Sals are staying. When's the last time you've seen the Sals?"

"I don't remember." She put the hood of

her sweatshirt up even though it was warm. Across the road, a spotless white truck stopped with a hiss in front of the bakery, and a man in an equally white uniform jumped out.

"How's Aunt Sally?"

"Better. In remission. Everyone's optimistic."

"Is Uncle Sal in the mob?"

"What?"

"Uncle Sal. Is he in the mob?"

"Not this again."

"I'm about to spend a lot of time with him, and I want to know. Besides, I have a right to know, in case I'm ever subpoenaed."

"He's not in the mob. And that's a stereotype. You're half Italian, and you're not in the mob."

"Dad, no one has ever known what he really does for a living. Every time I ask someone, I get a different answer."

"He's an accountant. Among, you know, other things."

"Other things?"

"Never mind. Drop it."

"Daddy-o."

I paused, thought about it, then said, "All right, okay. I guess you're a big girl now. Your uncle, he's, or at least was, a bookie. A big-time bookie. I don't think he does that

148

anymore though. I think he's out of it."

This appeared to impress her. She nodded at this disclosure. "A bookie. Sounds interesting. What do they do, exactly?"

"Make book. Take bets. Technically, it's illegal. I think he works, or at least worked, with some people in Las Vegas — that's all I know for sure. But he's also an accountant, a CPA. He works for legitimate restaurants and casinos. Does the books for them in Las Vegas and other places. Atlantic City, he does a lot of work there."

"So he's a numbers guy for the mob."

"Numbers guy? Where are you getting this from? He's not in the mob, okay? He may, you know, know some people, but trust me, he's not in the mob."

"He's in the mob, and I'm going to out him," Mindy said. "I going to force him to give it up, come clean once and for all. It will be good for him."

"He's not in the mob."

Mindy stretched out her legs and scooted down lower on the bench. "Well, whatever he does, he must do pretty well. Their house is huge. And he's always had tickets to everything. The World Series, the Super Bowl. And the summer home in Green Lake. That boat."

"A lot of that is your aunt's money. Sal

does okay, but your grandfather, Pappa Prio, he had the money."

"Is that why you married Mom, because she was loaded?"

"I had no idea your mother came from a wealthy family when we met. And I couldn't have cared less."

"Money doesn't hurt," she said.

"That's one problem we never had, I guess."

Mindy nodded toward Ethan, who was now swinging high, pumping his legs at just the right moment with just the right rhythm. "He's so good at that," she said.

"Yeah. Now, if I can just get him to take a shower by himself."

"I used to try to get him to do this. I tried forever. Look at him now, though."

I turned and smiled at her, happy she was proud of Ethan. "What's with the earring?" I touched the top of her ear. "I think you missed your lobe or something."

She leaned forward, resting her elbows on her knees. "Just an earring."

"We should probably go," I said. "I'd like to get to Asheville before dark. At the rate we're going, we'll never make it."

"Do you remember when Ethan had that seizure? When he was little?"

Her question came from deep left field,

and it caught me off guard. "What made you think of that?"

"Do you think that affected him? Made him worse?"

"No. That had no lasting impact on him. That's what they said."

"He almost died, didn't he?"

"Yes. He was five. Yes. That was a bad time."

"I found him on the basement floor."

"I remember. I know you did." I reached out and touched her arm.

"There's been a lot of bad times with him," she said.

"Some good ones too. But it's never been easy."

Mindy chewed on her lip and continued to stare hard at Ethan. "What's going to happen to him, Dad? Where's he going to end up?"

This question, soft and sincere, also shook me. "Why are you asking that?"

"I don't know, just wondering."

"I'm not sure yet. I'm not sure."

"What are you thinking? You must have some kind of plan, right?"

"We have some options we're looking at, yes."

"Like what?"

"Homes, different places. Anyway, we better get going." I stood abruptly. Ethan was swinging higher than ever, his smiling face up full to the sky.

"Up. High!" he yelled. "Up! High!"

"Let's go, dude-man. Come on, let's go." I made my way to the swings quickly, making sure to keep my back to Mindy.

6

The next morning dawned steel gray and cool. I stood at the window in my room and scanned the sky, looking for the hope of sun, then glanced down and took in the streets of Asheville, North Carolina. Unfortunately, my room overlooked the parking lot, so what I saw didn't reveal much other than the roofs of cars and a huge air-conditioning unit.

I finished my coffee and gazed up at a range of hazy blue mountains, humpback shapes brooding in the distance, and thought about what I would do if things were different, if I were on my own. I was in a strange and wild part of America, western North Carolina: forested mountains, hidden lakes, long and deep rivers, a place I had never been to before, and I doubted I would ever be in again. I imagined what I could discover if I were untethered, free to roam. When embarking on his journey some forty years prior, William Least Heat-Moon had written that a man who couldn't make things go right, could at least go. I felt a sudden urge to just go that morning, outrun my life and flee.

The day before had turned out to be survive and advance. Ethan had not wanted to leave the park in Homer's Den, and it took everything we had — threats, bribes — to finally get him off the swing. But things got worse back in the van, and we were forced to make an endless number of stops: at another park, a rest station, a Cracker Barrel, and a Walmart, before arriving in Asheville an exhausted and jangled pile of nerves.

Despite all that, Mindy had gotten up early, taken Ethan to breakfast at the Renaissance Hotel where we were staying (a Marriott property: thirty-five thousand points), and was now with him at the pool. This reprieve allowed me some much-needed alone time to think, strategize, and, of course, worry.

I put the time to good use. We would be in Charleston later that day, and a lot was waiting for me there — *a lot.* So I paced the room, checked my voice mail, listened to message after message from friends and relatives expressing surprise and shock over the wedding, deleted all of those messages, turned the TV on, turned it off, then, even though I had given up any hope of ever reaching her, called Karen.

She answered on the first ring.

"Hello?"

I stopped pacing. "Karen? Oh, hi, baby. It's me, Dad."

"Oh. Hi."

"How are you?"

I never heard her response. Instead I thought I heard Mindy screaming in the hall.

"Come in here now! Now! Move! Move! Move it, mister!"

It was definitely Mindy's voice, and she was definitely screaming.

"I'll call you back." I raced over and opened the door. There, as I feared, was Mindy trying to drag Ethan into the room. He was on his back, crying, his pale skinny body still wet from the pool.

"He didn't want to leave," she said. "I tried everything."

"You should have called! Come on, Ethan." I took his other arm.

"No!"

"Come on!"

"No!" He swatted at both of us. Mindy jumped away. "He pinched me in the elevator so hard, I thought I was going to bleed."

"I got him. Just let go! Take the key, open the door. Here, go on. Open it!" I knelt down. "Come on, Ethan. Stinky Bear is in the room. He wants to talk to you."

"You are so bad, Ethan!" Mindy yelled.

"Mindy, watch your voice, please!" It was then that I noticed she was soaking wet. "Did you fall in?"

"He pulled me in!" She opened the door wide. "Get up, Ethan!"

"No! Shut. Up. Idiot!"

"Come on, Ethan," I pleaded. "We'll call Mom if you get inside. We'll have a Sprite. We'll look at your photo album. All the pictures. We haven't looked at that yet."

"Don't bribe him. You bribe him too much! That's the problem!"

"I'm just trying to get him into the room, okay?"

Ethan was still on his back, so, with no other recourse, I grabbed both his wrists and dragged him inside the room. "Now, get up. I'm going to count to three. If you don't get up, we won't have a Sprite. One, two."

I felt his body go limp as his rage, and worry, dissipated. He stood slowly, crying, then reached out to hug me. I pressed his wet body against mine and ran my hand through his wet hair. I could feel his heart beating fast against my chest.

"It's okay. It's okay," I said over and over and over.

Back on the interstate an hour later, the world scotch-taped back together, Bing crooning "Little Drummer Boy," a Starbucks resting between my thighs, Ethan making calls on his old cell phone, Mindy wheeled on me.

"What's going to happen to him?" she asked.

(Note: Mindy's green eyes were fiercely beautiful, and when she decided to use their full power, max them out, she was capable of seeing through walls, pushing back tides. I felt those eyes on me now, felt them boring down, locking in.)

"Dad?"

I had sidestepped this at the park. I wasn't sure I could do it again. "What do you mean?"

"I mean, where's he going to end up? He can't live by himself. Who's going to take care of him later on, when you and Mom are too old?"

I paused before saying, "He'll be okay."

"He won't be okay forever."

"Why do you keep asking this?"

157

"Because I see what it's like. Plus, I remember."

"Everything will be fine."

"I'm, you know, worried, that's all."

"We'll be okay. Just a bad morning. This trip is rough on him."

I suspected this wouldn't do, and I was right. "I don't know, Dad. We need to start thinking about this now. I mean, we need a plan, an overall plan."

I drove onto the shoulder when she said that.

"Watch it!"

I swallowed, glanced in the mirror at Ethan, glanced over at Mindy, then let out one very big breath. I hadn't planned on doing this until Charleston. I had every intention of telling Mary first, but Mindy had opened the door about as wide as it could go, so I decided to walk through. I had kept this to myself for as long as I could.

"Well, actually, I do have a plan, kind of an Overall Plan. I'm taking him to a place. A home. It's in Maine."

I turned and watched Mindy's eyes grow large, and in that moment, in her red sneakers and black hoodie sweat shirt, I saw her as the little girl she will always be to me, my little buddy.

"What? What do you mean? Home? What

do you mean?"

"The place, the home, is called Ocean View. That's where he's going to live from now on. After the wedding, or whatever, I'm driving him up there, and . . . and that's where he's going to live."

"What are you talking about? Live? *Now?* What are you talking about? You're taking him *now?* What are you talking about?"

I spoke fast, hoping to overwhelm her with positive facts. "There are only thirty residents, and a three-to-one resident-to-aide ratio. Ethan will have his own room and his own bathroom. It has a gym, a full-size basketball court, and an indoor pool, which is great for him. He'll love it. The place is made for him."

"Wait! What?"

"It's right outside of Camden. Very scenic. Beautiful area. Have you ever been there? Beautiful. A tourist town. It's like a condo, in a way. We, I mean I, had to put a down payment to secure his space, so we own the room. I've been there three times. It's a state-of-the-art place. Four years old. Glowing reviews. It's very hard to get into. Very hard. He's going to love it. We were on a waiting list, but they had this sudden opening. If we don't take this now, he could wait for ten years, maybe longer."

Mindy put her hands up in front of her as if trying to ward off a blow. "Whoa! Slow down. Wait a minute! Maine? Are you kidding? *Maine?*"

I kept going. "There aren't many places in Illinois. Illinois is a terrible state when it comes to the disabled. The worst. The few good places have long, long waiting lists. So we looked at a lot of other places — in Kansas, Wisconsin, Virginia — and we're on the waiting list for all of them, but Ocean View called, and it's by far the best, by far. We ranked them top to bottom. The best one called first. The best one called."

"When did you decide this? I can't believe Mom never said anything."

This was where things got a little complicated. I briefly closed my eyes even though I was driving. "I haven't exactly told her yet."

"What?"

"Why. Mad?"

"No one's mad. Sit back, play with your phone. Here, here's mine. Be careful with it. Here."

"You haven't told Mom?"

"I shouldn't have put it like that. She actually does know. She's been there, and she liked it. We were put on a waiting list. She signed the papers and everything, so she knows, she knows. She just doesn't know that a spot opened up. We thought it would be years still. But they called and said they had an immediate opening for someone like Ethan, so I acted."

"Without telling her?"

I checked Ethan in the mirror again, saw that he was concentrating on my phone, and kept my voice low. "I almost told her a dozen times, but I wanted her to focus on the wedding, her daughter's wedding. I wanted her to be happy, enjoy the whole experience. She's the mother of the bride. She's had a rough few years. Sally's cancer . . . Ethan. Let's face it — me. Plus, I only had a week to decide, and involving her would slow things down. She probably would have wanted to go out there again, meet everyone again, which would have been hard with the wedding, impossible. Everything happened at once. So I went out there alone and took care of everything."

"I can't believe this. I can't believe you didn't tell us. Does Karen know?"

"No, no one knows. Listen, we had to act fast. It's an immediate opening, and there's a long waiting list. If we didn't take it, someone else would. The conditions of the agreement were that spots would be filled immediately. She, your mother, knows this.

Trust me, she's going to be okay with this. She'll be fine."

"I wouldn't be so sure about that. She doesn't like surprises. I think she's going to flip out."

"She might be a little upset, but she'll know it was the right move. It's easier to get into Princeton than a place like this."

I glanced back at Ethan again, wondering, what, if anything, he understood. My phone, forbidden fruit, was doing its job though, so I resumed the offensive: "You know, once people like Ethan turn twenty-two, once they age out, there's nowhere for them to go. No schools . . . There's nothing. No one cares. We've got charities for everything — AIDS, breast cancer, heart association, *slow food* — but no one cares about disabled adults. No one. You know how many autistic adults there are going to be in a few years with no place to go? Millions. Where are they all going to go?"

Mindy started to say something, but I kept pressing.

"Your mother and I, we're both getting older. We need to do this while we're still around, so he gets used to the place. If it doesn't work, we'll still have time to figure something else out, another plan. I don't want to wait until I'm eighty to be dealing with this."

"*Maine?* What, you couldn't find a place in Australia?"

"It's the best place; of all the places we saw, it's the best. They can deal with people like Ethan there. It was made for him. He'll be very happy there. I know him; he'll love it there."

"I can't believe you're doing this now."

"When exactly would I do this?

"Later, in a few years. And not right after Karen's wedding. I mean, that's crazy."

"She's not getting married anymore, okay?"

"I can't believe this. So you're really on the way there now? This whole trip was really to do this?"

"There's no point to wait. It won't get easier with time; nothing is going to get better. He's not going to improve."

"He's gotten better. He's gotten a lot better. He doesn't throw up now. You can go to restaurants and shop with him."

"He almost drowned you in the pool an hour ago. He's unpredictable."

She shook her head. "He's better. You just said, it's this trip that's making him bad."

"I know this is the right decision. If something happens to your mother or me, do you want to watch him, live with him?

Do you want to be doing Stinky Bear the rest of your life? Dragging him through hallways? Is Karen going to do it? You both live in New York now — you never see him anymore. You've forgotten how it is."

"I can do it."

"You know you can't," I said softly.

"So, so, some stranger is going to do it? You're going to leave him with some . . . some . . . minimum-wage guy a million miles away? Someone who will beat him up, or . . . or worse?"

"I thought you'd understand."

"I understand it's hard, yeah, but *Maine*. Now? I don't know, it's just —" She stopped. "There has to be another option. Some place closer to Chicago."

"There are other places, but we could wait ten or twenty years or longer."

"You can't do this, Dad. You can't just leave him. You can't just . . . *dump* him there."

Those words, *dump him,* set me off. "Do you think I want to do this, huh? Do you think I'm looking forward to it? No one loves him more than me, no one. But this is the best I can do. It's a good place. A good place!"

I braced for more protests, more anger, more questions, more guilt, but instead

Mindy did something I didn't expect: she covered her face with her hands and started to quietly cry. My little buddy.

"Oh, baby." I reached for her, but she brushed my hand away.

"You can't just leave him, Dad. You can't." Then she slid out of her seat and into the back with Ethan.

Sal was waiting for us on the expansive porch of the Jefferson Davis Inn. Despite nearing sixty, he remained a powerfully constructed person, with a barrel chest and thick arms that sprouted multiplying tufts of black hair. When he saw us approach, he flicked his cigarette into the bushes with his middle finger, a practiced and efficient move, and extended those beefy arms wide. Standing in white linen pants and a pink polo, smoke pouring through his nostrils, he looked like a vacationing Neanderthal, a Town and Country Caveman.

"Heeeere's Johnny!" he yelled.

I tried to smile, but I was sure it came off more like a grimace. "Sal."

Ethan bolted from me, racing up the steps, pencil arms outstretched. "Sal! Sal! Sal!"

His uncle warmly embraced him. "There he is! Ethan! Mr. Big. Hi! It's nice outside,

165

right? Look at that sun! Hot! Global Warning. Been sweating my ass off out here waiting for you guys."

"Sal, watch the language. He repeats things," I said.

Sal looked at me, then back at Ethan, and snapped his fingers. "Sorry. Jesus, right. Hey, Ethan, don't say nothing you hear from me, okay?"

"Nice. Outside!" Ethan shouted.

"Bet your fucking ass."

"Sal!"

"He may as well learn from his favorite uncle. Get over here." Sal opened his arms toward me. I closed my eyes as he hugged me hard.

"You're looking good, Johnny."

"Thank you." He released me. "You look . . . summery," I said.

He waved away my comment, took hold of both my shoulders, and looked intensely at me. "Hey, listen, all I want to say is, you're gonna get through this, okay? It's like when I had that gallbladder thing, that attack. Remember that thing? Thought that was it. I had the urn picked out. One day at a time, that's one thing that experience taught me." He raised a solitary finger. "One day at a time."

"I'll remember that."

"There she is!"

"Hey, Uncle Sal." Mindy dropped her bag on the porch. She'd been quiet the rest of the trip, and I sensed she was in no mood for Sal, normally a favorite of hers.

"Let me look at her! Little Miss Celebrity and everything! I saw you on the *Conan O'Brien Show* last month! There you were! I couldn't believe my eyes. My fucking niece! Come here."

"Your fucking niece." Mindy disappeared under another Sal embrace.

Sal patted her on the back a few times, then let her go. "So, what's he like? He an asshole or what?"

"Conan? Oh, tall. Conan is tall."

"Tall? Jeez, had no idea."

"It's a show-biz secret," Mindy said. "Don't tell anyone."

"Who the hell am I going to tell? Hey, where your things? Let me give you a hand. Don't give me nothing heavy on account of my back."

Without missing a beat, Mindy handed him her empty plastic water bottle. "Here, take this."

After a second of confusion, Sal laughed. "Look what she gives me." He wagged a finger at Mindy. "Look what she gives me! Empty bottle! I always said you would be

167

famous! Didn't I? Didn't I? Huh? All those plays in high school? Didn't I? Huh? The singing, the dancing. And you were home-coming queen, what: Twice?"

"That was Karen."

"Always knew you would make it. Always."

"You did," Mindy said. "You did. Well, I'm going to check in." With that, she quickly picked up her bag, grabbed Ethan's hand, and made her way inside.

Sal watched her leave. "She okay? She seemed a little quiet. She's usually all over the place."

"She's concerned about Karen. We all are."

"Jeez, John, but you gotta be proud of her."

"Karen?"

"The little one."

"Oh, I am."

"You can't teach what she's got. That wit. Quick on her feet with the zingers. Like Ali, stings like a butterfly."

"Yep, that's her. A stinging butterfly."

He lowered his voice. "I gotta be straight about one thing though. That thing with the adult diaper she does. That skit when her ass gets big, you know, inflates like that, whatever, the thing she did last week or whenever. I gotta say, do you think that's in

168

the best taste? Just between me and you, I know some people who gotta wear those, and it's nothing to laugh at. Intermittent incontinence isn't a joke; it can be serious and life changing."

I considered Sal's unusually earnest comment and concluded that my big, strapping bookie, maybe-in-the-mob-but-probably-not brother-in-law was possibly, at that very moment, wearing an extra-large diaper, and this saddened me. For better or worse, Sal was a constant in my life, indestructible, and I didn't like the fact that he might be running down.

"I don't think that's what she's making fun of. She's making fun of people who are so busy, they don't have time to go to the bathroom."

Sal studied me with his hooded black eyes. "See, I don't see it like that. I see it different."

"You should talk to her then. I know she values your creative input." I made a move toward the door.

"So," Sal said. "What you think of this place? Beautiful, huh? Despite the TV issue."

I paused and took in the historic Jefferson Davis Inn. It was, as advertised, an immaculate former plantation home, complete with the requisite white column pillars, porch swing, and screened gazebo. Situated on a shady lot populated with weeping willows and a row of arching cypress trees that lined the long entry road, it offered a fine view of Charleston Harbor. Gone with the Wind *comes to life,* the Web site said, and I had to agree. I walked to the end of the porch and stared out at the water, an unexpected sense of sadness, a gust of regret, hitting me. I had last seen the Atlantic on our honeymoon, thirty years prior; I was seeing it again under very different circumstances.

"Letting flies in here." I looked back. Sal was holding the door open.

"Oh, sorry."

We walked inside and entered a spacious foyer with a spiral staircase off to the right.

"Different," Sal said. "Unique in an historic fashion. You know who the place is named after?"

"Jefferson Davis. The Confederate President."

Sal looked disappointed. "Oh, you know that."

"Yes."

"Who told you?"

"I just know."

"Yeah, you're a teacher and everything, I

guess you would. You know, I'm kind of surprised they named this place after that guy. I don't get it. Didn't he get their asses kicked in the war? Didn't he own slaves? And they're naming a hotel after him? It'd be like, if we were staying in Germany in a place named after Hitler. The Adolf Hitler Inn, or the . . . the Hitler Hotel. Hey, I'm staying over at the Hitler. Or let's grab a drink at the Hitler. Don't seem right."

I looked at Sal's earnest face. I could tell he had given this issue considerable thought. "You've been here too long."

"Tell me about it."

"I'm going to check in," I said.

"Wait. One more thing." Sal stepped close and whispered, "The Jaw, that prick, is lurking around here somewhere. I seen him earlier out front, like some kind of predator. If I catch him anywhere near Karen, I'm going to bust him up."

"Sal, thank you, but I can handle Roger."

"I'm just saying so you know, you know?"

"The whole thing is disappointing."

"Disappointing? She's my niece. He disgraced her. He humiliated the family. I bought a new suit for this thing. Hugo Boss. You know what that thing set me back?"

"Where. Mom. Be?"

We both turned just as Ethan and Mindy,

hand in hand, entered the foyer. "She's coming, buddy," Mindy said. "And there she is now. Momma Pajama."

"Mom!" Ethan cried.

I looked up and saw Mary making her entrance down the staircase. As always, she was walking fast and with purpose, head up high. Her hair was back in a ponytail, and though I recognized a tired, tightness to her face, she looked, as I always thought, quite pretty.

"Hi, honey. Hi, honey!" She embraced Ethan at the foot of the stairs and held him for a long time, her eyes closed. When she let go, I saw her quickly wipe away a tear.

"Hey, Mom." Mindy walked over, and Mary reached for her next.

"How's baby girl?"

"Baby girl is fine. Just tired."

"I don't know how you made it this far. I don't know what you and your father were thinking."

"It was his idea," Mindy said.

"Yeah, I thought that was crazy," Sal said. "I told him."

Mary finally acknowledged me. "John." She hesitated, nodded once, then made her way over and, surprisingly, gave me a peck on the cheek. "I'm glad you're here."

"So are we. How's Karen?"

"She's in her room."

"Hey, Ethan, let's go outside and see the ocean," Mindy said. "Come on. It's nice outside."

"Don't you want to see your sister first?" I asked.

She avoided my eyes. "I'll take Ethan out for a while. He's been in the car all morning. Come on, buddy. Let's check it out."

"Bye!" Ethan happily scampered after Mindy.

"Hold on. I'll go with you," Sal said. "Show you around. I know every inch of this place." He pointed a finger at me as he passed. "Rooms got AC and their own minifridge. But the fridge is in the bathroom — would you believe?"

"Unbelievable."

"And don't forget the TV in my room. They just hooked up the cable. Maybe catch the Cubs game. New York and Boston tonight too. Giants, LA is the late game. Rivalry week."

"Sounds good."

Mary and I watched them leave and then turned back to face each other. She gave me an ex-wife, remember-I-kind-of-still-hate-you-look, then said, "So."

"So, how you holding up?"

She shrugged.

"Sal said Roger's here. He's not still staying in the Inn, is he?"

"No. Everett and Beth went back to Connecticut, but he's in another hotel somewhere. I'm not sure what he's hoping to accomplish."

"Is anyone else here?"

"No. No one. It's just us now. We caught most everyone in time. Some friends were here, the girls from college, but they left this morning."

"What's everyone saying?"

"Everyone's sorry, shocked, blah, blah. What are they going to say?"

"Is there anything else we have to do?"

"Everything's been taken care of. We called everyone."

"Like it never happened."

"Well, it never did."

"How long are we going to stay?" I asked.

"I'm leaving tomorrow. I decided to go back after all."

"Tomorrow?" My mind ignited. I would have to tell her about Ethan, the Overall Plan, tonight. "You sure? I thought we were going to stay a few days. What's the rush? We paid for the rooms. We should all be together."

"I want to go home. I'm sick of this place. I'll take him back on the plane. I'll give him

174

a pill — he'll sleep. Sal will sit next to him. It's risky, but we'll survive."

"He hates planes, you know that."

She gave me a hard look. "You have another plan?"

I swallowed. "All this is terrible. I feel bad for you. I know how hard it was. All the work."

"Don't feel bad for me, John. I didn't catch my fiancé screwing in the pool."

I was relieved she didn't say, *At least you did it in a hotel.*

"At least you did it in a hotel."

I nodded. The Jaw and me, fellow philanderers, blood brothers in adultery. The parallel was inevitable. "Anyway," I said.

Mary straightened her white sleeveless blouse and looked off to the side. "I'm sorry. I'm tired. I know you're upset. She's your daughter. You should go see her. She's on the third floor, 321. Knock."

"All right."

She turned and started back up the stairs.

"Are we going to get together for dinner?" I asked. "As a family?"

"Fine," she said as she marched up the stairs, not looking back. "Fine."

As the father of the bride, I had been given a spacious corner room on the third floor with a large bathroom (complete with aforementioned mini-fridge), small wet bar (complete with Jim Beam), white French doors that opened up to a small balcony, and a canopied bed. I took in the canopy and pondered its point. Why does a bed need a roof again? I then dropped my luggage into the closet where my rental tux hung, unlatched the French doors, and stepped outside.

I looked over the expanse of water stretching before me, inhaled a lungful of salty air, and remembered our honeymoon at Hilton Head one thousand years before. We had had a fine time, Mary and I: a week on the beach, sex in the morning, sex at night, seafood and wine in between. Mary was quite amorous back in the day, quite the love cat. We did it in on the floor, in the shower, and yes, even in the pool. I had forgotten about that. The pool. I couldn't help but laugh. I absorbed the view for a few minutes, wished I could stay longer, then headed off in search of Karen.

I found her room on the opposite side of the floor. I knocked and waited. Nothing. I checked the number, 321, and knocked again.

"Karen? It's your father. It's me. Dad. Daddy."

Still no sound. I knocked harder. "Karen? Are you in there?"

I heard a faint rustling, then finally footsteps. The door opened slowly, and there she was, Karen, my queen bee, messy-haired, pale-faced, red-rimmed eyes, Karen, my first baby.

"Hi," she said.

"Hi, honey." I squeezed her hard, felt a sudden fury at Roger, a rage. He had hurt her. He had hurt my child. Maybe I would unleash Sal on him after all, bust him up. Maybe I would unleash myself on him. Maybe he had it coming.

She stepped back and ran a hand through her blond hair. "I look like shit. I was sleeping."

"Can I come in?"

She moved aside and let me in her room, which I instantly recognized as an exact replica of mine. "Do you have a fridge in the bathroom?" I asked impulsively.

"What? Yeah, it's in there somewhere. Why, you want something? I have beer in there, I think."

"No, no, I'm fine. I'm fine." I sat on the bed.

Karen leaned against the desk with her arms folded. Despite the heat, she was wearing a big, faded orange-and-blue Illinois sweatshirt, which at one time, had probably been mine. She pulled the sleeves up to her elbows and brushed her hair off her face. She had grown it long for the wedding. I remember Mary telling me that.

"Well," I started, "I'm so sorry for you. This must be terrible. I'm just . . . I'm very disappointed in him."

She looked away, through her open French doors. "What can I say? He's a piece of shit."

I nodded. I wanted to say Roger was a scum-sucking bastard, but considering my own scum-sucking history, I had to tread carefully. "Was this the first time?"

"Does that matter?"

"No, it doesn't. You probably did the right thing."

"Probably?"

"You did the right thing."

She shrugged, kept looking outside.

"You sure he did it, though? You verified it?"

"I saw it. That's pretty good verification."

"So, you walked in and actually saw them doing it in the pool? This Penny, your friend? You actually saw them doing it? Having sex in the water? You're sure?"

"Yes. They were having sex. I know what it fucking looks like. It looks the same in the water as out of the water."

"Are they together now? Penny and Roger? Had this been going on long, this affair?"

"You know, Dad, I don't want to talk about it anymore. There's nothing to say other than I don't care what happens to either of them."

"You're right, you're right."

We were silent for a few seconds. Then she said, "Everything, it just . . . Everything sucks." She closed her eyes, and I thought she might cry, but she didn't. My queen bee never cried. "Everything sucks," she said again.

I just sat there, helpless, not sure what to say or do. Karen wasn't someone who needed help, wasn't someone you consoled.

"Is there anything you want, anything I can do?"

She opened her eyes, shook her head.

"You sure? You want me to talk to Roger?"

"Why?"

"I don't know. I think I should."

She looked down at the floor and spoke in a monotone. "I just have to get through the next few weeks. Return all the gifts. Put up with everyone feeling sorry for me. All that shit. It's going to be a pain."

"We'll help you through this. Your mom will. And Sally. And Mindy."

This brought a smirk. "Mindy. What black

hoodie is she wearing today? Her I-went-to-Princeton one or her I'm-on-*Saturday Night Live*?"

"Don't be like that."

"I bet she's having a field day with this."

"Why would you say that? She feels terrible. We all do."

"Right. Captain McBrag gets stood up."

"Don't say that. And you weren't stood up."

She shrugged again.

"You know, maybe I will have a beer," I said. "Do you want one?" I started to make my way to the bathroom.

"No. I just took a Valium. I better not."

I stopped in my tracks. "Valium? Who gave you that?"

"Mom."

"Your mother gave you Valium?"

"Yeah, she takes it."

"I didn't know that. You shouldn't take that. She shouldn't take that."

I changed my mind about the beer and sat back down on the bed.

"When did Penny and Roger do this thing again? When did it happen?"

"When we first got here. The first day. I got in earlier than they thought. They thought I was coming in late. I walked in on them."

180

"The pool is outside. They were doing it outside?"

"Listen, I don't want to talk about it. The details don't matter. I just want to sleep."

"Right." I glanced around the room, searching for something to say. "Do you remember . . . ," I began. "Do you remember when you didn't get into Princeton? How disappointed you were? You didn't know where to go, but at the last second, you just went to Illinois and you were so happy. Remember how everything turned out for the best? You joined the sorority, you became president, and you were a cheerleader. How you loved all the friends you made there."

"I met Penny there."

I scratched my jaw. "So, you want to take a nap?"

"Yeah."

"Sure. That's a good idea. Sure." I walked over and kissed her on the forehead. "I love you, you know that?"

She nodded.

"And you're always going to be my baby. Always. Always. Always."

She didn't say anything.

"We'll have dinner tonight. All of us. Sal will say something stupid, and we can all laugh at him. Family. Family. Family."

"USA," she said quietly.

"I'll send Mindy up in a bit. You guys can talk. She really wants to see you."

"Is Ethan here? Did he come?"

"Yes, of course. He's with Mindy. They're out somewhere."

"Just send him up then. I don't want to see anyone else. Just send Ethan. I just want to see him. He can stay in my room tonight. He can stay with me."

"Really? Oh. Okay. Ethan? Okay."

"Just send Ethan," she said.

A few hours later, after sitting on the balcony contemplating why bad things happen to good people, specifically Karen and, for the most part, me; and after I made a thorough examination of the pool/crime scene, looking for what, I don't know (the police chalk outline of Roger screwing Penny?); and after I declined Sal's first, then second, then third invitation to have a drink at the bar downstairs (third invite: "I'm buying, if that's an issue"); and after I spent more time sitting on my balcony considering my Overall Plan, trying to decide exactly how and when to tell Mary, we had dinner on the roof of a restaurant whose name I never got around to learning.

Under normal circumstances, I would

have been delighted with the evening. It was a warm, breezy summer night, we had a fine view of Charleston, the air smelled of salt water, and we were all together for the first time in what seemed like forever. I picked at my blackened grouper, checked my watch. Of course, these weren't what I would exactly call normal circumstances.

"It's. Nice. Outside."

Ethan was sitting between Karen and Mindy who, as far as I could tell, had yet to acknowledge each other. This disappointed me to no end. In light of everything, I had hoped for some kind of truce, if not the signing of an official armistice. Instead they both kept their heads down over their plates and took turns cutting Ethan's barbeque chicken into small then smaller pieces. Ethan, for his part, was having a wonderful time; in addition to Sal, he now had both of his big sisters fawning over him. He rocked back and forth in his chair to some private beat, a toothy smile on his face. A vibrant, rendition of "Family, Family. Family. USA" I feared, was imminent.

"Is there something wrong with your food?" It was Sally, Mary's older sister, a dour, quiet woman who had lurched from health crisis to health crisis for a good part of her adult life, the most recent being stage-two breast cancer. Resilient and humorless, she never had much patience for me, her underachieving, and unfaithful brother-in-law. During my marriage, we had politely coexisted, but since the divorce, rarely communicated directly with each other.

I looked across the table at her. She was a less pretty version of Mary, her nose a little too long, her eyes a little too narrow. Tonight she looked particularly thin and pale. I tried hard to muster up sympathy for her — she had been through a lot — but this was difficult. She was, and always had been, a first-class bitch. "It's fine," I said. "It's very good."

Sally kept her small eyes on me, so I made a point of eating a forkful of grouper.

"How was the drive in?" she asked.

I swallowed. "Uneventful."

"Sure took your time about it. It would have been nice if you were here."

"I would have liked to have gotten here sooner, but I had my hands full with Ethan. Everyone seems to be forgetting that."

"You should have flown. He's flying back with us tomorrow."

I gave her a very tight smile, returned to my food.

"Where. Pickle. Be?"

"So, you get to see any of the city?" Sal asked. He was as oblivious as Ethan to the mood of the moment, which was palpably tense. I glanced at my watch again.

"No. Just from the drive in. I ended up trying to take a nap."

"A lot of history. You gotta go to that fort. It's right out in the harbor. They gotta boat ride every hour. Pretty interesting. There was a battle, the first one of the war, but no one died. The South fired on the fort, and the North just surrendered. I have to say, I was disappointed to hear that. They didn't put up a fight or nothing."

"Pass the wine, John," Mary said. This was the first time she had spoken directly to me all evening, so I eagerly accommodated, quickly reaching across the round table for the bottle. I poured her, then me, another full glass.

"The wine is pretty good." I made a show of reading the label before setting the bottle down.

"Not bad," Sal said.

I tried to smile, looked over at Ethan, who was happily guzzling his second Sprite, and pushed my plate away.

"You done?" Sal asked.

"I'm not that hungry." I checked the time again. T-minus pretty soon before I had to inform Mary about Ocean View. I glanced over at her to assess her mood, but when we made eye contact, I immediately looked away.

This was not going to be easy. Mary was already dealing with a lot, and now I was going to take her youngest child to live in Maine forever. I never should have waited, never should have let it get to this point. I should have told her the moment I got the call. She was his mother. His *mother.* I reached for my wine, drained half the glass. Maybe I should wait until tomorrow morning. A good night's sleep. Coffee. Maybe tomorrow morning would be better.

"Hey, I saw our friend in the lobby," Sal mumbled in my ear.

"What?"

"You know, our friend the Jaw."

"Roger? What did he say?"

Sal waited until Sally asked Mary a question about the hotel before whispering, "Wanted to know where she was."

"What did you say?"

"I told him it was none of his goddamn business."

"Sal."

"He tried to shake my hand, all polite. Piece of shit."

"I wish he'd leave town," I said.

Sal leaned in, and I could feel his breath, hot in my ear. "I can make him leave town. Hey, I make a couple of calls, I can make him leave earth."

Before Sal said something that a district attorney could force me to repeat under oath in front of a grand jury, our waiter wheeled out the dessert tray. Sal actually rubbed his chin in thought before daintily pointing at the crème brûlée. Mindy ordered Ethan a hot fudge sundae.

"I don't think he should eat that," Karen said.

Mindy smirked. "Why?"

"Because he'll make a mess. You can't give him chocolate."

"If you're worried about your dress, move. Switch places. He likes chocolate."

"Where. Ice. Cream. Be?"

"Chocolate makes him hyper. You want him up all night?"

"Those two," Sal said.

"Chocolate doesn't make him hyper."

I finished my wine and poured one more glass. Though I wasn't keeping an official tally, I knew I had eclipsed my two-drink minimum and was now walking the very fine line that separates the buzzed from the bombed.

"You'd think the little one would cut her

some slack. All things considered," Sal said. He pulled out a cigar from his coat pocket.

"Sal," Sally said.

Sal grudgingly put the cigar away. "What's the point of eating outside?"

I reached for my wineglass again

"Dark. Outside," Ethan said.

"What the hell, I'm going to make a toast," Sal announced.

"What?" I looked at him, frantic. Though well intentioned, Sal's toasts had a tendency to devolve into Mussolini-like rants, complete with emotional declarations of family supremacy, vehement proclamations of love, and, on occasion, veiled threats against unseen enemies. "Don't," I said. "Sal, please."

Sal stood. "I was gonna give a toast at the wedding, so I'm gonna give one here. What the hell."

"Sit down, Sal," Sally said. She began rubbing her throat while nervously eyeing the other tables.

"Thirty seconds, that's all I need. I'm not running for president here. I'm her godfather, and I want to say a few things." He smiled at Karen, who stared at him, stonefaced. "Honey . . . ," Sal began. "All I want to say is, you're gonna be all right. You're gonna meet some great guy, and you're going get married. A doctor. A lawyer. Maybe a ballplayer. You're beautiful. Look at her, she's a damn model. I could fix you up in a minute. I got lots of friends. Good guys."

I thought I heard Mindy mumble, "You mean, Good *fellas*."

Sal continued. "So you're going to be all right. It's that prick's loss. He's a damn fucking prick, and if he comes near you, I swear to God, I will personally —"

He caught himself in midthreat, put his head down, then picked up his wineglass. "All I want to say is, I love all of you. All of you. And may we be together always . . . and always be together."

Other than Ethan, who said, "Where. Ice. Cream. Be?" no one responded. I gave Sal a half hearted thumbs-up and poured myself some more wine. It could have been worse.

"When the going gets tough, the wine gets going," Mary said. I thought this was an attempt at humor and started to smile, until I saw the look on her face.

"It's just wine," I said.

Sally stood. "I have to go to the bathroom. I'll be right back. Sal, watch my purse."

"No one's taking your purse."

Once she was gone, Mary said, "Don't you have anything you want to say, John?"

"No. I think Sal said it all. Other than we

all love you Karen —"

Mary cut me off. "Don't you want to tell us where you're taking Ethan?"

I didn't think I heard her right. I couldn't have heard her right. My throat tightened. "What?" I squeaked.

"Tell us where you're planning on going. Where you're taking Ethan, or at least, wanted to take Ethan."

I had heard her right. I tried to clear my muddled mind. "What do you mean?"

"You tell me what I mean."

I looked at Mindy, who shrugged. "I didn't tell her."

"What's going on?" Sal asked. "Where you taking him? Are you coming back on the plane with us? We have to take the noon flight. It's the only one."

"I got a call today, a few hours ago," Mary announced. "From the Ocean View Home in Camden, Maine. That's where John is taking Ethan. That's where Ethan is going to live for the rest of his life. They wanted to know if I had signed the final consent papers yet."

"Where. Ice. Cream. Be?"

"Home? Papers? What's she talking about, John?" Sal asked.

"John is taking Ethan to Camden, Maine, to live for the rest of his life, and he didn't

190

tell me."

"What the hell is she talking about?" Sal asked.

"Where are you taking him?" Karen asked. "What's going on?"

"He's taking him to a place in Maine. A home for people like him," Mindy said.

"To live?" Karen asked.

"Yeah," Mindy said.

"And you knew about this?"

"He just told me. I didn't know about it. He told me earlier today in the car."

"So you told Mindy and not me?"

"I said he just told me!"

I was woefully unprepared for this, woefully outnumbered and woefully drunk. I offered token resistance. "It's a good place," I said.

Mary deliberately pulled her napkin from her lap and folded it carefully before placing it on the table. "You didn't think they were going to call me?"

Everyone was staring at me, even Ethan. "It's a good place," I said again.

Mary glared and stood up. "The minute he was accepted, you should have told me. The *minute.* I'm his mother."

"I know. I'm sorry. I know. But . . ."

"We should have made this final decision together."

"I know, I know." I tried to walk toward her, but she pointed at me, so I stopped. "Don't. Don't," she said.

"Mary. Please, just listen, please."

She picked up her purse and stormed off, narrowly avoiding our waiter, who was approaching with the desserts. I watched as she disappeared through the doorway. Mary, Mary, sweet contrary.

"Where. Mom. Be?" Ethan asked as the waiter placed his hot fudge sundae in front of him. "Where. Mom. Be?"

I left right after Mary but did not give chase. Instead I wandered numbly through the crowded streets of Charleston, berating myself. I should have known they would try to contact her. It was a stupid and selfish plan. I was a stupid and selfish person. I walked for a long time.

I no longer remember how I made my way to the Inn, but somehow there I was, back on the balcony, alone again. It was a starless night, and I felt weightless in the dark, listening to the tide of the Atlantic.

"Dark. Outside," I said.

I swung my legs up on the railing and closed my eyes. Why had I decided this had to happen? I needed to think things through so I could explain them to Mary.

Over the past two months, I had been spending a lot of time with Ethan, much more than usual, as Mary immersed herself in the logistics of the wedding, and attending to Sally, who was recovering from her final round of chemotherapy. Since school was out for the summer, I had Ethan a good part of every day, a brutal stretch of survive and advance. Consequently, I was frazzled, exhausted, and constantly teetering on the edge of the Black Despair.

The day that Ocean View called about the opening had been particularly difficult. It was a Saturday morning and since C.C., our weekend respite worker and usual godsend, was on vacation, Mary had agreed to take him the entire day so I could recover. At the last second, just as I was getting Ethan into the car, Mary called to say she felt a migrane coming on and couldn't do it. A short, heated discussion followed that ended with us racing to be the first to hang up on each other.

A long lonely day ensued. We ran a series of mindless and unnecessary errands and made three separate trips to the park to shoot hoops in the hot sun. The tedium was broken up by a number of Tonto appearances and a licking festival of Woodstock proportions at the hardware store.

Ethan and I were in my small condo about to have an early dinner, when Dawn Elkin, director of admissions from Ocean View, called to inform me of an unexpected opening. Could Ethan be ready by the end of the month? I paused, then I heard myself answer yes.

I actually did call Mary right afterward, but she didn't answer, and I decided not to leave a message. I was exhausted, still angry, and in no condition to discuss the issue. I would tell her the next day. Sunday came and went, however, as did Monday and Tuesday, and before I knew it, I was packing the van.

Now I questioned why I hadn't told her.

The wedding was certainly a factor, as was the knowledge that Mary had given her tacit approval months before. There was another reason, however, a more honest reason: Ethan had to go somewhere, and I didn't want Mary interfering. I feared she would slow the process down, if not stop it entirely. And I wasn't sure I could wait any longer.

My life with my son had been anything but easy. The simplest things, taking a shower, emptying the garbage, checking the mail, could quickly turn into a terrible ordeal. I knew I was at the end of things and needed help. Ocean View was that help.

Ocean View was salvation.

I was sitting on the balcony, trying to juggle my bitterness and guilt, when I heard my phone ring. It was Rita.

I was in a bad way, desperate for a friend, so I actually considered, briefly, very briefly, picking up, but the wine was ebbing, and I knew I needed to face things. So I got a cold bottle of water from the fridge, pressed it against my forehead for a moment, and called Mary.

"Listen . . . ," I began. "I'm sorry I did it this way, I know it was wrong. But we couldn't wait. We have to do this now."

She was silent.

"Mary?"

"I won't let it happen. I won't sign it, the final consent."

"I know it's hard, but you agreed to this. We both did."

"I thought it would be five years, ten years. How did this happen so fast?"

"It just did. They said he's the right fit right now. Someone just like Ethan moved out or something, so . . . so I guess they're equipped for him, and . . . and they get special funding for him or something. I don't remember all the specifics. I have it written down somewhere. Anyway, we jumped way ahead on the list, years ahead.

I didn't ask a lot of questions."

"You should have."

"It doesn't matter. He's in."

"I'm not ready. He's not ready."

"They told us it could happen at any time. They told us that. That was one of the conditions. You knew that. They said we had to be prepared to move fast. We might miss our chance and go back to the end of the line. You knew this could happen."

"They said the likelihood of this happening was very, very small."

"But it happened."

She didn't say anything.

"Listen, you've been there. You know it's a good place. You loved it when we visited. And for years, we've talked about doing something like this. It just happened sooner than we thought."

"A lot sooner! You should have told me! Damn you, John! You had no right. I should have been part of this decision. What were you thinking? When, exactly, were you planning on telling me? When you got there? When he was already living there? When?"

"The day after the wedding. The next morning. It wasn't going to be ideal, I know, but that's when I was going to do it, tell you. I figured we would, you know, discuss it, and then you would agree and come with me. Us."

We were both quiet. A breeze picked up, and I felt it against my face.

I tried again. "I'm sorry. But I knew you were busy with the wedding, and Sally, so I took care of everything. I went back out there two weeks ago when you had him. I met everyone again, saw his room, met with his aides and therapists. Everyone was very nice, everything looked nice, so I made the down payment. I flew in and out in one day."

I waited for her to say something, but she didn't. So, with nothing to lose, I threw out a Hail Mary of scattered thoughts.

"We could wait for ten years, maybe longer. Do you want to wait for ten, twenty years? We always knew this day was coming. There's no place close to home. We've been over that. There's nothing available. Nothing. We're on all those other waiting lists, but that could be years, years, plus this one is the best — you know that. The best one called first. We got lucky, very lucky. So we have to do this; we have to try to do something now, while we're still relatively young and healthy. This is what we wanted, what we agreed on. You liked the place, you loved it. He's going to love it. I know he will. He'll have lots of attention, lots of structure. The pool, the gym. Now, I know the timing was or is terrible, I know I should have told you, I know I shouldn't have done this around the wedding, but I didn't know this would happen, any of this would happen. Their calling. I didn't know. Two, three weeks ago, I didn't know anything."

I stopped to catch my breath. "It's hard now, but it's the right move — you know it's the right move." I stopped and took a drink of water. My heart was racing. "Hello? You there? Hello?"

She finally spoke. "I've only been out there once. I need to go back and see it again. I planned to. I thought I had time. Years."

My heart leaped. I had hoped for this. "Come with! Drive out there with us. Ethan and me. Leave with us tomorrow! Tomorrow morning! Just come with us. We'll do this together."

She didn't say anything, so, hopeful, I pressed on. "Karen can come too. Why not? We can spend some time with her, get her away from everything. She was going to be on her honeymoon anyway, so she has the time. If nothing else, this trip will be good for that. We never see her anymore." Then everything caught up with me, the long trip, my Overall Plan, the past nineteen years, and I said something stupid — honest, but stupid — and when I did, I erased any progress I had made.

"I don't think I can do this anymore," I said. "It's just too hard. I'm sorry, but I don't think I can do it anymore."

I could feel her stiffen on the other end. "So this is all about you, then. Not Ethan, not me, not the girls. You." She hung up.

I stared at the dead phone in my hand and considered tossing it off the balcony. But I was a high-school English teacher, and I didn't do things like that. So I slipped it back into my pocket and sat there listening to the South Carolina wind for I didn't know how long. Eventually, I went inside and took my position on the free-throw line, made ten straight, then crept into bed and slept.

In the morning, I was awakened early by a loud knock on the door. It was Mary, wearing large round sunglasses, her hair pulled back in a ponytail, as always.

"The girls are downstairs," she said. "We're going."

I had been in a deep sleep and was confused, disoriented. "Home?"

"Maine." She turned and began to march down the hallway. "Get dressed."

I was suddenly wide-awake. "Really? You

mean, you're coming?"

"We all are." She was at the end of the hallway.

"Really? Karen too?" I yelled after her.

"We all are."

"Mindy?"

"All of us!" she yelled as she turned the corner.

7

I stood outside the airport with Sal as he blew a final plume of smoke and flicked his cigarette. "They got a helluva lot of strip joints in South Carolina. Not that that matters," he said.

"You know, it probably doesn't."

"Wish we were going with you."

"We'll be fine."

Sal put his hands in his pockets and jingled some change. His barrel chest inflated for a moment as he took in a big breath then slowly let it recede. He had already given Ethan a number of bone-crushing good-bye hugs (as well as five hundred dollars in cash) but was reluctant to leave. "This home, this place, you want me to make some calls? Ask around? Some of those places are pretty messed up. I read about them from time to time. You sure you checked it out good? Top to bottom? Thorough search?"

"It's a good place."

"What's the name again?"

"Ocean View."

He winked, then gave a half wave to Ethan, who was in the back of the van. "Got a view of the ocean, huh?"

"Yes."

"Nothing closer to home? I mean, Maine, Jesus. I don't even know where the hell it is."

I patted myself down, looking for my phone. "It's a good place."

"It's all so quick."

"It's not that quick." I found my phone in my back pocket, checked to see if it was juiced. "We've been talking about this a long time. We were out there last fall. Remember when Ethan stayed with you that weekend?"

"What's he going to do all day?"

"He'll be very happy there. They have activities. He'll be busy. He's going to love it. Hey, you're going to miss your flight."

"You got that cash, the money for Ethan? I want you to buy something nice for him. Or spread it around up there, give it to his teachers or whomever. Make sure they take care of him. Tell them I'll send more money. Every month. Cash. No one needs to know."

"We'll buy something nice for him. Thank you. And you don't have to send any more money."

"I'm going to miss the hell out of him, you know that?"

"I know that. You can visit anytime."

"Who goes to Maine?"

"He'll be home at Thanksgiving. And three weeks at Christmas. And three weeks next summer. It's like he's going to college. Think of it that way. Karen left, Mindy left. It's his turn."

"Everyone leaves." Sal jingled his change again, his dark eyes switching between me and Ethan. "So, she's on board with this all of a sudden? Your wife? Ex-wife? Seemed pretty upset last night."

I glanced at Mary, who was standing by the revolving doors, saying her good-byes to Sally. "She's fine with it," I said, but not very convincingly.

"Well, if he stays, if you decide that, I'm going to come out there and see him later this summer. Never been to Maine."

"That would be great."

"Sal! Come on!" Sally yelled.

"I gotta go. Get over here." He bear-hugged me.

"Thanks again, Sal. Thank you for the help with the wedding and everything, the calls."

"I'll be in touch." He squeezed me hard

one last time. "Take care of the girls. And you let me know if you see him —"

"I don't think we'll be seeing any more of Roger."

"Sal! Now! Come on. Now!"

"She's waiting. Go on."

He blew a final kiss in Ethan's direction, grabbed the handle of his suitcase, and trudged off. As I watched him walk away, shoulders stooped, I suddenly wished he were making the trip north with us. Despite his buffoonery, he was someone I could count on when it came to Ethan.

"Hey," I called out. "Salvatore."

He turned.

"Have a safe flight, all right?"

He shrugged. "Yeah, all right."

After we went to Enterprise and rented a brand-new red Honda Odyssey; and after I carefully transferred Stinky, Red, and Grandpa Bear, as well as other key Ethan accoutrements to the second van; and after I conferred with Mindy on the route, using my old-school Rand McNally atlas (Mindy: "What's with the map? What, you couldn't find a globe?"); and after I handed out water bottles and granola bars to everyone; and after I yanked Ethan's water bottle away from him when he started hitting Mindy on the shoulder with it, I slid into the original Odyssey and buckled up.

"Ready?" I said to Karen

She nodded/shrugged, kept her eyes in a book.

"Okay then." I readjusted the rearview mirror, cheerfully waved to Mindy in the rental behind me, and started off.

The plan was to drive to Myrtle Beach, about four hours away, Ethan time, and a straight shot up Route 17. Originally, I thought we'd drive northwest into the heart of South Carolina, toward Columbia, but I reconsidered after consulting my map. While Route 17 was a slower drive, it would be easier for Mindy to follow. There would also be more places to stop if and when Ethan acted up.

It was late, already approaching lunchtime, when we set off on the two-lane highway. I glanced at the sky, gray as a Confederate, then flicked on the radio.

"Can you turn it off? I'm getting a headache," Karen said.

"Sure. Sorry. Do you want some aspirin? I have some in the back somewhere."

"I already took some."

I turned the radio off. "What kind did you take?"

"I don't know, Dad. I just took aspirin. It

wasn't Valium. I know that's what you're thinking."

"How'd you sleep?"

"Fine."

"You looked tired."

"Thanks."

We drove a few more miles in silence. I kept glancing in the mirror, wondering how things were going in the other van. Ethan had been agitated at breakfast, licking the silverware and even yelping loudly once. I was sure he was finally sensing our tension, and was acting out.

"Too bad we couldn't all drive together, but this is better," I said. "We need a lifeboat, a quiet van, so we can take breaks. We got a good rate on the rental. Only sixty-five dollars a day."

Karen turned a page.

"Unlimited miles. And I can leave it in Maine for no extra charge."

Karen didn't seem all that interested in the specifics of the rental agreement. She kept reading.

"What book is that?"

"Gone Girl."

"I never read that. How is it?"

"Inspiring."

I checked the mirror again. Mary, who was in the passenger seat, appeared to be turning around. I thought I could see the back of her head. "Why is she sitting in front? She should be in the back with him."

"Ethan should have come with us," Karen said.

"He needs to spend some time with his mother. He hasn't seen her in a while."

"If you're going to keep checking the mirror every three seconds, he may as well have come with us."

I glanced over at her. Like Mary and, I just realized, Mindy, she was wearing large round sunglasses that made her face look especially pale.

"Did you guys all buy your sunglasses together?"

"What?"

"Nothing."

I drove another mile.

"So, any word from Roger?"

"No."

"Do you think it's over with him. Permanently?"

"Yes."

"Do you think you'll ever talk to him again?"

"No."

"You were with him for a long time."

"So. You were with Mom a long time."

I paused. "I'm not sure what your point is."

"I'm trying to read. That's my point."

"Sure. Read."

I switched lanes. While I certainly could understand her mood, I had hoped to put our time alone together, a rare thing, to good use. By nature, as I had mentioned, Karen was reserved, but I knew she needed to talk, and I was willing to walk the philandering line to help bring her out.

"So, how you feeling about everything?"

"Super."

"You know, talking about things helps."

"I want to read. If you want to ride with Mindy so you two can laugh and play with teddy bears together, be my guest."

"I don't want to ride with Mindy. I just want you to know that I'm here for you. We can sort things out together."

"There's nothing to sort."

"Okay, well, then fine." I checked the rearview mirror again. From what I could tell, everything seemed to be going okay in the other van, though Mindy was following me pretty close. I sped up. Just my luck she would rear-end me.

I tried a different tack. "Have you ever been to Myrtle Beach?"

"Yes."

"Really? When?"

"What?"

"When were you at Myrtle Beach?"

"I don't remember. A golf outing. Goldman flew us all down here."

"Golfing? When did you take that up?"

"I've been golfing since college."

"I didn't know you were still playing."

She closed her book. "How can you just leave Ethan at this place?"

I slowed down. "What?"

"This place in the middle of nowhere. How can you just do this?" She was looking at me now, her face blank. Then she hit below the belt. "An institution," she said.

I took my time before answering. "It's not an institution. It's a home."

"How can you?"

"I've given this a lot of thought, and it's for the best."

"You didn't even tell Mom."

"That was wrong, and I apologized. She obviously agrees with me now, though, or she wouldn't be coming with."

"I don't think she agrees with you at all. None of us do."

"Then why are you all coming on this trip?"

"Because you're making us. Forcing us."

"I'm not forcing anyone to come."

"He could stay with you for another twenty years."

Again I took my time before responding. "It's for the best. It's best for him, and it's best for everyone," I said evenly.

"You mean best for you."

"Is that what you think?"

"Yes. And not telling Mom, that was unbelievable."

"I said I was wrong and I said I was sorry."

"You're sorry? Just like when you cheated on her. You said that was wrong too, and you wanted everyone to forgive you. Some things aren't forgivable, Dad. Sorry doesn't work on everything."

"I don't know what you want me to say then."

"You're selfish."

"I'm selfish."

"Yes, you are."

"Is that what you think?"

"Yes. You're dumping Ethan, aren't you?"

I swallowed, felt blood rush to my head. "Dumping him."

"Yes. So you can be a free man. You dumped Mom, now you're dumping him. You're dumping him so you can do what you want, fuck other women."

With that, I put my turn signal on and pulled to the shoulder. I checked to make

210

sure Mindy saw me.

"What are you doing?"

I came to a full stop. "Please get out." I didn't look at her.

"What?"

"Please get in the other van. Please just leave. I know you're going through a bad time right now, but so am I, so it's best that we're apart. I don't need to hear about all of my faults right now. I need to be alone for a while. Alone."

I thought she might apologize, hoped she might apologize, but saying sorry wasn't my queen bee's thing. Instead she said, "Fine," unbuckled her seat belt, and got out.

I drove faster than I should have through some place called Francis Marion National Forrest. From time to time I caught glimpses of the ocean on my right, but I was inured to the scenery. Karen's words had stung, and rather than the usual guilt, I felt anger. She had no right to say what she had said. None. She spent, at most, what, a few hours with Ethan a year, and had long ago forgotten what it was like. I had nothing to apologize for and nothing to explain, especially to her. I had made this decision with everyone's best interests in mind, and I was sticking to my plan. This was the best

I could do.

My phone buzzed the moment I emerged from the forest.

"I think we need to take a break," I heard Mary say. There was some commotion in the background, and I had a hard time hearing what she said after that.

"What?"

"Things are getting bad!" she yelled.

"What? Oh. Okay. All right. Can you make it to the next town? It's not that far."

The noise intensified. Ethan, I thought, was crying.

"Will you *please* shut up? Shut up now! You're impossible!" Mary yelled.

"What's happening? What's he doing?"

"Pull over now!"

I flipped on my blinker. "Is he that bad?" I yelled.

Mary yelled back. "He's not the problem!"

"I'm sorry, but she's such a bitch," Mindy said.

"Can you watch what you say?" I glanced in the mirror instinctively, looking for Ethan, until I remembered he was still in the other van, then pulled back onto the highway.

I had envisioned this trip many times, constructed many scenarios, both bad and good, but none of my permutations, none of my calculations, had included this particular situation. My anger with Karen vanished as I assumed my familiar and permanently assigned role of the family — fixer, Mr. Make It Right.

Ignoring the fact that I had just thrown Karen out of the van, I said, "You have to be patient with her. She's under a lot of stress."

"I don't give a shit about her stress! I've been hearing about her stress since I was eight years old!"

"There's no point in yelling."

"I'm not yelling."

"I'm pretty sure you're yelling. Almost positive, in fact."

Mindy took out her phone then jammed it back into her hoodie pocket. "Why can't we get any service here? Where are we? I'm sick of this place. Bunch of Southern fucking rednecks."

"It's not the South's fault you had a fight with your sister."

Mindy sunk low in her seat, her bottom lip protruding, pouting, like a ten-year-old.

"Just curious . . . I know it's none of my business, but exactly what happened back there? Did she pull your hair or something, make a funny face?"

"Don't make a joke out of this."

"What happened?"

"She's just a bitch."

"Come on. You have to remember what she just went through, what's she going through, okay? She was supposed to leave on her honeymoon in a few days. Bali."

Mindy was unimpressed. She crossed her arms and closed her eyes.

"You and your sister have to make an effort. We're going to be together for a while. This was your decision to come on this trip. I didn't force you to come. So we may as well make it as pleasant as possible. A family vacation. We never took one."

"Do not use the word *vacation* on this trip. Do not."

I passed an exit for Georgetown, moved into the right lane, checked on the other van, purposely sighed so Mindy could hear me, purposely sighed again to make sure she heard me, and drove on.

I had no idea what had transpired in the other van. No idea what had transpired with Mindy and Karen, period. Years ago their relationship had somehow and without warning jumped tracks. Was it simply a bad case of sibling rivalry, jealousy, as Mindy said? Or had the strain and stress of growing up with Ethan played a part? Or was it my fault, the affair, the divorce? Was their relationship somehow a reflection or a consequence of my failings, my parenting?

The sad fact was, they used to be friends, best friends. When they were young, they used to take hikes together in the nearby forest preserve, have picnics in the backyard, share peanut butter-and-honey sandwiches, Pepsi from a thermos. They were sisters. Karen would walk Mindy to school, zip up her jacket, hold her hand when they crossed the street. She was very protective of her, a mother hen. For years they shared a room, clothes, toys, inside jokes. Mindy's first audience was Karen, not me.

To be sure, they never were particularly sweet girls. As I have mentioned, Karen was always distant, Mindy, sarcastic. They sprang from Mary's womb that way, their hardwire already in place. But when they were young, they had some sweetness in them, especially when it came to each other. I was there, I witnessed it. At night I would sometimes sing them the old Beach Boys song, "God Only Knows," and listen to their shared giggles. I would watch them say their prayers, hear them bless each other out loud. God only knows what happened to them.

Whatever it was, it wasn't right. They were

sisters. They used to share a room. They had been through too much together. What happened? What unraveled? How did the bond break? The bond should never break. Wasn't that the whole point of being sisters, of family? The bond should never break.

I drove fast, past another exit, the road vanishing underneath me, the gray sky looming low.

After Ethan had a meltdown because Karen wouldn't let him put his head through the open sunroof (we stopped at a rest area and drove around the parking lot for ten minutes so he could scratch that itch); and after Mindy had a meltdown because her phone kept cutting out when her agent called about her first movie offer (we stopped at a gas station so she could finish discussing *Upchuck Chuck,* a film about a food critic with stomach issues); and after Karen had a meltdown because the florist from Charleston called to say they were still charging her/Mary/me the full amount for the un-delivered flowers (we stopped at a Cracker Barrel parking lot where Karen told them exactly what they could do with their un-delivered flowers); and after we stopped at what I thought was an authentic southern BBQ restaurant but was really a dump (Me:

"Don't judge a book by its cover. I'm sure the food is great!"); and after we stopped to go to the bathroom at various gas stations and truck stops because the pulled-pork sandwiches proved to be a poor and turbulent choice (Me, yelling: "I didn't force anyone eat those sandwiches, okay? That was *your* decision"), we arrived exhausted at the Marriott in Myrtle Beach.

"I'm going to order room service," Mindy said as we trudged across the hot parking lot. "I'm going to order a fucking gun so I can kill myself."

"I am going to take a bath," Mary said.

"Swimming!" Ethan said.

"I'll take him," Karen said.

"You will?" I was surprised by this offer. "Thank you, honey."

She shrugged, grabbed Ethan's hand, and dragged him away.

I stopped to fumble with my luggage while everyone walked ahead of me.

"Hey, let's all meet for dinner at six thirty," I called out. "That sound good? We'll all have dinner together. Everyone! And enjoy the place. Costing me a lot of points. Enjoy it. It's like we're on vacation!"

At the hotel bar a few hours later, Mary said, "Do me a favor: don't use the word *vacation* anymore."

In a number of ways, and on a number of levels, my ex-sweet-sweetie and I were an odd couple, a mismatched pair of socks. I was optimistic to the point of delusional, she realistic to the point of grim. I was, at best, vague on details; she, at the at the very least, obsessed with specifics. I'm tall, blond, fair-skinned, blue-eyed; she's short, brunette, dark-skinned, dark-eyed. I like the Sox, she likes the Cubs. Our lives together for thirty-some years had been a testament to opposites attracting. And make no mistake about it: for most of those thirty-some years, we were crazy for each other. Love, go figure.

Sitting next to me at the crowded Marriot bar, in her blouse that showed off her toned arms, jeans that fit just so, hair pulled back to reveal her wonderful and slightly bemused brown eyes, I felt that age-old attraction, and hoped, despite the circumstances, despite everything, she did too.

"Okay," I said, "I won't say 'vacation' anymore."

We had spent the last few minutes tying up loose ends from the wedding, who we had heard from, what they had to say, who we still owed, who we didn't, while eating unsalted peanuts from a red plastic bowl.

An hour earlier Mary had surprised me with a call asking to meet for a drink. Reading too much into her offer, I immediately abandoned my plans to walk on the beach, threw on a new polo shirt, brushed my teeth, and obliged.

"I still can't believe that whole thing happened. Or didn't happen," I said.

Mary shook her head.

"How's she doing?"

Mary reached for a peanut. "You know her. Toughest girl alive."

"She doesn't look good. So pale."

"She's hurting, but she'll be okay. I think she had doubts about him all along."

Once again I wanted to call Roger a bastard, but I was under certain pot-calling-the-kettle-black constraints. Instead I said, "I'm disappointed in Roger."

"He's a bastard."

I nodded. "Are they coming down for dinner?"

She reached for her wine. "Oh, they're coming. They want to talk about the home."

"The home." I drank some of my wine. "I have to admit, I'm a little surprised by their reaction. I didn't think they would respond like this. They don't see him that much anymore."

"He's their baby brother. Always will be.

So be ready — they have a lot of questions. We all do."

"Be ready?"

"We'll have a little talk at dinner. The whole family."

"A little talk?" The prospect of being gang-tackled by the Nichols women gave me pause. I took a longer sip of my wine and cracked another peanut shell. "Well, let's start now. What do you need to know?"

"The timing, for one thing. We're supposed to leave him for a while. I remember something about that. They mentioned that on the phone too."

I sat up on my stool. "Yes, right, there's no contact for the first month. No calls, no visits, nothing. He has to get used to his new routine. No contact with him."

She turned away, toward the lobby. "So we just up and leave him and go home?"

"Yes, I know that will be hard, but yes."

She turned back to me. "Do you really think you'll be able to leave him? You get frantic when you don't see him for a day. Remember when he went to that camp? You called twice a day."

She was referring to a respite camp Ethan had gone to two years before. It was up in Wisconsin, and she was right; I had been frantic with worry and called constantly to check on him.

"I didn't call twice a day."

"More like three times." She sipped her wine. "So, we leave him for a month?"

"Those are the rules. I'll come back after the month is up. I'll drive back and stay a few days before school starts."

"Well, so would I. Why would you drive though? Why wouldn't you just fly back? A lot faster."

I stalled, glancing up at the Red Sox game on the TV behind the bar, then proceeded to fill her in on a small and admittedly sketchy part of my Overall Plan. "I was thinking of taking a trip around the country for the month. By car. Just, you know, driving, killing time. Probably head West."

"West."

"Yes. I've never been past the Mississippi. Just, you know, take some time off, explore." In addition to sketchy, this part of my plan suddenly sounded selfish, though I wasn't exactly sure why; I had to do *something* for a month.

Mary nodded. "Just drive around out West?"

"You know, thinking about it."

A little more nodding.

"Maybe do a some writing, or try to, I don't know. Just take a break."

Mary stopped with the nodding, firmly affixing her now no-trace-of-bemusement eyes on me. "This trip, you going alone?"

I responded too quickly. "Yes, of course, of course. Who would come with me?"

She didn't answer.

"I'm going alone," I said.

She digested this, took another sip of wine. "How long before you retire again, quit teaching?"

"Five years. I have five years, and then I'll get my full pension. I need to finish because I need the money. I need the full pension, the benefits, so I can help pay for the home."

"It's expensive," Mary said.

"It is. But I have that money from my parents, the inheritance. Wasn't all that much, but I never touched it, so that will help."

"You'll have to fill me in again on my share. If we do this," she quickly added.

I repeated my mantra — "It's a good place" — and ate some more peanuts while Mary searched through her large red leather bag, an item that was never far from her side and contained, I was sure, an extra phone charger, an extra pair of glasses, an extra bottle of Ethan's medication, an extra pair of sunglasses, and, I suspected, at least one trashy lonely-woman-meets-handsome-man-in-exotic-location novel, which she kept hidden at all costs. While she was rummaging, I noticed she was wearing her lucky half-moon earrings. It had been quite some time since their last appearance. She had bought them in Ireland on our only overseas trip, three years after we were married. I remembered those earrings. They had a story, and I took their sudden appearance as an encouraging sign.

"I wonder how old Father McDonnell is doing," I asked.

She kept fiddling with her purse, but I saw a smile. Father McDonnell was the priest who had provided a rambling, unsolicited blessing on the earrings in a smoky pub just south of Dingle. "That was the longest blessing," she said.

"Longer than the Old Testament."

"And you didn't want to tip him."

"You don't tip for blessings. Besides, we didn't ask him — he just started doing it."

"He was drunk."

"I'm not sure he was even a priest."

She almost laughed, but caught herself; while smiling was now officially allowed, laughing was still forbidden in my presence. She continued with her rummaging.

"Maybe we'll go back there someday," I said.

It was a bold statement, but before she could respond, Ethan walked into the bar.

"Mom! Mom! Mom! Hello! Hello! Hello!"

I turned in my seat as he made his grand entrance. Holding on to both his big sisters' hands, his toothy smile stretched wide, eyes shining, he looked as happy as Christmas. Having the whole family together was a huge dill pickle for him. Nothing could top it.

Ethan and Mary both reacted like it had been decades since their last meeting. She quickly scooted out of her chair; he broke free of the girls. "Mom! Mom! Mom!"

"Hi, baby." Mary kissed him on the forehead, held him close. "How's my best guy? How's my best guy?"

"Swimming!"

"Swimming, huh?" Mary closed her eyes, sniffed his hair. "Oh, I can smell the chlorine. You smell so clean! No bath tonight, maybe."

"Thanks for taking him." I smiled at Karen, who glanced away.

I turned to Mindy, who was sporting one of her many festive black summer hoodies, and said, "So, what did you do this afternoon? Beach? Spa?"

"Went whale watching."

I actually believed her. "Really? Wow,

that's great. Where?"

Mindy smirked, rolled her eyes.

I snapped my fingers, "Oh, right, sarcasm, right. Forgot how good you are at that. Anyway" — I finished what was left of my wine — "let me settle up so we can go eat."

I had my back to everyone, trying to flag down the bartender, when I heard Ethan say it.

"Sing."

I reached for my wallet and began a desperate search for my credit card.

"Sing!"

"What does he want?" Karen asked.

"Sing!"

"Oh, fuck! Not here. Place is packed."

"Sing!"

"We can't do that now, Ethan, not now," I heard Mary say. "Come on, let's go sit down. We'll sing at the table."

"Sing. Now! Sing! Now! Sing. Now!" Ethan began yelling this.

"Excuse me!" I called to the bartender. "Excuse me!"

"Ethan, honey, not now," Mary said. "Not now."

"Sing! Sing! Sing! *Siiiiiing!*"

The bartender took in the tempest that was taking shape over my shoulder, and tentatively handed me the check.

I winked at him. "Hold on a sec." I turned back around, scanned the bar, saw that Mindy was right — the place was packed — then saw Ethan's expectant, bordering-on-frantic eyes.

"Let's just do this," I said.

Karen, late to the game, now realized what was taking shape. "Oh, forget it. I'm not doing that, not here," she said, and attempted to walk away, but Ethan pulled her back.

"Sing!" Ethan yelled as if he were in labor.

People were starting to look at us. I knew all the elements of a bona fide scene were taking shape — an agitated Ethan, a crowded room, the nearest exit a good distance away — and felt a familiar sense of panic rising.

"Dad, come on," Mindy said. "Let's beat it."

"Just do it," I whispered. "What's the big deal? The things you do on TV."

"That's my job. I get paid to do that."

"I'll pay you later. Come on." I suspected the prospect of holding her sister's hand had more to do with her reluctance than anything. "Let's just do this. Come on." I herded everyone into a small circle. Mustering up as much dignity as I could, I began.

"Family . . ." I stopped and waited for the

others to join. Other than Ethan, no one did.

"Siiiiiiiing!"

"Come on, please. Act drunk if you have to. We're in a bar." I started again. This time I had accompaniment, though we sounded more like we were chanting than singing. "Family . . . Family . . . Family . . . U . . . S . . . Aaaaaa!"

Ethan made us sing this three times, an interminably long time to chant/sing in public. When we were finished, Karen and Mindy bolted into the adjoining restaurant while Ethan screeched, "Party! Party!" then fell on the floor and kicked his legs in the air, a finishing touch he saved for special occasions.

I tried to pull him up, gave up, and, against my better judgment, sheepishly surveyed the room. As expected, a lot of sunburned faces were staring our way. I offered a small wave to our audience — *that's all, folks* — and turned to the bartender, who had enjoyed a front-row seat to the extravaganza.

"Now, where were we?" I asked.

I was figuring out the extra-big tip, thinking our act was over, when I heard it again. This time it was just Mary and Ethan, their voices soft.

"Family . . . Family . . ."

I turned and saw that Ethan was safely back on his feet, Mary's arms wrapped around him. They both had their eyes closed as they swayed back and forth, cheek to cheek, on the crowded barroom floor.

I watched them for a moment. "Ready to go?"

"In a second," she said, holding Ethan tight.

After we sat down at a slightly wobbly table in the far corner, and after I got up and took Ethan to the bathroom, then sat back down, then got back up to take him to the bathroom again; and after Mindy realized she left her phone in her room and she stood up, and after Mary said, "Sit down, you don't need your phone, can't you live without your phone for an hour"; and after Mindy sat down, picked up her menu, and issued a massively aggrieved sigh; and after Mary, trying to ignore sighing Mindy, said there was a draft coming from somewhere; and after Mindy said, "What's with you and drafts; I don't even know what a draft is," using quote marks with her fingers when she said the word *draft*; and after Karen left to go to the bathroom for a ridiculously long time, then came back and said she was going up to her room and wasn't coming back; and after Mary said, "Sit down, we have to talk," and Karen asked about what and Mindy said, "What do you think, climate change?"; and after Karen sat down, picked up her menu, and issued a massively, aggrieved sigh; and after the waitress told me they didn't carry Jim Beam; and after Mindy said, "Oh boy, Dad, are you going to get the shakes now or what"; and after I smirked and said, "Yeah, right, the shakes," then secretly began to worry about getting the shakes, I picked up my glass of ice water and made a kind of toast.

"I want to thank everyone for coming along on this vaca— trip," I said.

"We're not doing this for you," Karen said.

"Thank you anyway."

Karen leaned across the table and spoke hotly. "We don't agree with what you're doing. We think it's wrong."

I took a deep swallow of my water. *I can handle this,* I told myself. "I'm sorry you feel that way . . . ," I began. "I know it's going to be hard, but it's the right thing to do."

"The right thing for you, maybe," Karen said.

"No. It's the right thing for Ethan. He's

going to be very happy there. They have a
—"

Karen cut me off. "Tell him what you think, Mindy."

Mindy finished draining her glass of water. "I don't know, Dad. I mean, you could have waited a few more years. He's only nineteen."

I switched on my teacher's voice, a combination of patience and condescension. "Unfortunately, Mindy, there's never a perfect time to do this."

"I can't imagine a worse time though."

This came from Mary, and it surprised me. Based on our talk at the bar, and the fact she was even in Myrtle Beach with me, I assumed she had moved over to my side.

"Where. Pickle. Be?"

"Pickles are coming," I said. "Do you have to go to the bathroom?"

"You already took him twice," Karen said. "Don't run off."

I smiled. "Who's running off?"

"Let me save everyone a shitload of time," Mindy said. "We don't want you do take him there. That's it in a nutshell, Dad."

"Okay, now I'm confused. I thought you said you were willing to come up and look at the place."

"We never said that," Karen said.

This was a bit of head-scratching, so I actually scratched my head. "Well," I said, "I think the fact that you're here, on the road with me, sitting here at this restaurant, at this hotel, implies that. You've also been driving all day in case you've forgotten that. I thought we agreed we would all go up there together and then make the final decision."

"We changed our minds," Karen said. "There's no point in driving all the way up there. It's going to take forever. So let's just save the time and head home. If anything, he should be at a place in Chicago."

I issued what would be my last smile of the evening. "First of all, in case you've forgotten, neither of you lives in Chicago anymore, so I don't know why that matters." I turned to Mary. "Isn't that right?"

"She has a valid point, John. Chicago is our home. I don't think we've exhausted all the possibilities."

I could feel my smile retracting. "There's nothing available in Chicago, you know that. We've been through this. And I thought you agreed to come up there with me and take another look. I don't understand. A minute ago you were asking what the place cost. I'm sorry, but this is all very confusing."

"Mom," Karen said.

Mary straightened her silverware, briefly touched her throat. "You just sprang this on me, us. And I think the girls have good points. Maine is too far. We don't need to drag him up there if we're just going to say no."

"Wow, the girls really got to you, didn't they?"

"No one got to me," Mary said.

"It's pretty obvious what you're doing." This from Karen.

I sat back in my chair and looked down at the table. "Okay, and what am I doing?"

"You're taking him as far away as possible so you don't have to see him," she said. "It's pretty obvious. If he were in Chicago, you'd have to see him all the time, visit, get involved with the place, the home. This way you won't."

I had had enough. It was now my turn to lean forward. "That is *not* true. That is *not* true at all. First of all, this is far and away the best place we saw. Far and away. And, as soon as I retire, I'll go out there. I'll spend summers out there. And he'll come home for all the holidays and —"

"I have to agree there, Dad," Mindy said. "Out of sight, out of mind."

I felt my skin turning hot. "That is *not*

232

true," I said again.

"Maybe Mindy and I can split watching him. I can afford help. We both can. She makes a lot of money."

"I don't make that much money," Mindy said. "You probably make more."

I tried to keep my voice even and low, but I wasn't having much success. "I appreciate the offer. But you two can't even *look* at each other, much less raise Ethan together. Maybe if I had different daughters. Maybe if we were a normal family, things could have been different."

"A normal family," Mindy said.

"So it's our fault?" Karen asked.

"It's no one's fault," I said. "But your relationship played a part in your mother's and my decision."

"I haven't decided anything," Mary said.

"Normal family? You're the one who left our family, Dad. You're the one who went off and fucked that other woman," Karen said.

"What does that have to do with this?" I threw my napkin down on the table and stood up.

"Where. Dad. Going?"

"Sit down, John. You're upsetting Ethan."

"I'm not upsetting —"

"Sit down, John!"

I sat back down.

"Why. Mad?"

Ethan was getting agitated, his bottom lip jutting out, a sure indicator of a pending meltdown. I pulled my phone out of my pocket and handed to him. He eagerly took it, his lip receding.

"Let's talk about this later," I said. "When he's not around. This is not the time."

Mary actually laughed. "We don't have time. You're forcing this decision."

"So are you with them or me?" I asked her.

"I'm with Ethan. I want what's best for him. This isn't about you," Mary said. "We're just having a discussion here. Everyone gets their say. We should have had this discussion all along. Maybe we should go home and decide there, talk more. The girls have valid points, and they should weigh in."

"We're going to lose the spot! They'll fill it. There's a waiting list. All the good places have waiting lists years long. This is the right time."

"The right time for what? To write your next book? Fuck another woman?" Karen said. "You think your entire life is going to get better once you dump him. You blame him for everything. It's not his fault. It's

234

not his fault that you never wrote another book, Dad."

"I don't blame him for anything."

"You kind of do," Mindy said. "You blame him for the affair, you blame him for not writing, you blame him for being a high-school teacher your whole life even though I know you don't like teaching anymore, for not traveling, for drinking."

"I like being a teacher. And I don't drink that much."

"Ethan has been your excuse for years," Karen said.

This was obviously a coordinated attack, an ambush, and much worse than I could have anticipated. Mary, with her half-moon earrings, had lulled me into a false sense of security at the bar. I stood back up. "Do you know how hard my life has been? Do you?"

"Save it, Dad," Karen said. "He's been your excuse for everything. You're always walking around in an Ethan daze. You weren't even going to make my wedding. You were going to be late, probably miss it."

"That's kind of a moot point," Mindy mumbled.

Karen wheeled on Mindy. "At least I date men. At least I'm capable of having normal relationships. At least I don't have to go on TV and wet my pants in some kind of pathetic attempt to get attention. At least I live in the real world and I'm not some bitter, cynical, class clown who hates everything and everyone. So fuck you."

"You fuck you," Mindy said.

"Stop it! Both of you! You're acting like little girls. And that goes for you too," I said, pointing at Mary. "All of you. I'm the one who pays the price if he stays."

"Pays the price!" Mary said. "He's with me half the time."

"He's with me a lot more than he's with you. You know that! You always have some excuse. Your headaches. Sally."

"That's true, Mom, it seems you don't see him that much," Mindy said. "Maybe if you took him more, we wouldn't have this problem."

"You punt him off on Dad," Karen said.

"Punt him off?" Mary's eyes flared.

"Yeah, punt him," Karen said. "Every time I call, he's at Dad's."

"I have him as much as your father does, probably more! I don't know what he's telling you!"

"I'm not telling them anything."

Mindy: "You're always bitching, Dad."

Karen: "You're always hiding behind Ethan."

Mary: "You're always complaining. And I'm *sorry* my sister has cancer!" Now it was she who stood. "Let's go, Ethan."

Ethan, who had been absorbed in the phone, looked up and bounced his eyes between Mary and me. "Where. Go?"

"To our room. We can eat dinner there. Come on."

"No! Eat. Pickle!"

"Yes." She tried to take his hand, but he pulled free.

"No. Eat!"

"Fine," Mary said. She snatched her red bag and stormed off. A second later the girls pushed their chairs back.

"We're leaving at eight tomorrow," I managed to say.

"Why. Mad?" Ethan asked. "Why. Mad?"

The girls left with their mother; I watched all three of them march away in a military file.

"I'm not mad," I said between clenched teeth. "I'm not mad."

8

The next morning, since we were no longer speaking and since driving hundreds of miles together was apparently no longer a realistic or desired option, Karen and Mindy, independently and unbeknown to me, arranged to have two rental cars dropped off at the hotel. With the exception of Ethan, everyone now had their own vehicle.

We gathered silently in the lobby around eight, presumably, I hoped, for a détente breakfast, when the cars pulled up. As soon as I saw the drivers hand Mindy and Karen their keys, I realized what was happening, and I lost it.

"Your own cars? Are you kidding? This is nuts! You two are impossible!" I expanded my glare to include Mary. "All of you! Do me a favor, and don't come."

"Fine!" Karen said. "Just leave Ethan."

"No, he's coming with me!"

"Then we're coming," Mindy said.

"Go home! Everyone!"

"John, let's talk."

"I'm done talking, and I'm done with all of you." With that, I grabbed Ethan's hand and bolted from the hotel.

"I'm surprised Stinky Bear didn't get his own car," I said as we pulled onto the highway.

My plan was to drive to I-40, then eventually hook up with I-95, which would take me all the way to Maine. From now on, it was straight-shot interstate, no sponging *Blue Highway* moments, no side trips or authentic southern BBQ restaurants, no resort hotels. I wanted to get there as fast as I could. I wanted to get this ordeal over with.

"Just you and me again," I said to Ethan. "Just you and me."

"Stinky. Bear."

"And Stinky Bear."

"Red. Bear. Grandpa. Bear."

"Those guys too. Forget everyone else. We don't need them. I hope they all get flat tires. Ha! Can you imagine Mindy trying to change a tire? Karen? Ha! The little princesses. Your mother too. All of them!"

I drove with insane intent, never bother-

239

ing to check on how the convoy behind me was faring. My free throws the night before had not helped, and I had slept little, fuming in my pillow, my anger, my hurt (as well as my guilt), escalating over what had transpired at dinner.

I suspected I wasn't acting rationally, suspected I was at a breaking point, in fact, maybe had already broken, but I didn't care. I moved up my seat close to the steering wheel, pressed the gas, and tried to lose myself in the rush of road: sixty, sixty-five, seventy miles per hour. The land was flat, uninspiring, the day gray and indifferent. I was, by nature, a slow and distracted driver, but I wanted to fly now. Ethan amused himself with an Etch A Sketch and I kept both hands on the wheel and we sped on.

Seventy-five, eighty.

The girls' words had drawn blood. Was this how they saw me? Selfish? A drunk? A failure? Was I that big of a disappointment? Had they a right to expect more? Had they a right to judge me?

Eighty, eighty-five.

When we passed the exit for Wilmington and my phone went off, I silenced it. When I thought I heard honking behind me, I ignored it.

I had not asked for this life. Ethan had

happened, and everything after that had followed. I did the best I could. Every day, every minute, every second, I did the best I could.

"Do they think I want to do this? Do they?" I said this out loud, my voice tight.

Ethan glanced up from the Etch A Sketch.

"This is a very, very tough decision, very tough. But someone has to make it. Sooner or later someone has to make it. So I made it. I made it. I'm your father, and I know what's best. No one loves you more than me, no one!" I shook my head, pounded the steering wheel, the Doubt and Guilt overwhelming me. "I don't want to do this, but I have to, okay? I have to! It's the right move, the right move. It's a good place, a good place."

"Why. Mad?"

"I'm not mad. I'm not mad."

I wiped away a tear, and Ethan went back to the Etch A Sketch.

We stopped at a gas station to fuel up and go to the bathroom. As Ethan and I made our way back across the parking lot, Mindy popped out from behind my van. I jumped when I saw her.

"What's with the driving?" she said. "It's like a bad chase scene."

I scanned the lot, saw Karen in her Honda, sitting low in her seat like a gang-banger, giving me the evil eye. "Where's your mother?"

Before she could answer, I cut her off. "I don't know why you're all even following me. I'm taking him there. This isn't your or Karen's decisions. So, if you think you're going to talk me out of this, you are very mistaken. So leave us alone. Go back to your celebrity world with big-headed Will Ferrell, and let me handle Ethan. I know what's best for him. And this is best, this is best!"

Mindy scowled, then stormed back to her car and slammed the door. I thought she might have given me the finger, but I wasn't sure because the sun was glaring off her window.

"Mom!" Ethan yelled. "Hello! Hello! Hello!"

Mary jumped out of her van. "Exactly what is your problem? Are you trying to get us all killed?"

I tried to stare her down, but despite my anger, I couldn't, and just looked at the ground. "I'm in a hurry."

"A hurry? Do you think you can outrun us? Is that what you're trying to do? You can't do this unless I agree, so there's no point to that."

"I'm going," I said. "I'm taking him up there, and you'll sign everything."

"You're acting crazy!"

"I don't care."

She assessed me through round sunglasses before saying, "He's coming with me. Come on, Ethan. You drive with me. Mom."

"He's staying with me."

"Not the way you're driving. Come on, Ethan." She extended her hand.

"No." I wrapped an arm around his shoulders. "He's staying with me. We're fine. He wants to stay with me, don't you, Ethan? Don't you want to stay with me?"

"Yes!" Ethan looked at Mary who still had her hand out. "No!" he said.

Mary moved over a few feet, positioning herself between my van and me while I tightened my hold on Ethan and tried to think things through. Having a shouting match in a parking lot with my ex-wife, the woman I was still very much in love with, the woman I was secretly hoping to woo back, was another scenario I had not envisioned in my Overall Plan.

"Could you please move?" I tried to get around her, but she blocked me, arms folded across her chest.

"What's going on? What are you doing?"

It was Karen. She and Mindy had somehow materialized and, along with Mary, formed a circle around me. I was surrounded by grim-faced women in large round sunglasses.

"Why. Mad?"

"He won't let Ethan go," Mary said.

"So you're kidnapping him?" Karen asked. "So we're doing that now?"

"I'm not kidnapping anyone."

"So let go of him. Give him to us."

"Sun. Out."

Cornered, I bared my fangs. "You know, I can't tell you how disappointed I am in all of you. Look at us!" I stopped and waited for a response but got nothing. Everyone stared back at me, jaws thrust forward. Finally I said, "You think this is easy? I want to do this?"

"Don't do it then," Karen said. "Mom, you can stop him."

"She doesn't want to stop me because she knows I'm right."

"We need to talk about this some more, John," Mary said.

"Why are you flip-flopping? We just talked about it last night! We've talked about doing this for years! We're through talking, finished with it!"

"You're forcing this decision," Mary said.

"We need more time."

"I'm not forcing anything!"

"Hey, Dad, chill out," Mindy said.

"Poo-poo!"

"Don't tell me to chill out."

"Poo-poo *bad.*"

"Let's stop someplace and figure it out," Mindy said. "That's all we want to do. We shouldn't drive any farther until we discuss everything. We didn't get a chance to last night. And you ran out of the hotel this morning — you escaped. We just want to talk, Dad."

Under normal circumstances, I would have welcomed her conciliatory comment, agreed to talk things through, but I was in a bad, angry place, a place without reason.

"Talk? Talk? If you wanted to talk this morning, how come you went out and got rental cars?"

Mindy shrugged. "Fallback plan."

"We can't even sit in a van together, much less talk. And there's nothing to talk about anyway. I'm doing this because it's the right thing to do. There's nothing to discuss. We're doing this. I'm doing this. I'm not making you two come. It doesn't matter to me if you come." I looked solely at Mary. "I don't care if you come either. I'll send you the forms. You'll sign them, I know you will.

You know this is the right decision."

"I'm not signing anything."

"Yes, you will." With that, I grabbed Ethan's hand and pushed past my family.

I have never been good with anger, never knew what to do with it, and I was angry now. The names of towns flew by, but I had no interest in exploring. I had no sense of where I was and made no attempt to calm down.

When you had a child like Ethan, bitterness was a constant temptation. It was always there, scratching at your door, trying to lure you to dark places. Over the years, I had done my best to resist its call, but many, many times I succumbed and allowed myself a good wallow. I was knee-deep in a serious wallow now, I knew that, but made no effort to pull myself out.

"I'm doing this for you," I said to Ethan. "I know you don't understand, but I am."

I pressed the gas and switched lanes, Mindy and the others following close. When I made an abrupt move around a car, they all stayed right with me.

Ethan remained oblivious, transfixed at first by the Etch A Sketch and later by my phone, which, unlike his unusable one, had lights, buttons, sounds.

I drove faster, the van pulsating. In that moment I wanted to lose my family, leave my life behind. I wanted to escape, literally and figuratively. The girls, Mary, Ethan. It was more than anyone could bear.

Sixty-five, seventy, seventy-five, eighty. I gripped the wheel with two hands and sped on.

In the parking lot of the truck stop, Mindy staged another ambush, this time with her car. She swung so close to me that I had to jump back, spilling some of my coffee.

"Watch it!"

She lowered her window and peered over the top of her sunglasses. "This isn't funny anymore."

"Mindy! Hello! Hello! Hello!"

"I'm not trying to be funny. That's your job."

"Mom can't keep up."

"Where is she?"

"Where. Mom. Be?"

"She's in front of us now. She missed the exit and pulled over onto the shoulder. She's waiting for us."

"Where's the other one?"

Mindy pointed at Karen's car at the far end of the parking lot.

"Hey, Ethan," she said. "Do you want to

come with me? We can get pickles."

"Yes!"

"Knock it off," I hissed.

"Pickles!"

"Don't try to bribe him; don't do that. Just leave. I can take Ethan and do this myself. Even though I'm such a bad father, even though I'm such a pathetic, self-absorbed, whiny drunk, I can handle it."

"Mom has to sign the papers."

"Trust me, she'll sign them."

Mindy raised her window and drove off.

About an hour later, inside a North Carolina visitors' center, Karen accosted Ethan and me by the maps.

When he saw her approaching, Ethan jumped up and down with excitement, almost dropping the can of Sprite I had just bought him. "Karen! Karen! Karen! Karen!"

"Funny running into you," I said.

"You're an asshole, Dad."

"Please try to watch what you say." I wiped Ethan's mouth with the back of my hand, then returned to the large wall map that confirmed that we were just a few miles from Virginia.

"You're a selfish person," she said.

"*I'm* selfish? I'm the one who takes care of

him. I feed him, I bathe him, I wipe his ass. And *I'm* selfish. You know, you could come visit him more often."

"You're going to get us all killed!"

"No one is getting killed, okay, so cut the drama!"

A young overweight mother wearing plaid shorts and pushing a stroller stopped and stared at us. This was not surprising, since Karen and I were more or less shouting at each other.

"Is everything all right?" she asked in a soft Southern accent.

"Everything's fine," I said.

Karen pointed at me. "He's taking my brother to an institution!"

I looked wildly at Karen, then back at the woman, and felt compelled to explain. "It's not an institution. She's wrong. It's a home."

"It's an institution," Karen said. "He's dumping him!"

"I'm not dumping him. Stop saying that."

"Yes, you are!"

The woman's eyes bounced back and forth between Karen and me before settling on Karen, who apparently appeared more sane.

"Do you need help? Should I call the police?"

Karen fell silent, as if considering this option. "No," she finally said. "But he's taking him to an institution, and we're trying to stop him."

"It's not an institution!" I yelled. "It's a home and it's very nice!"

Ethan jumped up and down. "It's. Nice. Outside!"

The woman hurried off.

"Where. Mom. Be?"

"Where's your mother?" I asked.

Karen took off her sunglasses and stepped close to me. "What do you care?"

I took a step back. "You're right; I don't. Tell her she should go home. All of you should. I can do this alone. I don't need anyone's help."

"You're right. You're the only one who cares."

"Sometimes I think I am. You couldn't move away fast enough. Ethan has always been my problem, always. You and Mindy check in when it's convenient."

"You're his father," she said.

"Sprite! More!"

"That's why I'm doing this. I know what's best."

"We all deserve a say."

"This is my decision."

Karen stepped close again. "You know,"

she said in a surprisingly even tone. "Ethan is part of all of us." When she said that, her bottom lip began to quiver with what I could only assume was anger because, as I have noted, Karen never cried.

"So? What's your point?"

She searched my face with her blue eyes, looked away, then looked back at me.

"And just in case you've forgotten," she said. "Just in case you don't remember how things were, we were there, Dad. We were there with Ethan and you and Mom." Her eyes were reddening now, and when I saw that, when I realized my queen bee was starting to crumble, something began to break inside me.

"Karen." But it was too late; she was through the doors and gone.

"Why. Mad?"

Back in the van, I forced myself to remember things I had forced myself to forget.

Karen was standing next to me that day the neurologist called to tell us the official result of the MRI. ("We confirmed the initial reading. He has global brain damage.") I remember her asking, "What's wrong, Daddy?"

That day in the supermarket, when Ethan gagged so badly that he threw up in the crowded checkout lane in front of Mindy and Karen.

That day in the Six Flags parking lot when he refused to get out of the car so we had to go home. Mindy cried the whole way back, Karen's arms around her.

That day he fell to the floor at Mindy's grammar school graduation and refused to get up for an hour.

That day.

That day.

That day.

There were hundreds of them, thousands of them. Every day was a that day. For me. For us.

I squeezed the wheel and checked on Ethan, now sitting in the back. He was quietly eating a bag of potato chips, sipping a Sprite, oblivious to the drama, his "Why. Mad?" detector switched off. I glanced at Stinky Bear in the passenger seat, eyes all-seeing, picked him up, and pressed him close to my cheek.

What happened to you, happened to all of us, I heard him say.

This hasn't been easy on anyone, he said.

They were there, he said.

Then: *She's right. Ethan is part of all of us.*

"Okay," I said out loud. "All right."

I moved my foot over to the brake, began

to slow. Eighty-five, eighty, seventy-five, seventy, the anger seeping out of me, a trailing, noxious fume.

"All right, okay." I put Stinky down and switched into the right-hand lane, waiting for my family to catch up.

"So," I said to Mary. "Another quiet day on the road."

We were standing at Taylor's, a crowded restaurant off the interstate, waiting for the girls, when I started in on my not-very-rehearsed-but-nonetheless-sincere apology. I figured I was going to spend the rest of the evening saying I was sorry, and I wanted to get a jump on things.

"I'm sorry for the way I was driving. That was stupid. This whole thing has gotten out of hand. I'm very sorry. That's not like me, you know that."

Mary didn't immediately respond. Instead she picked up a menu and started to read. After a minute she said, "Next time you have a nervous breakdown, try not to do it in a speeding car."

"I'm sorry."

"We'll talk when the girls come. Have a drink. It's been a long day for everyone."

My relief was tinged with confusion. I'd been bracing for a good beatdown, if not a hard punch in the stomach. "I am sorry," I said again. "About everything. I didn't handle any of this right."

"I. Starving!"

I massaged Ethan's shoulders. "Yes, we'll eat, we'll eat." While Mary continued to scrutinize the menu, I allowed myself a peek around Taylor's. It was classic supper club: dark and small, clean and homey. Large framed photos of a sturdy-looking, alpha-male-dominated family in various acts of sport — hunting, fishing, skiing, but mostly hunting — hung on pine walls. There was a formidable salad bar in the middle of the place, deer heads and antlers on the wall, and a small but inviting bar in the back. "Place looks kind of neat. It has a motel too. Maybe we should just stay here tonight."

Mary finally put the menu down and glanced around the restaurant. "Fine," she said.

"Pee-pee. Now."

"I'll take him," Mary said. "You've had him all day. Come on, buddy. I'll wait outside while you go."

"No, it's all right. I got him. Let's go, dude-man. Come on." I led Ethan to the men's room and, after he was done, thoroughly washed his face and hands and

254

kissed him on the top of his head.

"You've been a good guy today. Thank you. Everyone else has been bad but you. Even I've been bad. I've been very bad. But you've been great."

"Shut. Up. Idiot."

"You should have told me that earlier. Would have saved me a whole lot of trouble. Come on, let's go."

When we returned, all three women were sitting at a table by a window with checkerboard curtains. I paused, approached tentatively. Mary's benign response notwithstanding, after the Great Chase, I wasn't sure how I would be received.

I gave everyone a sheepish wave. "Hello." Karen and Mindy didn't look up from their menus.

"Eat. I. Starving."

Ethan and I sat down next to each other. "I'm hungry too. We all are. Put your napkin in your lap. Come on."

Karen did it for him. "Here," she said. "Leave it there, Ethan. Don't play with it."

I drew a deep breath and jumped right in. "First off, as I told your mother, I'm sorry for what I did back there. My driving like that. I'm sorry. It was inexcusable."

The girls, like Mary, seemed more interested in the menu than my apology. Mindy said, "Let's order first, then you can grovel, Dad."

"All right, okay." I smoothed down Ethan's tangle of hair, looked around the restaurant again, felt my spirits modestly rise. I liked being off the road, liked this homey place, and I especially liked the fact that, at least for the moment, we weren't all screaming at one another. "Table all right? No drafts?" I asked Mary.

"It's fine." Mary slipped on her glasses, a sure sign she was tired. The half-moon earrings were nowhere in sight.

"You feeling okay?" I asked.

"Yes, I'm fine."

"You look a little tired."

"We're all tired." Mary glanced over at the girls. "And I think we're all sorry about what happened and what was said, aren't we?"

Both girls shrugged, mumbled, "Yeah, sure."

"Apology accepted." I picked up Ethan's napkin, which had already fallen to the floor. "Anyway, the motel looks fine. We may as well stay here. Call it an early night. They have a pool."

"Swimming?" Ethan shouted.

"Maybe. Yes. After we eat. There's one outside. I saw it. It has a diving board."

"Nice. Outside."

"It's very nice out. Hot."

The girls were quiet. They ordered their dinners in low voices. No one asked for any drinks, so I resisted the urge, though I could certainly have used one.

"So," I said after the waitress left.

"So," Mary said.

"I was thinking," I said.

"Where. Sprite. Be?"

"It's coming." I handed Ethan my glass of water, since he had already drained his. "Once again, in addition to the way I was driving, which was dangerous, very dangerous, I also want to apologize over some of the things I said. You weren't the only ones saying horrible, spiteful things."

No one responded, so I went on. "Also, and much more important, I was thinking that maybe I was wrong about this whole thing. Maybe I *am* forcing things. Maybe you're right: maybe I made the final decision too fast. I should have included you all in it. We all should have had a say. Maybe I can call them and say we need more time. I'm willing to do that."

Everyone continued to be quiet.

"Isn't that what you want?" I asked.

Mary took off her glasses and rubbed her eyes. "We're willing to cut a deal," she said.

"Cut a deal," I repeated.

"The girls and I have been talking."

"Talking? Really?" I looked at Mindy and Karen. "You two talked? When did that happen?"

"Phones, Dad," Mindy said. "They work in cars now."

"Oh." My modestly rising spirits stopped rising. I had no idea where this was heading, and I feared another group mugging was imminent. "What deal?"

"A cease-fire," Mindy said.

"Truce," Karen said.

"We'll stop the resistance if you stop being crazy," Mindy said.

"No more kidnapping Ethan," Karen said.

"I wasn't kidnapping him."

Karen said, "We'll go up there peacefully and if, *if* we like what we see, he can stay there for six weeks on a trial basis. Six weeks. All of us have to agree to this though. If we all like it, he can stay. I'll go up there and check in on him. I can make it to Maine one or twice."

"You can't see him for a month," I said.

"I can check in with his aides, or whomever, get reports. Doing it firsthand is better than over the phone."

"Me too," Mindy said. "I'll check too."

I thought about this. "Okay," I said. "What

258

happens after six weeks, though? Then what?"

"Then we'll evaluate things, make the final decision," Mary said. "If we feel like it's not going well, he's coming back home, and we'll wait for a place closer."

"Where. Pickle. Be?"

I searched the bread basket, found a soft dinner roll, and handed it to Ethan. "We'll lose a lot of money if we take him out then. Just so you know."

"Money isn't an issue," Mary said.

"And we could wait ten more years for a place in Illinois."

"So we'll wait," Mary said.

I sat, quietly digesting things, a little suspicious of their offer. Just hours ago they certainly would have lynched me if a suitable tree branch or lamppost had been handy. Now this. "May I ask, what prompted the change of heart?"

"It's not really a change of heart. It's a change of perspective," Karen said.

I wasn't sure what that meant, but since it sounded conciliatory, I slowly said, "Right. Okay."

"If nothing else, you and Mom could use some time off," said Mindy.

I thought some more. "Right. Okay."

"At this point we're just agreeing to a trial

run," Karen said. "Nothing is officially decided. We're just agreeing to try it out. No permanent decisions."

My mind kept processing. "Right. Okay."

"Can you, maybe, say something else?" Mindy asked.

"Do we have a deal?" Karen asked.

I took in the serious but beautiful faces around the table: the women in my life.

"Okay," I said. "I guess."

"You guess?" Karen asked.

"Okay, deal."

"No more drama?" Mindy asked.

"No more drama."

"No more kidnap attempts?" Karen asked.

"Pretty much got that out of my system." I smiled.

Karen extended her hand first, and we shook firmly. Then I shook Mary's and Mindy's hands.

"Me!" Ethan cried.

I shook his hand. "You're all going to like this place," I said. "You'll see." I faced Ethan and began talking fast, the words gushing out. "Especially you. It has a pool and hoops, and a bike path and computers. And you should see the sunrise over the ocean. Big. The home is up on a hill, and it has an amazing view. And it has good food too. We ate lunch and dinner there. Pickles.

Lots and lots of pickles. All you can eat. Well, not all the pickles you can eat, but pretty much everything else."

Neither Ethan nor anybody else was particularly interested in my sales pitch.

"It's going to be a long trip," Mary said.

"We'll have fun being together. And it's a good place."

No one responded, so I dropped the spiel and decided to order a drink after all. I flagged down the waitress and ordered a Jim Beam.

"Make that two," Mary said.

"Make that three," Karen said.

"Four!" Ethan yelled.

"I'll have some of his," Mindy said.

9

The next morning, after Ethan and I split the "Big Hunter" omelet while sitting directly underneath a large, glassy-eyed deer head (Ethan pointing at deer head: "Why. Mad?"); and after I brushed his teeth while singing "Joy to the World" like Alvin the Chipmunk; and after Stinky Bear surprisingly confessed that he had a sexual addiction; and after Grandpa Bear led him in a tearful prayer ("Oh, Lord, give him strength. His penis is in your hands"); and after Red Bear encouraged the use of condoms ("I never leave home without them."), Rita called.

"John?"

I tossed Stinky to the other side of the bed, cursed my stupidity for not checking the number, and wondered if I had inadvertently channeled Rita through my sex-addiction routine. "Oh, hello," I said.

"I've been trying to reach you. Where are you?"

"In Virginia. Off the highway. In a hotel. Motel."

"Did you get my messages?"

"Yes. I did. But I'm with the whole family, so it's hard to call back. We're taking Ethan to a home in Maine. To live. We all are, Mary, the girls. All of us. Mary."

Rita either didn't hear me or didn't think the fact that I was taking my disabled son to live halfway across the country or with my ex-wife important or interesting enough to comment. Instead she said, "I've been thinking of you."

My heart sank. I had no patience for this, no patience to cover old you-are-my soul-mate, we-were-good-together, don't-you-think-we-were-good-together ground, so I played my always reliable trump card: "I have Ethan here, so I can't talk."

"When are you coming back? I need to see you."

I glanced at Ethan and prayed for some kind of divine intervention, some kind of wall-rattling outburst so I could escape. Instead, possibly for the first time in his entire life, he was utterly calm, studying pictures in a magazine, *Explore Virginia*. "Rita, this isn't a good time. He's in one of

263

his moods."

"I've been thinking about you," she said again.

"Well." I stabbed Ethan lightly in the leg with my big toe, hoping to activate him. He ignored me and quietly continued his Dalai Lama impersonation. "Please try to think of something else."

"When can we talk?"

"I'm not sure there's anything to talk about."

"I need to see you."

"I thought we were clear on things."

"When can we talk?"

In the hall, a door opened and then slammed. Mary's room was right next to mine, so a knock on my door was a firm possibility. I jumped out of bed. "Tomorrow. I'll try to call you tomorrow. I have to go. Good-bye."

"John, don't run from me. Something's happened."

"I have to go. Bye."

I hung up, waited for the knock that never came, and cursed myself again. I knew I should have dealt with Rita then and there, insisted that she stop with the calls, been adamant. But adamant had never been my forte. Besides, I had some guilt there. The affair had been my fault, my responsibility. I had invited lovely and lonely Rita into my crazy life then unceremoniously dumped her. I probably deserved this and more.

I peered out the peak, confirmed an empty hallway, then lay back down in bed, sifting through the grainy residue of my philandering ways. I indulged in a good ruing of my many mistakes (meeting Rita, screwing Rita), as well as an intense evaluation of my character (final analysis: I was two-parts decent guy, one-part slime bucket), while Ethan continued to quietly leaf through the magazine. I beat myself up for a while, really went at it from every angle, until spent, I pushed out of bed to go run his bath.

After the girls had breakfast, and after we arranged to have some of our things shipped back to New York and Wilton, we slowly caravaned to the Richmond Airport, where we dropped off two of the rental cars.

In the parking lot, I pulled out my old-school Rand McNally to determine our route and destination for the evening.

"Fredericksburg," I said, pointing. Mindy and Mary were uninterested in the planning process, but Karen was fully engaged. She intently studied the map, checking then rechecking it against some app on her phone.

"We should go farther; that's too close," she said.

"I know what he can handle, and I think Fredericksburg is as far as we can get today."

"That's crazy. We should get to DC, or even Baltimore. It's only a few hours."

"We'll never make it," I said.

"Yes, we can. I'll drive with him. I'll sit with him the whole way."

"The whole way."

"Yes."

"And I won't have to sit in the back and play games, or do the bears or pretend to make phone calls with him?"

"No. Absolutely not. I guarantee."

"You guarantee."

"Yes."

"Okay, well, if you can do that, then we might be able to make it to DC."

"Baltimore," Karen said. "We can make Baltimore for sure."

"We won't make it to Baltimore."

"Yes, we will."

"Trust me, we won't."

Three minutes into our drive, Karen, who, as her teachers constantly reminded us, was programmed to achieve, who always thought big, who ran her first marathon after five weeks of training (Karen: "It's just running"), who always thought she could do things other people couldn't (note: she usually could and did), decided that the middle seat of a minivan, in the middle of a two thousand five hundred-mile road trip, was the perfect place and time to do something dozens of therapists and teachers (not to mention Mary and I) had tried and failed to do: teach Ethan Nichols to read.

"What does this spell? E-A-T."

"Shit."

"It doesn't spell that, Ethan. Think now. Come on. I know you can do this. Come on, what does this spell?"

"Shut. Up. Idiot."

"I need you to focus, Ethan. E-A—"

"Where. Stinky. Bear?"

"He's not here. Now come on, think."

I lowered Dolly Parton's version of "Silent Night," checked the mirror, and saw Karen furiously jotting down words on a yellow legal pad. Watching her, I felt a range of emotions: as always, love — she was my queen bee after all; sadness — she was supposed to be getting ready for her honeymoon; and finally irritation — she could be so goddamn stubborn.

"Hey, sweetie. He probably doesn't want to do that."

She kept writing. "So? You should make

him do it."

After a few minutes I glanced back again. She was still determinedly going at it with the pad and marker, hair hanging in her eyes, while Ethan picked at his nails, thoroughly uninterested. "Hey, sweetie, I appreciate what you're doing, really do, but you might want do yourself a favor and play with the bears. He's not really into that. But thanks for trying. You're the best."

She continued to assault the pad like a coach diagraming an intricate, last-second, inbounds play. "Stuffed animals won't help him," she said. "He needs to be challenged."

"Teach him new fart noises then." I smiled in the mirror.

"You treat him like he's a child. Are you still dressing him in the morning? Are you still giving him a bath?"

I didn't say anything but kept up with the smile.

"Dad, you need to stretch him."

"That's a little easier said than done, sweetie. Play with the Etch A Sketch. He likes that."

"That's not going to help him. You have to teach him new things, help him be more independent. You've given up on him."

"I haven't given up on him. I teach him things."

"Like what? What's the last thing you tried to teach him?"

"Well, let's see. Oh, just last week, I taught him how to play the French horn. He picked it right up."

"I. Starving."

"You're not hungry," Karen said. "You just ate a big breakfast. Now, come on. Let's do some reading. What am I pointing at?"

Karen's prodding inevitably activated Question Mode.

"Where. Mindy. Be?"

"She's in the other van."

"Where. Mom. Be?"

"She's with Mindy."

"Where. Sal. Be?"

"I don't know where Uncle Sal be. Here, see what I wrote? That's the word *pickle*. You like pickles."

"Where. Sally. Be?"

"She's with Sal."

"Where. Mom. Be?"

"I just told you."

This kept on until Karen broke down and gave him a can of Sprite.

"Going to the Sprite pretty early in the game," I said.

"Just drive."

The Sprite bought her all of four minutes. As soon as Ethan finished, I knew what was coming.

"Pee-pee."

"You don't have to go," she said.

"Pee-pee. Now!"

"Ethan, we've only been driving for fifteen minutes. Here, now let's do the alphabet. I'm going to write a letter, then you're going to circle it. I'm going to use capital letters, since they're easier to recognize."

"Pee-pee now! Now! Now!"

"You don't have to go!"

"Yes. Pee-pee. Pee-pee. *Bad!*"

"Dad, does he really have to go?"

"You just gave him a can of pop. What do you think?"

"It can't run through his system that fast."

I put on my blinker. We were coming upon an exit. "He has a very unique system."

We stopped at one of those sprawling mega truck stops that offered all of life's basics: food, clothing, showers, books, booze, massages, and, much to Mindy's enormous delight, guns.

"Now. We. Are. Talking," she said.

In the men's room, Ethan relieved himself of the Sprite, urinating a solid, gushing stream that could have put out a forest fire.

"A lot of pee-pee," I said softly.

After he was done and after he made a

careful inspection of all the open stalls ("Wow! Stinky!"), we wound our way back through the eighteen-wheelers' metropolis, passing by a large magazine rack that ran half the length of an aisle.

"Hold on a second."

I perused the paperbacks, picked up a trashy romance novel for Mary, *Betrayed Love,* thought about it, and selected another, *Forever Love.*

On the way to the checkout line, we passed the gun department, where I spotted Mindy leaning over the glass counter. She was sporting a new oversize Bud Light cap and talking to a bald, pinched-faced older man.

I took in the crowded truck stop; the bald man; the guns; my condescending, professionally provoking daughter, and concluded that this was a volatile and potentially violent mix. I cautiously approached.

"Tell me why the Glock is so great again," I heard her say.

"Squeeze off more rounds with it."

"Squeeze off more rounds," Mindy said, nodding. "Great, I'm going to be doing *a lot* of shooting."

I tapped her on the shoulder. "Ready to go?"

She ignored me, her eyes glued to the

guns under the glass. "Do you have anything else. Any Uzis? I heard they're pretty good."

The man assessed her with small, watery eyes. "No, but I got an AK-47. Got it out back."

"An AK? Perfect. I lost mine."

The man squinted at her.

"Yeah, left it on the bus. Really stupid."

I took Ethan's hand and scurried away.

After paying for the book and a couple of Hershey bars, we made our way outside and headed toward the rental van. I wanted to make a grand presentation of *Forever Love* to Mary, who was sitting up front, checking her phone.

When I held up the book, she lowered her window and smiled the cute little sweet-sweetie I'm-embarrassed smile that made me fall in love with her when I first saw her across a hot classroom in Lincoln Hall at U of I close to a lifetime ago. It had been a while since I had seen that smile. "What's that?" she said.

I held the book up so she could take in the cover in all of its glory: a young, shirt-less man kneeling on the ground, gazing up at a young woman who looked queen-like in a flowing white gown. Both the man and woman's hair was swept back to reveal beautifully stoic faces. Behind them, a moon was rising over a restless sea.

"Tolstoy's last book," I said.

She took the book, then slyly snatched one of the Hershey bars out of my hand.

"Enjoy," I said. "And let me know how that book ends. It sounds very pro-love."

When we reached our van, I was not really surprised to find Karen sitting in the driver's seat.

"What do you think you're doing?"

"I thought I'd drive for a while. Give you a break."

"We've only been driving for twenty minutes."

"I drive faster than you. Where's Mindy?"

"She's buying a machine gun. Come on, I'll drive."

"No, I think we should revise our seating strategy."

"Our seating strategy. Revise it."

"Yes." She stared straight ahead, both hands on the wheel. "I think we can accomplish more with this configuration. Be more productive."

"But I thought you may want to teach Ethan Latin. You know, stretch him. He's expressed an interest."

Karen started up the van.

"Fine," I said, sliding open the side door. "I can confirm our reservations for Fredericksburg from back here."

Back on the road, I launched into a classic episode of *The Stinky Bear Show,* featuring scenes from famous movies. Offering exaggerated accents, acts of simulated violence, and extravagant body functions, it was one of Ethan's favorite routines.

"Fredo! I know it was you. You broke my heart!" I said as Grandpa kissed Stinky roughly on the lips. "You broke my heart!"

Stinky Bear then farted loudly.

"That's from *Godfather: Part Two,* minus the fart," I explained to Ethan in my John Nichols voice. "Heartbreaking scene. Fredo wasn't a bad guy. Just stupid."

"More!" Ethan cried. He pounded the seat with delight.

"Ooookay! More it is!"

My next scene featured Stinky Bear doing sit-ups while Grandpa Bear angrily looked on.

"Now, why would a slick little hustler like you sign up for something like this?" Grandpa demanded.

"Wanna fly jets, sir!" Stinky shot back.

"My grandmother wants to fly jets! Now I want your DOR!" Grandpa Bear yelled. "I want your DOR!"

"I ain't quitting!" Stinky Bear yelled as I

furiously bent him backward and forward at the waist.

"Give me your DOR! Spell it. D-O-R!"

"No, sir!" More sit-ups from Stinky Bear.

"That's it, then. You're out!"

Stinky stopped with the sit-ups. "You can't do that! You can't do that!" he yelled.

"Why not?!"

"Because I got nowhere else to go!" Stinky cried. "I . . . got . . . no . . . where . . . else . . . to . . . go!"

Grandpa Bear then farted.

"Officer and a Gentlemen," I said to Ethan. "Lou Gossett Jr. is a sergeant trying to get Richard Gere, a recruit, to drop out of the air force officer's school. Great scene, great line. And just so you know, in the actual movie, Lou Gossett Jr. did not fart. Or, if he did, it was a silent one."

"More!"

"Sure. Sure. I have all day. Nothing but time, nothing but sweet, sweet time." I began to pummel Grandpa's face with Stinky's furry little paws while loudly humming the theme from *Rocky*.

"Dad, can you knock it off? I'm getting a headache."

I stopped with the pummeling. "Sure. But can I drive?"

Karen was quiet.

"I said, can I drive?"

More silence.

I leaned forward and raised Stinky close to her ear. "Yo! Adrian!"

"They don't serve booze at the Cracker Barrel," I informed Karen. "Sorry, but no wine."

Her worst fears confirmed, Karen slapped her menu down on the table and disappeared in the direction of the equally alcohol-free Old Country Store.

"What's with her?" Mindy asked.

"What do you think?" I pushed my menu aside. I had no appetite for anything but alcohol and aspirin.

We were sitting in a booth by a window just off another exit, still buzzing from the road. That day's ride had been particularly brutal, a death march of Bataan proportions. We stopped an agonizing six times, the last at a desolate water-filtration plant somewhere in northern Virginia, where I'd attempted to play catch with Ethan/Tonto in an empty parking lot. It was hot out and, much to Ethan/Tonto's intense delight, the parking lot was asphalt, always an intriguing surface to explore since it heated up so well. It took us a full hour to coax Ethan/Tonto back into the van.

I drained my water, tried to gather myself. Everyone was exhausted and on edge.

"What a nightmare," Mary said.

"It wasn't so bad. We got through it," I said.

"That fucking Tonto thing."

"It comes and goes," I said.

"It really came today," Mary said. "It really came today."

I looked around the half-empty restaurant, searching for poor Karen, then made the mistake of saying, "Poor Karen," out loud.

Mindy glared at me. "Poor Karen."

"Come on. Try to remember what she's going through, okay? She was supposed to be getting married. Instead, she's eating here. How would you feel?"

Mindy gave an especially slow shrug. (Note: as you may have discerned by now, the Nichols women are frequent shruggers. They're also very good at it, world-class. They raise their shoulders deliberately, holding them up high and tight for an exaggerated second, before carefully lowering them back to standard, Greenwich Mean position. It's an effective and sometimes dramatic way of conveying a "not in my job description," "I don't know," or, in Mindy's case, "I don't give a fuck" sentiment. I was never sure of its origins, but over time the gesture had become an ingrained part of our family's culture, a primary form of communications. Even Ethan did it occasionally.)

"She's never been able to spend any time with Ethan," Mindy said.

"That's not true," I said.

"It is so true. I always babysat him. She never did."

"Well, she was always on a date or at a party or something. You never left home." That last part kind of slipped out.

Mindy's pale pixie face turned evil, her lips curling upward. "And what's that supposed to mean?"

"Nothing. Where the hell is our waitress —"

"What did you mean by that?"

"I. Starving."

"He didn't mean anything. Let's eat and find a hotel," Mary said.

"I went out. I had friends."

"I know you did." Then, since the hole I was digging apparently wasn't quite deep enough, I said, "You and Karen emphasized different things, that's all."

"What does that mean? Different things?"

"Just drop it," Mary said.

"Well, she liked athletics, for example, and you loved animals."

"Okay, here come the hamster jokes again."

"I never said anything about the hamsters. You know, we're all tired right now. . . ."

"You never let me have a dog. All I got were the stupid hamsters."

"We couldn't have a dog because of Ethan, you know that. That would have been a bad combination. And those hamsters were great, they were great. I mean that. I miss them. Lassie, Benji, Lassie-Who-Won't-Die. That one lived forever, remember that one? It just wouldn't die." I looked hopefully across the table at Ethan. "Do you have to go to the bathroom?"

"No." He had gotten ahold of Mary's phone and was punching numbers.

"Are you sure? I can take you. You had a lot of water at the water plant."

"No."

"You sure?"

"Shut. Up. Idiot."

"I wish this fucking place served booze," Mindy said. "Why are we here?"

"Watch the language. And there's nothing wrong with Cracker Barrel," I said. "Their food is actually pretty good. And he likes to browse the store; they have a lot of knick-knacks."

"You mean they have a lot bullshit. This

whole restaurant is built on bullshit. They should call it the Bullshit Barrel."

"Hey, watch the language," I said again. "We don't need him picking up on any new words."

"I just want a glass of wine. Today was nuts."

"I think you could use a break from the booze," I said.

"Okay, Dean Martin."

"Where. Karen. Be?"

"Good question. Where is she?" I asked.

"Who gives a shit?" Mindy said. With that, she stormed off toward the Old Country Store, the very epicenter of bullshit.

I watched her leave. "We raised a couple of sweet angels, you know that? Yes, sir, we did something right. Nothing but love in those girls. Nothing but love."

"Where. Mindy. Be?"

"Maybe the girls should just go home," Mary said.

"Come on. We had a bad day, that's all. Things will get better. We'll have dinner, find a nice hotel, maybe all go for a swim, maybe go out for ice cream. It'll be fine."

"Everything will always be okay," she said.

"It will be."

"Wish I had your attitude." She went back to her menu.

"Hey, I'll lend it to you. You can have it for a week."

Mary shook her head, but smiled a little.

I was giving serious consideration to reaching for her hand when my phone went off. Rita. *God damn her!*

"Who's that?"

I fumbled to turn it off. "Sal."

"Aren't you going to get it?"

"I don't want to talk to him. I'll call him later."

"Let me talk to him then."

"Sal! Me. Talk!"

"No, not now. We're eating. We'll call him later."

Ethan made a grab for my phone. "Sal!"

I jammed my phone in my pocket. "No! We're eating."

"We're not eating," Mary said.

The girls miraculously saved me by marching back into the restaurant like a pair of Imperial Stormtroopers. Mindy sat down, pulling her chair close to the table, but Karen remained standing.

"You taking our order or what?" Mindy asked.

"I'm meeting someone," Karen said.

"What?" I asked. "Who?"

"I have a friend here from college, Donna Schrader, and I'm meeting up with her for dinner. She just called."

"Here?" Mary asked. "I don't even know where we are."

"You have a friend in Fredericksburg?" I asked.

"Yes. She was a DG, and we're meeting up at a place in town. So, can I have the car?"

"I thought we could all eat together," I said.

"I've had enough family time today," Karen said. "There's a Hampton Inn five miles from here. They have rooms. There's no Marriott. I'll meet you back there later tonight."

"How late are you going to be?" Mary asked.

"I don't know." She turned to me. "Can I take the other van, the rental?"

"Ask your mother."

Mary studied Karen, her face impassive, Buddha-like. "Don't be too late. We have another long day tomorrow."

Karen snatched the keys from the table, and left.

"Where? Karen. Be?"

"She'll be back," Mary said.

"That's strange," I said. "Who the hell is this Donna?"

"She's meeting the Jaw." Mindy said this

282

from behind her menu.

"What?" Mary asked.

"Roger. She's meeting him."

"Roger?" I took a hold of Mindy's menu and lowered it so I could see her face. "What are you talking about? Roger."

Mindy avoided my eyes. "I just heard her on her phone in the bathroom. She talks so loud. They've been talking the whole trip, I think. They're going to meet somewhere."

"Roger? Really? Are you serious?"

"That's what I heard." Before we could bombard her with more questions, Mindy stood abruptly and said, "I got to make a call," and jetted off.

"Where. Mindy. Be?"

"Roger? Do you believe that? That's crazy!" I said. "And why would she want to see him?"

Mary looked a little stunned. "I don't know what's going on."

"You think maybe he's following us? He must be! How else can they be meeting?"

Mary gazed intently out the window, her mouth a straight line. "I said, I don't know."

"I'm going to try to stop her." I stood. "I can catch her."

"No, you're not. Sit down." Mary pulled her red purse onto the table and began searching through it. "She's almost thirty years old."

"Are you sure?"

"She's a big girl. Sit down."

"Where. Karen. Be?"

I sat back down and looked out the window, at the highway, and watched cars and trucks move by. My daughter was probably already on that highway, heading to meet up with a man I detested. I didn't like this turn of events, I didn't like it at all.

After Mindy returned to the table and Mary and I interrogated her on exactly what she heard; and after I ordered the chicken-fried chicken but didn't eat any of it; and after I asked, "She said the name Roger, you're sure of that, I mean, you heard her say the name Roger?"; and after Mindy said/ yelled, "yes, yes, yes!"; and after I cut up my chicken-fried chicken into small pieces and gave them to Ethan because he was still hungry even after his chicken-fried steak; and after we were all quiet, lost in our own, presumably-worried-about-Karen, wonder-where-she is thoughts; and after Mindy said, "What the fuck is a cracker barrel anyway?" and I said, "You know, you should be thinking about Karen"; and after I started wondering what the fuck a cracker barrel was; and after Mindy asked the waitress what it was; and after the waitress said she wasn't sure but that it might have been a barrel used in "olden times"; and after I ordered another chicken-fried chicken dinner because despite my worries over Karen, I realized I actually was hungry; and after Mindy snorted and said, "Olden times, what the fuck?" under her breath; and after I said, "Stop acting so New York"; and after Mindy said, "What does that mean"; and after I said, "You know what I mean"; and after Mindy said, "No I don't"; and after I said, "Yes, you do, Miss Always Dresses in Black"; and after Mary slammed the table with her hand and yelled, "Will you two please stop it!"; and after Mindy and I stopped it; and after I finished my chicken-fried chicken and briefly considered ordering the fried ice cream for dessert but instead asked for the bill (which wasn't fried), we checked into the Hampton Inn, where I gave Ethan his bath.

"Oh, man, poor Karen," I said, drying him off with a towel. "I hope she knows what she's doing."

Ethan, who seemed to understand that Karen's disappearance was cause for concern, looked at me with wider-than-usual eyes and held up his hands in question. "Where. Karen. Be?"

"She's with Roger, we think. Who apparently isn't gay, by the way."

"Call."

"Call? You mean, Karen?"

"Yes! Me. Call."

"Oh, sure." I gave him his old cell phone, then sat on the bed while he punched numbers, pleased that he was doing something in context of the situation.

"Karen?"

"Tell her to come home," I said. "Tell her Roger is a dirtbag. Tell her, once a cheater, always a cheater. Wait a minute — don't tell her that. That's not necessarily true."

"Hi. Karen!"

"Tell her come home!"

"Home!"

"Tell her we love you!"

"Yes!"

"Tell her, she will get over this. Tell her to forget the Jaw."

"Forget. The. Jaw!"

I stopped, surprised. Those were new words for him. Ethan's vocabulary was very limited, and any new words, any addition other than possibly the f-bomb, was cause for celebration. "Right! Exactly! Forget the Jaw! That's great! Do you know what a jaw is?"

He reached out and touched my jaw.

"Right! Yes!" I wished Karen were here to witness this breakthrough. I was teaching him, stretching him after all. He would be reading and writing soon, then going to college, maybe just a state school, but still. "Very good! Roger has a big jaw. And he's a cheating slime bucket, but then again, who am I to talk, huh? I'm in an awkward position here, very awkward, don't you think? I got Rita calling me now. Rita! What's that all about, do you think? Rita's going to ruin everything. Stupid Rita!"

"Reeeeta!"

I froze. Another new word. But not a good one. In fact, of all the words in the King's speech, all of them, this was the one I never wanted my verbally challenged son to master and then yell eighty to ninety times a day.

I paused, knowing my next move was crucial. If I emphasized the wrongness of this word, admonished him for saying it, overreacted, it would be forever ingrained in his lexicon. I had made that mistake years ago with *shit, shut up,* and *idiot.* I simply could not make the same mistake with Rita.

"Hey, I got an idea," I said. "Want to watch the Illini game?"

He pointed a finger upward. "Yes!"

"Good. Illini! Yes, let's do that. Let's

cleanse our minds with that! Let's forget everything else, wipe the slate clean. Perfect!" I put on his pajamas and grabbed my laptop.

Years ago my beloved Fighting Illini had staged the most memorable comeback in NCAA tournament history, scoring fifteen points in a frantic, four-minute span to force overtime against the University of Arizona. They would go on to win and advance to their first Final Four in sixteen years. I had attended that game with Sal, we had great seats, and had since watched tapes and rebroadcasts of it dozens and dozens of times with Ethan, the excitement and mounting disbelief of the announcers' voices, the insane cheering of the crowd, holding his attention like few things could.

I found the last ten minutes of the game on YouTube. By now, Ethan and I both knew every steal, every basket, every deflection, every syllable of the announcers' breathless narrative. Over the years this game had fused to our consciousness, and we never tired of seeing it one more time.

"There's Deron — watch him now," I said. "He's going to hit the three."

When Illinois's star guard, Deron Williams, sidestepped a defender at the top of the key and drained his game-tying shot, a shot that had filled me with the purest form of joy, a shot that reaffirmed my optimistic outlook on life, a shot that helped me get to sleep more nights than I cared to admit, Ethan pounded the bed with his fist and screamed, "Three!"

"Three!" I yelled.

"Go. Illini!"

"Yes, go, Illini!"

We watched the game to its amazing conclusion and slapped each other five several times. The game, the shot, had once again served its purpose, washing me clean of all worry, albeit just for a while.

I gave Ethan a glass of water and watched him drink. He looked relaxed and happy, his eyes shimmering — Ethan at ease. Seeing him so content, I thought the time might be right to share something else with him.

"Hey, I want to show you some pictures. Come on, sit down."

I returned to the laptop and found the Ocean View Web site. While I had mentioned the home to him in passing a handful of times, I had not made a concerted effort to discuss it, or his future, in any detail. Since I was never exactly sure what he was grasping, I didn't want to unnecessarily raise his anxiety. I did know that it was best to tell him about upcoming plans with as little advance notice as possible. I thought this might be a good time to start preparing him; we were just days away.

"Here's where we're going," I said, pointing to a picture of Ocean View. It showed a stately, redbrick building with black shutters and a long porch dotted with white wicker rocking chairs. I touched a photo of one of the chairs with my finger. "You can rock back and forth on those chairs. And you can see the ocean from there too. Very pretty."

Ethan stared at the picture.

I swallowed. "You're going to stay there. Live there. Maybe."

Next I showed him the spacious gym with hardwood floors and six different baskets. The gym was a key factor in my decision, a selling point.

"You can shoot hoops there," I said. "They just built it."

"How. Many. Me. Make?"

"Fifty."

"How. Many. Dad. Make?"

"Twelve. You win." I paused. "But you'll be playing with other people too."

"Go. Illini!"

"Right." I clicked on the link for the swimming pool. "You can go swimming every

290

day there. It's warm. Heated. You can do that after you play hoops. Hold on to the sides, though. Be careful."

"Yes. Ma'am."

Since he still seemed interested, I moved on to a photo of a bedroom. It was nondescript, with a twin bed, dresser, classroom-style desk, and a small TV. A vase of flowers was perched on the dresser, a burst of yellow-and-purple colors that made the rest of the room seem stark by comparison.

"This isn't a very good picture. The rooms are nicer," I said. "They're very comfortable and sunny, and you have two windows that overlook the back where there're hoops and places to play catch every day and run and take walks. And they have cable, of course, so you can watch *SportsCenter* and some Illini basketball games."

"Go. Illini!"

"Right. And there's a computer room where we can Skype you every day. Every day we can talk and see you on a computer. I'm going to call you every day, see you every day. Every day that you're gone. Every day."

I quickly shut the computer, cleared my throat, and stared straight ahead at the blank TV. We would be there soon. In a few days we would be there. I let this sink in. Then I reached over and grabbed Ethan and hugged him as hard as I could.

"Why. Mad?" he asked. "Why. Mad?"

The next morning we found Mary sitting alone in the lobby, her head hunched over her phone.

I pulled out a chair for Ethan. "Good morning."

"She didn't come home last night."

"Who? Karen?"

"She didn't come home. I was up all night. Finally I went looking for her."

"You drove around last night?"

"Yes. It's not a very big town. I thought I'd see the van, but I didn't."

"Eat. Starving. Eat. Now!"

"Wait a minute. Just wait." I walked over to the windows, scanned the mostly empty parking lot. "Is the van here now? Is she back?"

"I said she didn't come back."

"Where is she? Do you think she's all right? Did you call her?"

"Eat!"

"Please, Ethan, wait! Did you call her?"

"I left her a message. Get him something. I'll sit with him."

"Juice!"

"Get him some juice," she said.

I walked in a fog over to the small buffet in the center of the lobby and grabbed a banana, yogurt, and juice, my mind on Karen. Why would she do this? Why would she rush off to see him? Why didn't she come back? Why wouldn't she call? When I returned to the table, Mindy was sitting there, nursing a small Styrofoam cup of coffee. Despite the weather, she was wearing her black Princeton sweat shirt, the hood up. Her eyes were puffy, her face pale.

"This coffee sucks," she mumbled.

I placed Ethan's food in front of him.

"Tell him," Mary said.

I remained standing. "Tell me what?"

Mindy took a deep gulp of her coffee, grimaced. "What time is it?"

"Eight thirty. Tell me what?"

Mindy took another swig of coffee. "Karen is meeting us in Washington, DC. She's already there."

"She's in Washington?"

"She just texted me. She said she's at the Marriott by the airport. Can you sit down?"

"She contacted you?" I asked.

"Yes. She knew I wouldn't ask any follow-up questions, and she was right — I didn't."

"Well, I am." I took my phone out.

"You really think she's going to answer?" Mindy asked.

I put the phone down on the table, and Ethan immediately snatched it up. "Is she with Roger?"

"Probably, I don't know." Mindy swirled her coffee. "So, when are we leaving?"

"Soon," I said.

"I have to shower," Mindy said.

"Then go. Hurry."

"Okay, okay." Mindy slowly got up from the table and disappeared down the hall.

"Where? Mindy? Be?"

"She'll be back, honey. She's taking a shower."

Ethan returned to his yogurt and my phone, pressing numbers with sticky fingers.

"You don't think they're getting back together again, do you? After what he did to her?" I asked.

Mary took off her glasses and rubbed her eyes. She looked exhausted. "I can't believe she would."

"This just pisses me off. It's very selfish of her to leave us like this, make us worry like this. Like we don't have enough on our minds? We should be focused on Ethan right now. This is a very hard and very important thing we're trying to do, and she's doing crazy things like this, distracting us."

Mary gave me a sad mother's smile. "Distracting us?"

"Yes. You're out there all night looking for her. I was up half the night worrying about her. Maybe I can understand their wanting to talk, but to disappear and not call? To take off like this?"

"She's going through a lot right now. We have to give her some space."

I paused. "Okay, yes, all right. But she could have told us. A quick call, at least. A text."

Mary hoisted her bag over her shoulder. "You have to remember that it's not just about Ethan," she said. "It's about all of us, John, all of us." She stood and headed toward the door. "I'm going to wait in the van."

"Did you even eat anything?"

"I'm not hungry."

As soon as we got on the road, Mary put her iPod on and slumped down in her seat. Out of the corner of my eye, I watched her head lean, then gently fall against the window. I knew she was worried and beyond tired, and I wanted to take her hand, reassure her, but that was a privilege I was no longer allowed. I switched lanes.

A few miles down the road, I checked on

Ethan, who was happily sharing his photo album with Mindy in the middle seat.

"Pretty amazing, Dad," Mindy said.

"What? You mean the book?"

"Incredible."

I smiled. I had spent quite a bit of time putting a photo album together for Ethan, carefully selecting each picture, writing captions I knew other people would read. It was essentially a composite of his life, including photos of everyone and everything that was important to him: the local Dominick's supermarket, his favorite place on earth, where people were particularly patient and friendly. The Wilton Panera, where he and I had breakfast every Saturday; Rafferty's Bar, where we had dinner on Fridays; Auerilo's pizza, where we ate on Saturdays; Denetha the deli woman, Chuck the bartender, Sally the waitress, all the people who made his life, our lives, a little easier. They were all in there, as well as photos of the Sals, Mary, me, the Bears, and, of course, Mindy and Karen. I had planned to give it to him at Ocean View, but decided to dig it out of a box that morning.

"How long did it take you to do this? There has to be, like, a hundred pages. It's huge."

"One hundred and four pages. I've been

doing it for a while," I said proudly. It took a lot to impress Mindy.

"Who are all these people?"

"Ethan's friends. Different people. People who work at the supermarket, the restaurants, neighbors, people like that."

"Who's this, Ethan?"

"Denetha!"

"The grocery store," I said. "We went there every day. She worked in the deli and gave him a piece of cheese. It was the highlight of his day."

"And who's this, Ethan?"

"C.C!"

"She was his aide at school. She watched him for years. She also came over to the house."

"He's going to miss them," Mindy said.

I swallowed. "He can come home whenever we want and see them. And he'll make new friends."

Her comment stirred the Doubt and Guilt, so I stopped talking and switched my attention back to the road, passed another Honda van, then a beer truck. Signs for towns with *Blue Highway* names — Stafford, Garrisonville — flew by.

"Oh my God. Why do you have this picture?"

"What? Which one?"

"The one of Karen and me. Going to that dance. God, look at my hair."

"It's historic. Your big double date. She was a senior, you were a sophomore. See, you went on dates."

"I couldn't believe she let me go with her. She must have been doing community service or something."

"She wanted to go with you."

"We had fun I think. Something happened though."

"You got drunk and threw up on your date."

"Right. Tom Murphy. I knew it was something highbrow."

"See? That picture is proof positive that you two can get along. Exhibit A."

I expected some kind of cutting response, stings like a butterfly, but Mindy fell quiet. A minute later I saw her still studying the picture, her brow furrowed.

"Why. Mad?" Ethan asked her.

"She's been crying," Mindy said.

"What?" I turned down the Christmas carols. "Who's crying?"

"Karen. She's been crying a lot. I've heard her. Our rooms are right next to each other. Most of the night, she never stops. I hear her."

"Karen? Crying? Are you sure? Karen?"

"Yeah, I hear her," Mindy said. "She's crying. A lot."

The rest of the way to Washington was a blur. Whether Ethan behaved, whether he stomped his feet, shrieked, or quietly conjugated verbs on the legal pad that Karen had given him, I no longer recall. All I could think about was Karen.

"Slow down," Mindy said.

"Just keep him busy."

There was guilt, and then there was the more serious form, father's guilt, and I was experiencing the latter. With her words from the other night — *You walked around in an Ethan daze when I was growing up* — now ringing in my ears, I came to the conclusion, long suspected, that I had never really been there for my queen bee. Self-sufficient, independent, and strong since the day she was born, she was the third adult in our house, someone who made her own choices, did her own thing. In short, someone who never asked, so never received. Mindy, a precocious child and, of course Ethan, were other stories, demanding time, attention, and energy. But Karen never needed my help, ever. That was, of course, up until now, and when she finally had asked for it, finally had reached out, what had I done? I had ignored her calls, cut her short, dismissed her running off to see Roger as a distraction.

Ethan had a lot to do with this — he was a huge responsibility — but while that might be an explanation, it was no excuse. Over the years I should have made time, found time. In the end, was one child, regardless of his or her needs, any more important than another?

"Why didn't you tell me she was crying?"

"I don't know. It's a pretty private thing."

"You should have said something."

"I just did."

"Call her or . . . or text her. Tell her to meet me in the lobby in twenty minutes."

"She was just crying."

"Just do it! Please! Just tell her I'm going to be there as soon as I can."

When we arrived at the Marriott, Mary finally woke up, pushing off the door groggily, and asking, "Where are we?" Her hair was matted down on one side, her face flushed red.

"At the hotel. I'm going to find Karen."

"Swimming!" Ethan cried. "Me. Out!"

Mary cleared her throat and fumbled in her bag for her glasses. "Are we getting out here?"

"No, I'm going to find Karen, and we're leaving. Everyone, just wait here. We're not staying."

I jumped out of the van and hurried across the parking lot, my intentions still unclear. I wasn't sure what I was going to say or do when I saw Karen, wasn't sure what I was hoping to accomplish. Apologizing, admitting negligence, and offering love and support were all options. One thought was clear, though: for once, I was going to make her a priority.

I worked my way through the lobby, weaving through small packs of people wearing plastic name tags. A conference of some kind was obviously taking place, and there must have been a coffee break because a crowd was growing and it was hard to walk, much less locate, Karen.

After circling the noisy room for a few minutes, I ended up at the front desk, where I asked the clerk to ring Karen's room. Apparently, though she had already checked out.

"When did she do that?" I asked.

"I really can't give out that information, sir."

"But I'm her father."

"I'm sorry."

I checked my phone for messages, then

surveyed the room again. The place was packed now, mostly with young men talking and gesturing animatedly. I was about to plunge back into the crowd and resume my search, when somehow, over the din, I heard the all-too-familiar sound of Ethan in distress.

"Swimming! Now! Swimming! Now!"

The center of the crowd parted, and there he was, crawling frantically on his hands and knees toward me. Mindy followed, clutching Stinky and Grandpa Bear in mad pursuit.

"Excuse us! Excuse me! Watch it, move it, don't step on his hands!" Mindy yelled. "Come on, Ethan, get up. Excuse me! He's all right. He just lost a contact."

I watched the scene unfold with a sinking heart. Not this, not now.

"Swimming! Swimming!"

When Ethan saw me, he stood, his face red, wild, helpless. I ran over to him and took him in my arms. His body was rigid, so I rubbed his shoulders to calm him. "It's okay, it's okay," I cooed. From a safe distance, a group of men looked on with confusion, and then, inevitably, sympathy.

"He just bolted out of the van. I couldn't stop him," Mindy said.

"It's okay. He's all right."

"Is she here?"

"I don't know. I don't think so. They said she checked out."

Mindy handed me Stinky Bear. "She said she was here. She just texted me."

"She did? I can't find her." I gently pressed Stinky against Ethan's cheek to dry his tears, while the crowd drifted back to its meeting. As the room began to empty, a placard in the corner came in to view: YOUNG UROLOGISTS SOCIETY OF AMERICA.

"Dick doctors," Mindy muttered. "A whole roomful."

I kissed Ethan on the top of his head, smoothed his hair. "You okay now? Everything okay? You shouldn't crawl like that. You're a big guy. Big guys don't crawl on the floor. You have to stop doing things like this. You have to."

I felt his body stiffen again. "What's wrong? Relax. Everything's okay. All done. Just relax."

"Karen!" he yelled.

"What? Karen? Where?"

"Karen!" Ethan pulled away from me and bolted, stiff-legged, arms flapping, toward the entrance of the hotel.

I followed his path, and he was right, there she was, Karen, standing in front of the revolving doors dressed in sweat pants and a blue T-shirt, her hair pulled back in an unfamiliar ponytail. Mindy and I quickly made our way to her.

"Hey, Karen, over here!"

When she saw us, she gave a small and decidedly unenthusiastic wave, murmuring, "Oh, hi," when we reached her. Ethan hugged her hard while she absently rubbed his hair.

"Swimming!"

"Yeah, swimming. Sure." Her voice was flat.

"Are you okay?"

"I was going outside to look for you. I just checked out."

"Is Roger here? Are you with Roger?"

She ignored my question. "Where's Mom?" she asked.

"She's outside."

"Pee-pee."

"Just wait, Ethan!" I snapped.

"Pee-pee now!"

"I'll take him," Mindy said.

"He doesn't have to go." I scanned the lobby asked again. "Is Roger here?"

She shrugged.

"Listen, don't go back to him. Whatever you do, don't do that."

"Who said I'm going back to him? Who said that?"

"Then what are you doing here?"

As if on cue, the man of the hour, Roger, appeared, looking like Thurston Howell III had dressed him that morning: dark blue blazer, white button-down shirt, chinos, loafers. The eternal fraternity man, a future, if not already, Master of the Universe. I stared at his jaw, as big as a pelican's. I did not want my grandchildren to have a jaw like that. I did not want pelican grandchildren.

"Hello, John." He said this casually, without a trace of embarrassment, as if we had just run into each other in the locker room of the club, towels wrapped around our trust-fund asses. He smiled and extended his hand, which I appropriately ignored.

He nodded and smiled at Ethan, then turned to Karen. "Can we talk?"

"We're done talking," Karen said.

"Just another minute."

"Nice. Outside. Hot."

"My family's here now. I'm going," she said.

"She's done talking to you," I said.

"Karen," he said.

"You heard her."

He turned to face me full on. He was about three inches shorter than me, and had a loose, athlete's air about him, a fluidity that I, for the first time, noted. "John, in all due respect, this doesn't really concern you."

"Anything involving Karen concerns me."

He gave me a dismissive smile and then reached for Karen's arm. She tried to pull away.

"Come on, babe."

"Let go of her!"

I took a step toward him. (Note: I am not a violent man. Far from it. But I am six-foot-three and, at least at one time, was a competitive athlete. Big Ten. Big stage. I spent the formative years of my life, the years you draw on in moments of crisis, the years that shape your response mechanisms, exchanging elbows, pushes, hacks, and charges with boys and then men much larger than me on the basketball court. I've thrown blind picks that have sent men flying; I've exchanged trash talk with gangbangers; I've played hurt. These experiences, combined with the fact that I loved my daughter, were dealing with a torrent of recently released guilt, were functioning with massive sleep-deprivation and had-been-in-a-van-with-Ethan-Nichols-for-close-to-a-week, a period of time that would have pushed Gandhi over the edge, probably explain what happened next.)

I swung at Roger with the hand that was still clutching Stinky Bear, hitting him directly in his pelican jaw. Even though Stinky buffeted the blow, down Roger went, flat on his back, my hand stinging.

"Dad!" Karen cried.

"Get up, you big pussy!" Mindy yelled before stepping behind me.

I stood there, breathing hard, aware that dozens of young urologists' eyes, the future of America's urine, were once again on us, or more specifically, on me.

"Why. Mad?"

"Jesus!" Roger said. He got to his feet and began to back away.

"Don't you ever touch my daughter again. Don't you ever see her again. Do you understand me?"

"Just settle down, John." Roger rubbed his jaw and then examined his hand.

"Don't tell me to settle down!" I moved in on him again, but this time, rather than risk breaking my hand on the Pelican, I began swatting him in the face with Stinky Bear.

"Dad!" Karen yelled. "Stop it!"

"Wow! Wow!"

Roger turned his head, and I noticed a strip of white adhesive, a large bandage, running along the base of his neck. I took square aim at it.

"John, please. I just wanted to talk to her!" Roger yelled. He kept backing away in search of safe quarter, but I pursued, banging away with Stinky.

"John, stop it!" First Mary's voice, then Mary. She was standing by the doors, holding Red Bear.

"Hit him, Mom!" Mindy yelled. She raised Grandpa Bear menacingly over her head. "Come on! Finish him off! Family, family!"

"USA!" Ethan shrieked, delighted.

Mary approached, her eyes ping-ponging from me to Roger, from Roger to me. "What is going on here?"

"Nothing." I stopped with the swatting, caught my breath, and appraised my almost-son-in-law. Despite the fact that he had just been severely beaten at close range by a teddy bear, his blond hair still looked perfect, and this perfectness infuriated me even more. I stepped toward him and raised Stinky.

"John!" Mary yelled. "Put the bear down. Now!"

I lowered Stinky, backed away. "You stay away from my daughter, you understand me? And don't call her 'babe' anymore.

She's not your babe."

"John, please," Roger said. He was holding the back of his neck.

"You stay away."

"Why? Mad?"

Roger started to say something, but I put a finger to my lips and stared him down, ex-philanderer to philanderer. Then I took Karen and Ethan each by the hand and walked out, head high, Stinky tucked under my arm.

After a fast-and-furious ride, during which I refused to answer any of Mary's questions or explain my actions; and after I yelled, "Shut up, will everyone just shut up?" several times at the top of my lungs; and after I refused to go back and get Karen's things at the hotel or pick up the other van; and after I raised the volume of Alvin and the Chipmunks singing "We Wish You a Merry Christmas," then raised it even higher after Mindy screamed that the fucking music was eating her brain; and after I almost ran another minivan off the road because they were driving too slow and/or I was driving too fast; and after Mary grabbed my arm and yelled, "John, you're going to get us all killed," and I yelled, "No one is getting killed, okay, no one's getting killed";

and after I turned off the music and thought, *I'm probably going to get us all killed,* we stopped at a Cracker Barrel, where drained, exhausted, and slightly dizzy, I worried if I was finally having the major breakdown that I was destined to have on this trip.

"Put the bear down, John," Mary said after we were at our table. "Let go of the bear."

"Put it down, Dad," Mindy said. "Nice and easy, nice and easy."

"What?" In my frenzy, I hadn't realized that I had been clutching Stinky Bear since the fight. I slowly placed him on the table where Ethan snatched him up.

"Stinky!"

I cleared my throat.

"What was that all about?" Mary asked. She was genuinely worried, her eyes searching my face, and this long-lost look of concern made me want to start crying, bury my face in her soft shoulder. I was about to lose it.

Karen saved me the sentimentality. "You know, it was really stupid what you did back there. Hitting him. Leaving my things at the hotel. Leaving the van. I don't need rescuing. This has nothing to do with you. Nothing!"

Though I had thought I was done with histrionics, I pounded the table and hissed, "What do you want me to do, huh? Shake his hand?"

"You acted crazy!" Karen said.

"She's right, John. You shouldn't have hit him," Mary said.

"Yeah, Dad, that was kind of Nicholas Cage of you," Mindy said.

"Crazy? Crazy is running off to a man who cheats on you days before your wedding. Crazy is . . . is . . . lying about where you were going like some, silly, teenage girl. We were worried sick about you!"

My outburst caught Karen by surprise. She looked down at the table, and I saw her swallow hard. This wasn't exactly the father-daughter moment I had envisioned earlier that day.

"Hey, I'm sorry. This whole trip, everything. I'm just tired." I reached for her hand, but she pulled it away.

"I'm sorry," I said again.

Karen looked up, then back down again and said, "I wanted to make sure he was okay."

"What?" I asked. "Are you kidding? Who cares about him?"

"I hit him. I hit him pretty bad with a bottle. The glass broke. He was bleeding. I

311

thought he was going to die."

We were all, understandably, confused by what seemed to be some kind of confession. I shooed the waitress away and asked Karen, as calmly as I could, what the hell she was talking about.

She kept her eyes on the table as if she were reading from a script. "We had to go to the emergency room. He was cut pretty bad. His neck. He turned when I swung at him. Turned his head. They were going to call the police, the doctors were, but Roger talked them out of it. I thought I'd killed him when I first did it. Blood was everywhere. I hit him hard."

It was Mary who responded first, speaking softly. "Honey, what are you talking about? When did this happen? Last night?"

"Sprite!"

"When we were in Charleston. The night I found them. That night. He and I, we had a fight. In the suite upstairs. You were in your room."

"Jesus," I said, and reached for her hand, which she now let me hold.

We all sat there in silence for a second or two. Then Karen started to cry.

"Oh, baby," I said.

She covered her face and, between terrible sobs, said, now in a high soft voice I hadn't heard in years, "I thought I loved him and I almost killed him. I was going to marry him. Marry him! Why did this happen? I thought I loved him. Look at me. Look what's happened. All of this, why did this happen? How do you plan for something like this? I was supposed to be married. *Married.* How do you plan for this?" She rushed out of the room.

"Oh God." Mary threw her napkin down and chased after her.

"Where. Mom. Be?"

"She'll be back. She'll be back." I handed Ethan my water and looked at Mindy. Her eyes were wide, her cheeks puffed out. "Did you know anything about this? Police? Emergency room?"

She shook her head, her bottom lip protruding. I thought she too might start to cry. Instead she pushed her chair back and stood.

"Where you are going?"

"Check things out," she mumbled.

"What?"

"See what's going on." She took a quick drink of water and then left, surprisingly, to join her sister.

Later, at the Hampton Inn just outside of Dundalk, Maryland, after I had given gave

313

Ethan his bath, his meds, and the bears, and after I took him down the hall to Mindy's room for the night, I called Mary.

"There's no bar here," she said.

"Hampton Inns don't have bars."

"Then let's not stay at any more Hampton Inns."

"Okay."

"Do you have any of your private stash?"

"Yes. A little."

"Meet me in the lobby."

I found her sitting by the large-screen TV, staring vacantly at a baseball game, her hands clasped in front of her like an obedient schoolgirl. She had two paper cups, already filled with ice, sitting on the small table. I pulled out a chair.

"Hit me," she said.

"Probably not the best choice of words around me." I poured the bourbon. "So, how is she?"

"She'll be all right. She cried for a while."

"Did she say anything else? Any more details about what happened?"

"No. She just cried. Let it out. It was good for her."

I sat back. "Pretty disturbing."

"Yep."

"Did Mindy follow you? Was she there with Karen?"

"Yes, she was there."

"Kind of a surprise."

Mary shrugged. "She loves Karen."

"You're kidding, right?"

"She loves her sister."

"Not so sure about that."

"She does, trust me. She does."

"You're not seeing or hearing what I am then."

"It started with Karen, the whole thing. The fighting. It started with her."

"Really? I thought it was more Mindy's issue."

Mary rubbed her eyes. "You have to remember, Karen used to be like a mom to her. Took care of Mindy. And Mindy worshipped her. Let's face it, Karen was pretty perfect. *Is* pretty perfect. But Mindy got into Princeton after Karen didn't. Mindy gets on TV. Suddenly Karen isn't needed anymore. So she starts ignoring Mindy, not returning her calls, all that. Little things at first. But one thing led to another. Karen attacks. Mindy retaliates. That magazine thing didn't help, that interview."

"Captain McBrag."

"That too. The whole thing has gotten out of hand. It's ridiculous."

"They'll work it out," I said, though I wasn't completely convinced they would.

"They will," Mary said.

I stretched my legs, tried to get comfortable in the small hard chair. "I can't believe I did that."

"What?"

"Roger. Punching him."

"I can't believe you did that either. Never seen you like that."

"I lost it."

"You and Karen."

"What can I say, we're a violent family." I took a drink, the bourbon stinging the back of my throat. "God, Karen's story. That could have been tragic."

Mary shrugged again. "The things I used to see in the DA's office, that wouldn't even register. I know a good therapist, though. Maybe she can refer someone in New York for her."

"A therapist? How do you know him?"

"It's a she. I went to her after the divorce."

"Oh." I glanced away.

Mary looked out the window. It had been overcast all day, and the rain had finally come, a soft, steady drizzle. I finished my drink and watched Mary watch the rain in the summer twilight and all at once I felt myself sagging. This trip had led us all to this strange and sad and complicated point, and I wondered where it would take us next.

"You know," Mary said. "After he was diagnosed, it was hard. But I remember thinking things would get better. I remember thinking that there would be a time when everything would be fine, or at least close to fine. Ethan would be happy and better, the girls be happy. You and me —" She stopped. "I kept thinking that if we stuck together, we would eventually get to where everything was going to be fine. That we were going to make it, all of us. We were going to arrive someplace together and be fine. You used to tell me that all the time. A happy ending. You used to say that. We're going to have a happy ending." Her voice caught, and she briefly put her hand to her mouth.

"We're going to have a happy ending."

"No, we're not. Not this time."

"Everything will be fine, especially for the girls. They have good lives. They're smart, successful. Come on, they're pretty amazing when you think about it. What they've already accomplished."

"They're not happy. They're both angry all the time, and they drink too much, especially Mindy. Maybe it was me, or you, or maybe it was the stress of Ethan, I don't know. Maybe we didn't spend enough time with them."

"We did the best we could. You did, especially. And they're fine, they're fine."

"They deserve to be happy. I know I'll never be happy again, but I want my girls to be happy. That's all I want. At least let them find some happiness in this shitty world."

"It's not a shitty world."

"What's good about it? Look at us, in the middle of nowhere, the wedding off, taking my autistic son to some godforsaken place a thousand miles away, some institution."

"It's not an institution."

"And then I'm going to go home and be alone in that big house. Sally sick, the girls gone, Ethan gone, you . . ." She waved her hand.

I glanced at the front desk, saw the clerk was gone, then inched my chair closer and tried to put my arms around her, pull her toward me, but she brushed me away.

"Anyway." She picked up her big bag from the floor, stood. "What time are we meeting tomorrow?"

"Where are you going? Sit down. Come on."

She ran a finger under an eye. "I hope Karen's things get here in time."

I took in my ex-sweet-sweetie, standing in the lobby of a roadside hotel on a rainy night, broken and lonely, but decided not to push things. "They should be here by nine."

"What about the other van?"

"They're going to pick it up. We don't need two vans anymore. It's more of a hassle."

"It's going to be crowded."

"We'll be fine."

"Okay, well, I'm going to bed then."

"Good night, Mary."

"Okay."

10

Karen's things didn't arrive until after eleven, so rather than lose more time deciding what to ship, we jammed everything into the remaining Odyssey, making things very tight. Mindy sat in the far back, a bag on her lap, while Karen and Ethan were barricaded by boxes in the middle. Up front, Mary had bags wedged tight against her feet, and even though it was warm and sunny, I was forced to wear my jacket because there was absolutely no room for it anywhere.

"This is crazy," Mary said.

"We'll ship some more stuff at the next stop."

"Why didn't we ship it now?"

"Because I want to get going. We're losing time. We're supposed to be there in three days."

Back on I-95, Tony Bennett singing "Little Drummer Boy," the road clear and the sky a deep blue, the morning gradually settled. Though she had skipped breakfast, Karen seemed no worse for the wear. Ethan was fine too, alternately playing with the Etch A Sketch and his cell phone while Mary and Mindy read newspapers. There was no residue of last night's drama, no shadow of what had transpired. One thing life with Ethan had taught us all was that yesterday's issue, for the most part, was yesterday's issue.

"It's nice outside," I said.

No one, not even Ethan, responded, so I drove on in silence. As we made our way up the interstate, I tried to take advantage of this burst of peace, tried to put my William Least Heat-Moon hat on and sponge up what I could of the Eastern Seaboard, but instead was diverted by a memory from the War Years. We were having dinner, all of us, an unusual occurrence since Ethan, while a saint in restaurants, was a hellion at the kitchen table. Consequently, most of our attempts at family meals disintegrated into street fights, complete with food throwing, milk spilling, and my escorting Ethan from the table. But this one evening, for reasons unknown, he was calm, eating slowly and quietly, his head down over his plate. Mindy and Karen talked about their days at school.

Mary asked me if I wanted more meat loaf. We even had ice cream, chocolate chip, for dessert. I remember Mindy taking in the bucolic scene and saying, "Wow, look at us, we're like a normal family." That was all we'd ever wanted. Moments like that, moments like this.

The quiet was broken, but not by the likely source and not by a likely sound. It was Karen, and it was her laugh. I glanced in the mirror to confirm this Halley's-Comet occurrence and saw Mindy leaning forward holding her phone over Karen's shoulder. They were both watching something and smiling.

"Pretty hilarious, huh?" Mindy said.

"Yeah, funny," Karen said. "Do you know that guy?"

"Yeah, he's kind of an asshole, but he's funny."

"Yeah, he is."

Mindy sat back, pleased. Ethan remained transfixed by his Etch A Sketch and phone. Mary yawned and turned a page of her paper. I turned up "God Rest Ye Merry Gentlemen," and we drove on. Just like a normal family.

Normal family ended up having to make an abnormal number of stops throughout the day: for lunch, gas, poo-poo, pee-pee, Sprite, pee-pee again, and then again (this time for me). Finally, after a very late lunch (or very early dinner), we surrendered and checked into a Courtyard Marriott where, after a PBS–style-fundraising bear marathon on the bed ("Thanks to Bears Like You"), I took Ethan swimming.

The pool, as I was beginning to suspect all indoor hotel pools were, was empty. After getting him safely situated in the shallow end, I made a show of jumping in with a rebel yell and furiously swimming a lap, believing that one burst of exercise, that twenty seconds of frantic activity, would undo the havoc that the Cracker Barrel was wreaking on my body. When I was done, I stood in the deep end, gulping mouthfuls of humid chlorinated air.

"Why. Mad?" Ethan asked. His eyes were fixed on me as he carefully worked his way around the pool, holding on to the side. Occasionally, he stopped and kicked his legs with a huge grin on his face.

"Just having a heart attack. No biggie. Keep kicking."

"Mom!"

"Mom?" I turned. As advertised, my ex-sweet-sweetie was standing by the steamy glass door, wearing an unfamiliar black one-piece.

"Swimming! Mom! Hot!"

"She sure is!" I yelled this in Stinky Bear's voice.

Mary smiled, kicked off her flip-flops. "It is hot in here."

"What are you doing?"

"What does it look like I'm doing?" Without another word, she jumped in and disappeared under the water.

"Swimming! Mom!"

When Mary emerged, she splashed Ethan, and he happily splashed her back, smiling his wide, toothy grin. He didn't associate his mother with fun — no one in our family did — and he was beside himself.

"Mom! Wow! Wow!"

I watched the mother and son battle for a while, let them have their moment, then swam over and joined the fray, choosing no sides. After taking a few direct hits to the face, Mary surrendered.

"No mas!" She tried to escape, but I grabbed her foot. We ended up on the other side of the pool, laughing, breathing hard.

"What prompted this?" I asked.

Mary shrugged. She looked rejuvenated, her hair tucked back behind her ears, her face glistening. She gave me one last splash.

"I needed this."

"You look good in that suit."

She didn't respond to that. Instead she scooted low in the water and checked the clock above the door. "He can sleep with me tonight. I have a suite with two rooms. It was the only room they had."

"A suite, eh? Does it have a Jacuzzi?"

"It does, actually. Not sure why. I bet no one uses it."

"Let's use it tonight." Then I added, "For Ethan. I'll run out and get some wine for us."

She offered a smile. "Wine."

While this wasn't exactly an invitation, it wasn't exactly a don't-even-think-about-it, so, sensing an opportunity, I moved toward her. She let me stand close, so close that I could feel her breath warm on my face, see tiny streams of water dripping down the tops of her breasts.

"Another pool," she said.

I took her hand and was just beginning to think this was the culmination of two years of waiting and praying, that I was finally getting the nod to return from the desert, when I heard Ethan scream.

Mary jerked free of me and dove toward the center of the pool, where Ethan was thrashing away, half underwater. Before I could move, she was pulling him up, sputtering, coughing, gagging for air. I swam toward them as fast as I could.

"You're all right," she said. "You're okay. You can stand here. It's not that deep." Ethan was in a panic, yelling and throwing his arms about, his eyes filled with terror. As far as I knew, it was the first time he had been underwater.

I took a firm hold of an arm, Mary took the other, and we watched him cough for a minute before slowly leading him out of the pool. "You shouldn't have let go of the sides. Never let go. But you're okay, you're okay, Ethan, settle down, settle down," I repeated.

We dried him with separate towels while he stood, shaking, his coughing dying down. When he finished, he looked up at me.

"No. Swimming!"

"Okay, no swimming." I kissed him on the top of his head and felt his wet hair against my mouth.

"You can't leave him alone for a second," Mary said. "Not one second. You'd think we'd know that by now." The light in her eyes was gone, and the exhausted, worried Mary was back at her post.

"He's fine. He just went underwater. It's not a big deal. Why don't you go back in? I got him."

She laughed, but not happily. "I'm done." She put on her flip-flops.

"You sure?"

She wrapped the towel around her waist, tied the ends together in a hard knot. "Just bring him to my room."

"You sure?"

"Yes, I'm sure," she said, walking toward the door.

Even though he had just been swimming, I decided to wash Ethan's hair, so I gave him a bath. After I put on his pajamas, I brushed my teeth, slipped on a clean shirt, then hustled him down the hall to Mary's room. I still had hopes.

Those hopes died an immediate death when Mary opened the door in sweat pants that perfectly matched her worn-out expression.

"You get lost?" she asked.

"I gave him a bath. Sorry."

"Say good night, Ethan," she said. No hint of Jacuzzis, wine, the extra bedroom where Ethan could sleep while Mary and I quietly made long overdue love.

"Where. Stinky Bear. Be?"

"He's inside. Come on. Say good night."

Ethan shot me a resigned look that made me wonder if, on some basic male level, he had sensed his father's intentions. "Leave. Now," he said solemnly.

"Good night," I said.

"Leave. Now."

Mary took his hand and closed the door without so much as glancing at me. I lingered for a moment, all-dressed-up-with-nowhere-to-go, considered knocking, considered serenading her, but thought the better of it. Instead I issued my official one thousandth sigh of the trip and turned away.

I resisted the temptation of the lobby bar and instead returned to my room to map out the remainder of the trip. I pored over the Rand McNally and, factoring in dozens of poo-poo, pee-pee, Cracker Barrel, and Tonto breaks, tried to determine an ETA for Maine. With so many intangibles (conclusion: poo-poo is one of life's great intangibles), it was impossible to say exactly when we would arrive.

Off duty for the night, I pulled out *Blue Highways* and reread a few pages, marveling at the contrasts between our two journeys. William Least Heat-Moon had touched, seen, and tasted America. I had touched, seen, and tasted Cracker Barrels. He had hit the road to escape a failed marriage. I had hit the road and taken my failed marriage with me.

I scanned the room for Stinky Bear. I needed to talk things out with him, seek his wisdom, ask him about love and life, but remembered he was with Ethan. I only had old Grandpa Bear with me, and he was sleeping.

Sensing I was ripe for a visit from the Doubt and Guilt, I turned on my laptop and went to the Ocean View Web site. I needed to remember why I was on this trip.

Built at the turn of the twentieth century, Ocean View originally had been the summer home of the Doyles, a well-off Boston family with ties to the shipping industry. Seven years ago, with real-estate prices in free fall and with the last of the Doyles long gone, the sprawling estate was put on the market and purchased at a fire sale price by a group of far-thinking and deep-pocketed parents who were frustrated by the shortage of suitable housing options for disabled adults. The founding families, all Boston Irish Catholics, found a small order of nuns to oversee the care of their children in exchange for a comfortable place to live and worship. The nuns accepted, with the stipulation that a small chapel be built on the grounds and that 10 percent of the yearly contributions the families made be donated to their order.

Only twenty residents lived at Ocean View, with ten more higher-functioning adults living in three group homes down the hill in Camden. I had toured one of the group homes, and while impressed with the arrangement — the residents were thoroughly integrated in the communities and even had jobs — I knew Ethan would do better in a more structured environment.

For parents of disabled children, Ocean View was the proverbial shining city on the hill. But it came at a steep price: a one-hundred-thousand-dollar down payment, thirty thousand dollars a year, and a pledge in writing, certified by an attorney, that Ocean View would be beneficiary of your will and that that inheritance would be a minimum of three hundred and fifty thousand dollars.

It was expensive, but there were few choices. America has many attributes, but the care of its growing population of disabled adults is not one of them. I was fortunate that I could afford this steep price, fortunate that I worked in an affluent school district that paid me well, fortunate that I would get a good pension for the rest of my life. Mostly, I was fortunate that David Prioletti, Mary's father, had started a rock quarry business some sixty years ago in southern Illinois and that that quarry would one day be sold in excess of forty million dollars.

Other families, I knew, did not have such resources, such options. To most, Ocean View, with its swimming pools, airy gymnasium, on-site medical staff, and bright and cheerful café, was a dream. I knew this and felt some guilt, but there was little I could do about the inequities of life. Simply put, Ocean View was more than good place: it was as I have mentioned, our salvation.

I browsed the site for a while longer, checked the weather in Camden (cloudy and sixty-five), then clicked off the computer and climbed into bed. I had high hopes for a dreamless sleep.

I had just drifted off, when the hotel phone rang. I groped in the dark to answer, heart racing. Good news, I knew, did not come in the form of late-night calls.

"Yes? Hello?"

"Dad, it's me, Karen. You need to help. We're locked out."

I sat up, glanced at the clock. It was one thirty. "Karen? Where are you?"

"Outside the hotel. In the parking place. We forgot our keys. Mindy's puking."

I sat up. "Is she sick?"

"She's drunk. Wasted. And she's throwing up. Heaving. It's gross."

"Okay, I'll be right down. Give me a second."

"Daddy-o?"

I was on my feet, searching for my pants. "What?"

"I'm really drunk too. I mean, really wasted too."

"What? Well, don't move. Don't drive. Stay there! Just stay there!"

"Whatever you say, Daddy-o."

Mindy was on her hands and knees in the parking lot, a small pool of vomit in front of her. A streetlight was bathing everything in a bluish-white glow, and in that glow, my daughter looked unearthly, a zombie dog on the prowl. Karen was standing over her, gently petting the top of her head. Under normal circumstances, I would have been heartened by this, applauded her big sister efforts, but Karen had her shirt off and was standing there in a black bra.

"Really hot out," she said when she saw me.

"Put your shirt on! What is wrong with you?"

"She's airing her tits out," Mindy said,

wiping her mouth with the bottom of her shirt.

"Yeah," Karen said. "Men don't know what it's like. Tits sweat."

"Put it on."

"She loves showing her tits off," Mindy said.

Karen started struggling back into her blouse. "You're the one who took your shirt off in the bar."

"You took . . . ?" I walked closer, giving the vomit pool a wide berth. "Get up. Stand up. Watch where you're walking. Don't step in it."

From of the corner of my eye, I spotted a very short man wearing a tight black T-shirt and a plethora of gold chains. In a heavy Spanish accent, he shouted, "Hello!" and smiled.

I jumped. "Who's he?"

"Manny," Mindy said. She was sitting on the ground, eyes deranged.

"Who?"

"Manny," Mindy said, "He bought us tequila. So I was going to have sex with him. It's the least I can do. He bought us a lot of tequila."

Manny nodded his confirmation, smile widening. "Hello!"

I discerned from his size and just-happy-to-be-here smile that he didn't pose a real threat. "Thank you, Manny, for walking them here," I said. "I can take it from here, though. I'm their father. You can go now. *Gracias.*"

"I think he wants a blow job," Mindy said. She heaved air, a dry gravelly sound. "He implied that at the bar. He bought us tequila. Shots."

"Be quiet. Don't talk. Just be quiet." I turned back to Manny. He kept smiling and nodding in a way that suggested English wasn't even a second language. *"Vamos,"* I said. *"Gracias* though. *Gracias* very, *muy mucho."*

"Dad, he's not going anywhere until one of us blows him," Mindy said. "You might have to do it," she said to Karen.

"My blowing days are over," Karen said. Her eyes were closed, and she was wobbling, her arms out to her sides like she was surfing.

"Hello!"

"Dad," Mindy said. "Would you mind blowing him? Take one for the team? I don't think he'd mind."

That was it. I pointed at Manny. "Go! Beat it! Get out of here. *Vamos!* Run!"

The tone of my voice did not require a UN translator. Manny's smile quickly disappeared. He gave the girls one last furtive look and skulked away.

"And I thought he was the one," Mindy said.

"Get up. Come on, it's late."

We crossed the lot slowly, Mindy stopping every few feet to dry heave and then marvel at the night sky. "So many stars. So many stars. We don't have them in New York. We have, like, nothing in New York. I don't think we even have a sky. It's like a big nothing."

"A void," Karen said.

"A what?" Mindy said.

"A void."

"Yes! A void! That's it! There's nothing above us there. Nothing above us, just, like, nothing."

"That's weird when you think about it," Karen said. Then they both started laughing very hard for some reason.

"Have you done drugs?" I asked.

"No, why? Do you have any?" Karen asked.

"Keep moving. Both of you."

Just outside the hotel door, Mindy came to a complete stop, stuck her neck out like an ostrich, and threw up. This started an ugly but not unpredictable chain reaction. Karen covered her mouth, gagged, then threw up an amazing volume of spew, some of which splattered on my pants. Surrounded now by an inlet sea of puke, with vomit shrapnel embedded in my jeans, my own gag reflex, which was historically at threat-level orange, kicked in. I ralphed right alongside my daughters.

"Family! Family!" Mindy yelled, pumping her arms upward.

"USA!" Karen screeched.

"I feel bad Mom and Ethan are missing all this," Mindy said, wiping her mouth again with her shirt. "We do so little together as a family."

I wiped my mouth with the back of my hand, disgusted. The night had devolved from making love with Mary to this. I opened the door wide. "Get inside. Come on. Take the damn stairs. The stairs. Over to the right. Hurry. Second floor. Come on, I don't want anyone to see us. You're going to my room."

It took us a while to manage the stairwell and hallway, which had to be the longest in the vast Marriott chain. Every few feet, Mindy sat down on the floor and had another acidlike revelation. ("Indoor carpeting is nice. Think about it, I mean it's *nice*.") When we finally made it into my room, she stumbled over to the queen-size bed and fell on it, face-first.

"Take off your shirt!"

"That's what that guy at the bar said," Karen said.

"That's why I did it," Mindy said.

Karen flopped down next to Mindy, but at least had the good sense to stay on her back. Both girls had puke on their fronts.

"Take your shirts off. Both of you."

They sat up obediently and pulled off their tops while I rifled through my bags. "Put these on." I handed them each a T-shirt and watched as they wrestled with them. Karen was trying to force her head through the arm sleeve.

"For God's sake, how much did you drink?" I helped untangle her, then threw their shirts in the tub, rinsed out my mouth, and returned with two clean washrags.

"Sit up. Both of you. Sit up." I started in on Mindy first, wiping her face and doing the best I could with her hair. "What did you drink?"

"Tequila," Mindy said.

"Anything else? Anything else?"

"More tequila," Karen said.

"Yeah, that's right. That was it. Tequila, and then we had more tequila. They go good together."

I kept at Mindy's face. "Where did you go?"

"Pinky's," Karen said. "Down the street."

"How did you get there? I know you didn't drive."

"We used, you know, our feet to get there," Karen said. "Our feet."

"We walked."

"Right, that's the word I was searching for. So good with words, are you."

I moved over to Karen, scrubbing down her cheeks and chin and neck. Then I propped them up with pillows, made them each drink a full glass of water, and pulled a chair close to the bed.

"What are you doing?" Mindy asked.

"Just close your eyes and try to sleep."

"You worried we're going to choke on our own vomit, aren't you?" Karen said.

"No. I'm worried you're going to choke on each other's vomit," I said.

"You're funny, Daddy-o," Mindy said. "You're officially a funny person. I've always respected your comedic abilities. You've been a secret inspiration of mine. You could write for the show. We have some shitty writers. I mean, they're shitty."

"Where's Ethan?" Karen asked. Her eyes were closed.

"With your mother."

"Are you two getting back together?" Mindy asked.

I pulled the top of my shirt over my nose. Despite my efforts, both girls still had a fine stench wafting off of them. "Not that I'm aware of. Unless you know something I don't know."

"She still loves you, you know," Mindy said.

"Yeah," Karen said, "I concur with that sentiment. I sense the love. Chemistry. You two still have it. It's electric."

"You should repropose," Mindy said. "Someone in this family should get married."

"Yeah, Mom can have my dress," Karen said. "It's in the van. No, I shipped it back, that's right."

"You can get married at a Cracker Barrel," Mindy said. "We got to reunite the family, get the band back together."

"You know, Dad, you know, we broke your car window that time, after you left Mom," Karen said. "Did you know that?"

"What? What are you talking about?"

"After we found out about your mistress," Karen said. "You know, the woman, the slut."

"Yeah, Miss Slut Hooker Whore, our almost stepmom," Mindy said. "We smashed the windows of your car in honor of her of amazing sluttiness. I was home on break, and Karen you were there, weren't you? Yeah."

"Yeah, that was me."

"Yeah."

"Yeah. We used my golf club. A seven iron, my favorite club. Distance and height. Distance and height. My favorite club."

"Yeah, Tiger Woods's wife got that idea from us," Mindy said. "Remember, you called the police, and they thought it might have been that kid across the street. That kid, that basketball-playing kid. Looked like Opie."

I wasn't surprised by this confession. "I knew it wasn't Kyle. I realized later it might have been you two."

"Yeah, suspicions confirmed," Mindy said. "I mean, I mean, wouldn't you do that? You left our mom. Mom Nichols. Mrs. Mom Nichols. You left her. Momma Pajama."

Karen belched. "You mean Mama Drama. She was pissed."

"Just for the record, I didn't leave her. She threw me out, technically."

"Same thing," Mindy said.

"Try to sleep."

"Do you ever regret what you did?" Karen asked. "To Mom?"

"Of course. But I can't do anything about it."

"Why did you do it then?"

"I was stupid."

"Men are weak," Mindy said.

"Men are the root of all evil. They suck," Karen said. "Especially Roger."

"He really sucks," Mindy said. "It doesn't surprise me what you said about his dick."

"The crooked banana? Yeah, that was weird. I used to close my eyes when he got a boner. It was scary."

"You know, I don't need to hear all this. Go to sleep."

"I can't sleep like this," Mindy said. She was sagging toward Karen.

"You two are both going to feel like hell tomorrow."

"We'll survive," Karen said.

"Yeah, my big bad older sister is tough. She's a tough bitch. I wish I were as tough as my big, bad, bitchy, bossy, beautiful, bitchy . . ."

"You said that already," Karen said.

"Older bitchy but beautiful older sister who's bitchy."

"You said that already."

"You're the one who should have gone into show business. I should have followed my passion."

"Passion?" Karen mumbled.

"Hamsters. Hamsters love me. I could have been like that woman with all those apes. Living in a jungle with, like, all these jungle hamsters. A herd of them."

"Jane Goodall," Karen said.

"Yes. Her." Mindy burped. "You know, I never told you this, but I think it's time I do."

Karen was slipping down her pillow. "What?"

"In high school, at WT, I used to sell your panties to guys on the football team."

Karen's eyes snapped open. "What?"

I pulled the shirt away from my mouth. "You did what?"

"Yeah, I made like ten bucks a pop, or pair. Those guys were such fucking creeps."

"That's why I never had any," Karen said.

"Yeah. That's why."

I was understandably horrified by all of this. "What is wrong with you? Why would you do something like that?"

"I needed the money. Someone had to support those hamsters. I wanted them to go to college."

"I never had any panties in high school," Karen said. "Mom was always yelling at me, asking me what I was doing with them. I thought I was going crazy. Mom used to make me write my name on them to keep track of them."

"I know. I got, like twenty bucks for the signed ones. I mean, autographed panties from Karen Nichols, head cheerleader. Come on, it was a steal."

"I can't believe you did that," Karen said.

"I can't believe you never figured it out. Didn't you think it was strange that I always wanted to go panty shopping with you? Who wants to go panty shopping with her sister? Who wants to go panty shopping, period?"

"I don't remember. I don't remember anything anymore. Which is good, sometimes. We had pretty fucked-up lives at home."

"Really fucked-up. Like, reality-TV fucked-up."

"Your lives weren't that bad," I said.

"We had a crazy house, Dad. A crazy house," Mindy said. "Do you remember Silent Nights?"

"Yes," I said softly.

Mindy was referring to the darkest part of the War Years, when the blitzkrieg raged. We were experimenting with Ethan's medications, and things weren't taking. His tantrums were worse than ever, and the slightest thing would set him off. Desperate, we agreed to keep all noise — TVs, radios, and even talking — to a bare minimum. Consequently, we turned into a house of mimes, pointing to things we wanted, rubbing our stomachs when we were hungry, waving hello, good-bye, clasping our hands together and holding them close to our heads when we wanted to sleep. The whole thing was tragically ridiculous and, to make matters worse, it didn't work.

"We survived," Karen said.

"Kind of," Mindy said.

"You two both turned out fine." I reached over and turned the lights off.

"Who do you love more?" Mindy asked. "Be honest. Karen can take it."

"Lie down now. Lie on your stomachs." They slid down on their backs so I had to turn each of them over.

"Good night, girls." I kissed them both on the tops of their heads.

"Where's Stinky Bear?" Mindy said, her voice muffled by the pillow. "Where Stinky. Bear. Be?"

"Go to sleep."

"I miss Ethan," Karen said.

"Yeah, so do I. Where's his room?" Mindy said. "Get him in here. I miss the big galoot. He always smells so clean."

"Because I'm always giving him baths."

"I love him," Mindy said. "Every time I

think I am incapable of love, I think about him. I think, man, I love him, like a pure love, so there, I'm not as fucked-up as I think. Ethan kind of makes me normal. He makes me be nice. I'm not a nice person, but around him, I'm not that bad."

"Yeah, I know what you're saying. That's his thing," Karen said. "He gives you a chance to be nice. Ethan gives everyone a chance to be nice."

"Sometimes I think that without him, we'd all, like, fall apart. He's, like, our center or something. Hey, Dad, do you really think you can leave him? Just leave him like that?"

"I'm not going to just leave him, but, yes, he's going to stay there, yes. We all agreed we were going to give this a try. It's a good place."

"No, you're not," Karen said. "When it comes down to it, no, you're not."

"He's your whole life." Mindy said this softly, like she was dreaming.

"This whole trip is a joke," Karen whispered.

"When it comes down to it, no way are you leaving him there, no way, not for six weeks. Not for one day," Mindy said. "We're just waiting for you to realize it and go home."

"This whole trip is a joke," Karen whispered again. "A big, fat, joke."

11

The next morning began much too early with a knocking, followed by the sound of Ethan's excited voice: "Hello! Hello! Hello!"

I sat up in a fog. I had had my Ethan-is-talking-normal dream again, but couldn't remember specifics, just that we were together and that he was speaking, clearly, in complete sentences. I did not like those dreams, didn't like them at all; after I woke, a feeling of loss would cling to me.

"Hello! Hello! Hello!"

"Okay. Hold on!" I suddenly had a strong desire to see him, give him a squeeze. I got to my feet and wobbled, stiff-legged over to open the door. And there he was, standing next to Mary, bright-eyed bushy-tailed, Mindy's Bud Light cap on backward. He may as well have been wearing a T-shirt that read, CARPE DIEM! I leaned down and kissed him on his forehead, then gave him a solid hug.

"My man," I whispered.

I smiled at Mary. She looked summery that morning: sunglasses, a soft yellow sleeveless dress, sandals. I wondered how far we were from the ocean.

"Where. Girls. Be?" she asked.

I released Ethan, put a finger to my lips, and motioned with my head. "Enter."

Ethan walked past me, followed by Mary. When she saw Karen and Mindy lying side by side, facing each other, breathing heavily out of their mouths, she took off her sunglasses and said, "I don't even want to know."

"Stinky!" Ethan cried.

"You don't."

"Girls!" Ethan said, pointing and smiling. "Girls. Sleeping."

"Girls," I said. "Right. Very hungover girls. Girls who were out very late last night."

Mary's face wrinkled up. "What is that smell?"

"Girls who threw up last night. Girls who drank too much tequila."

"Stinky!"

"Oh God." Mary cupped hand over her nose. "How did you stay in this room?"

"I think they need to sleep awhile," I said.

"How long?"

"Labor Day."

Mary shook her head, reached for Ethan. "Let's go, buddy. You want to go swimming?"

Ethan jumped up and down. "Swimming!"

"All right," I said, even though swimming was absolutely the last thing I wanted to do at that hour. "Let me get my suit. I'll meet you down there."

"You stay here. I'll take him."

"Dad. Come! Swimming!"

"Come on, Ethan," Mary said. "I'll take you. Let's give your old daddy-o a break. I think he had a rough night."

I gave Mary an appreciative look. "Thank you. I'll take him after that. Maybe play hoops somewhere. Find a park."

"Hoops! Now!"

"No. Swimming now. And hold on to the sides," I said.

"Let's go, buddy," Mary said. She gave Mindy and Karen one last look. "Our sweet girls," she said.

"Yes, sir, we did something right."

Of all the cities and towns we had been through, Wilmington, Delaware, was probably the place I had the least desire to explore because, in all honesty, I had never heard of it. In its defense, it did seem like a nice, solid mini-city, just orderly and clean enough to make it unremarkable. For all I knew, it might have had a deep and rich history. George Washington might have slept there, possibly Lincoln too. It might have had a vibrant arts community, or a thriving underground music scene, but I never made an effort to find out. All I really learned about Wilmington, Delaware, was that it had a pretty good outdoor basketball court.

After his swim with Mary, Ethan and I found a quiet, shady park at the end of a dead-end street. It had a small court with real cloth nets, not the chain nets many parks had, and this was a plus. Sometimes the rattling sound of the chains upset Ethan; the cloth nets were soft and silent.

I took a few shots, then sat on a nearby bench and encouraged Ethan. He was particularly deadly that morning. He immediately hit five in a row, pushing the ball two-handed from his chest, jumping a bit as he released. I was amazed, as always. He was as good as me, as good as anyone.

As he shot away, I wondered, not for the first time, if things had been different, if his chromosomes were normal, what kind of player he could have been. Would he have made the basketball team, would he have played? Started? Would he have been a point guard, or the shooting guard that I was? Would I have been one of those ex-jock fathers who lived vicariously through him? When you have a child like Ethan, you have to contend with a fair amount of "what if" moments, and though they diminish over the years, they could and would still ambush you at odd times and at odd places. Like a park in Wilmington, Delaware.

"Nice shot!"

"More!"

"Okay, shoot more. Take your hat off — you'll shoot better. Your hat, take it off."

I sat back, squinted up at the sky, relaxed. This was a good morning: the girls were burying the hatchet, I was inching closer to Mary, and Ethan was in a fine mood. What was more, he hadn't uttered the name Rita in close to twenty-four hours. Based on experience, I knew the word had not stuck. The danger had passed.

Eventually, Ethan walked over and buried his head in my lap.

"What's going on? You tired? Need a break? Halftime?"

"Play," he said softly. He was being shy and tentative because I often turned this particular request down. I knew what he wanted to do.

"Play what?"

"Play."

"What game do you want to play? Chess?"

"No!"

"Um, Monopoly? That's always fun."

"No!"

"Oh, I know, poker! That's it. I bet Sal taught you."

"No!"

"Then what game, dude-man, what game? You have me wondering here."

"Illini," he said, his voice muffled.

"What?"

"Illini."

"Oh. Wow, never would have guessed that. Never. You want me to play Illini?"

He sat up, eyes gleaming. "Yes! Yes! Yes!"

"Illini, huh?" I surveyed the park: the court was still empty, and while there was a cluster of children and parents by the swings, they were a good distance away. I stood. "Sure, why not? We haven't played that in a long time. Okay, Illini!"

"Dee!"

"Right, you be Dee. Okay."

From time to time, at Ethan's request, we would reenact the final minutes of the famous Illinois–Arizona game. I, of course, took on the heroic role of Deron Williams, and he of star guard Dee Brown. It was a ritual that required energy and enthusiasm.

Fortunately, I had enough of both in the tank that morning.

Back on the court, I stretched, touching my toes a few times, before launching into the well-worn narrative.

"Wow, a close game throughout. Arizona has *exploded* into a fifteen-point lead. Once again the first double-digit deficit the number-one team Illinois has faced all season! This crowd is stunned."

"Shoot!"

"Okay." I officially commenced the comeback by hoisting a shot from the top of the key that was nothing but net. "Deron Williams gets three of those fifteen points back! This game is far from over!"

Ethan retrieved the ball and bounced it back to me. I dribbled off to the left of the basket and continued the long-since-memorized play-by-play. "Brown feeds Williams. Williams for three. Got it! Deron Williams with the biggest three of his life!"

"Face!"

"Look at his face! The look of determination!"

"Back!"

"He's putting the Illini on his back right now!"

Ethan gleefully jumped up and down and yelled, "Go, Illini!" then bounced another pass my way. This time I dribbled to the free-throw line, faked my invisible defender, and took another shot. This too went in. Like Deron had been years before, I was on fire. "Right between the — !"

"Eyes!" Ethan screeched with joy.

We kept this up for a good fifteen minutes under a hazy sun, Ethan feeding me passes while I provided the running commentary, which climaxed with, "The Illini are going to the Final Four! The Illini are going to the Final Four!" Afterward we went to a McDonald's for Sprites, where we sat happily in a booth celebrating the amazing victory.

"Wow!"

"Wow is right. That game was wow!" I said, squeezing his hand. "I remember Sal hugging the crap out of me after that. He hugged me so hard, he hurt my back. I was in pain for a week."

"Sal!"

"Yeah, Sal. One of the world's all-time huggers. He actually practices hugging."

"Me!"

"You what?

"Me!" Ethan stood up and extended his arms.

It took me a moment to realize what he wanted. This was new. "What? Oh, sure, sure." I stood and, in the middle of the crowded McDonald's, we hugged hard.

"Done!"

"No, not yet," I said, burying my face in his hair.

"Done!"

"No, not yet," I said.

When we returned to the hotel, we found the girls slouching in oversize chairs in the lobby. With their large round sunglasses and chalky faces, they looked like strung-out rock stars waiting for their limo. Neither one said anything as we approached.

"Well, well, well, if it isn't Thelma and Louise," I said.

They remained silent, staring straight ahead, heads not moving.

"Oh, I almost forgot," I said. "We just had brunch with Manny. He sends his regards. *'Hola, muchachas bonitas'* were his exact words. I hope you don't mind, but I gave him your home addresses. He's goes to New York a lot on business, he said."

More silent staring.

"You guys come straight from the health club? Get a good workout in? You seem tired. Hey, where's your mother? Did she work out with you?"

"I'm over here." I turned just as Mary walked up, bags in tow. She was still wearing that cheerful little dress and had, I noticed, a slight spring to her step, a perky spark in her eyes. I found this interesting, if not encouraging. There was no Valium in that woman's system, at least not this morning. "Ready to hit the road?" she asked.

"Hope so. Our teenagers' binge threw us off schedule though, so we're going to have to make tracks, limit our throw-up breaks. Do either of you have airsick bags? Might save some time."

"We're right here, Dad," Mindy said. "You don't have to yell."

"I'm hardly yelling." I, of course, was talking very loudly, enjoying the pain and torment each decibel inflicted. "And remember, we're in one van now, so get ready for a commercial-free Stinky Bear marathon. And let's not forget the new Red Bear reality show, *Hard of Hearing*! Everyone talks really loud in it."

"Oh, fuck," Mindy said.

"Hey, watch the words, please," Mary said, motioning to Ethan.

"I just remembered, I think I left Red Bear at the bar last night."

"What?" I stopped with the mocking. "What are you talking about? You think you left Red Bear at that bar? What bar, that tequila place? That place?"

"Yeah. I'm pretty sure I left her in the bathroom, I think. Or somewhere."

"You *think*?"

"You were dancing with her on the bar," Karen said.

"I was?"

"You were?"

"Yeah, then you threw her to that guy. Remember? That guy who bet you wouldn't take your shirt off?"

"I did?"

"You did?"

The cavalier way they were discussing the abuse and abandonment of Red Bear outraged me. "What is wrong with you? Why did you even bring her there?"

Mindy shrugged. "She wanted to come."

"She's not your bear. You had no right to do that." I eyed Ethan, not sure how much of this he was taking in, worried how he may react. He was picking his nails, unconcerned; he'd never thought all that much of Red Bear.

"We have to get her." I checked my watch. "It's eleven thirty. The place is probably open now."

"John, it's just a bear," Mary said. "You just said we're running behind. We'll buy another one."

"Another one? What are you talking about,

357

another one? We can't leave Red Bear. That's Ethan's bear. He'll be asking for it. He needs his bear. That bear is important. What kind of people do that, leave bears?"

I felt everyone's eyes on me, but I remained steadfast. I admit, my attachment to the bears was probably fodder for a therapist, but I didn't care. For years they had been an important part of our lives, had helped me through some long days, and we weren't about to leave any one of them, even Red Bear, the Ringo Starr of the group. "Go over there and get him. Her."

"You're kidding," Karen said.

" 'No Bear Left Behind,' that's our policy," I said. "I mean it. Those bears are . . . are family."

"Family?" Karen repeated.

"Just, go, go!"

Both girls emitted sighs and heaved themselves up and out of the big chairs.

"Take Ethan with you."

"What?" Karen said.

"Take him with you. He'll keep an eye on you."

Mindy groaned. "I cannot believe this. Come on, dude-man."

Ethan looked up from his nails, confused and alarmed. "Where. Going? What. Doing?"

"We're Saving Private Red Bear," Mindy said. "Come on."

I watched them leave, Ethan walking between his sisters, holding their hands. The girls took baby steps, their feet barely leaving the ground, shuffling more than walking. I heard Ethan ask, "Why. Mad?"

"They're acting like they're fifteen," I said.

"They're just blowing off some steam together," Mary said. "Hey, I'm going to get some coffee. Why don't you get your things and meet me at the restaurant."

"Coffee?" I turned around and that was when I saw Mary's smile, big and sweet. Exactly why she was smiling, I wasn't sure. It may have been the bears; for years, I suspected, she secretly got a kick out of my devotion to them. It may have been the girls; she too was glad they were reconnecting. Or maybe, just maybe, she finally realized she was as in love with me as I was with her. (Note: that last one might have been a stretch.) Regardless, if she was happy, then I was happy. "Coffee? Absolutely. Yeah, just give me a few minutes," I said, and hurried off.

Just when you think you're getting somewhere, life intrudes. I was pretty sure someone had written that line somewhere, and it came flying back at me when my phone buzzed a few minutes later. I was in my room, quickly packing and riding the wave of Mary's smile, and once again answered without first checking who it was.

"I need to see you," Rita said, her voice husky, urgent.

I froze, caught a glimpse of myself in the mirror, an ex-philanderer-in-the-headlights, and said, "Oh. Hi."

"I need to talk to you. I need to see you."

"This isn't a good time."

"Don't say that to me."

"Rita, I'm in Delaware with the family. I can't talk. Everyone is here. I told you that. Maybe we can talk when I get back, though, truthfully, I'm not sure why." She didn't say anything. "Is there something wrong? Is there a problem?" I asked.

"Chase died."

"Chase?"

"Chase. From the club. He died two weeks ago."

"I'm sorry. Chase?"

"You know, Chase. Chase Hart."

"Oh, right. The tennis player. Him." Chase was the quintessential aging arch-conservative, someone I avoided, particularly in the locker room, where he was known to launch into unprovoked political tirades while naked, his testicles dangling frighteningly low. "I'm sorry to hear that."

"It's so sad. Heart attack. They couldn't revive him."

"Did you know him well?"

"Very well. We had become very close. Very close."

I glanced at the clock, reluctantly sat on the bed. Mary, smiling, happy Mary, was waiting for me, and I was discussing the demise of Chase Hart, a man whose balls used to upset me. "How old was he?"

"Sixty-seven. Just gone like that, just gone."

"I'm sorry to hear that. How are you holding up?"

"I don't think I can go on. I really don't."

I looked down, focusing on the carpet. "Well, it's sad."

"I miss you."

I wasn't exactly sure of the exact connection here, how Chase Hart's dying resulted in her missing me, so I said, "I don't think you miss me."

"How do you know what I feel, how I feel?"

"Rita, have you been drinking?"

"Yes."

"It's not even lunchtime."

"I'm not drinking now."

"Oh."

"But I will be. Soon."

"I have to go."

"I need you. I need to talk to someone. I'm very alone right now. I hate being alone. I hate it. When are you coming back?"

"You're not alone. You have lots of friends, you have family. Your cats."

"I'll come out to meet you. Tell me where you are. I can leave today."

The image of Rita bursting into a Cracker Barrel made my heart seize. "That's not going to work. It's not. And you know, you really shouldn't call me anymore. We've been done for two years now. It's over between us. You know that."

"I don't want to die alone."

"Rita, just stop it. Stop it, come on. No one's dying."

"Chase died."

"Well . . . right . . . okay . . . but you're not."

"I need to see you. Why is that such a big thing? Why can't you do that for me?"

I took a breath. "Because I'm getting back together with Mary."

Silence. Then, "You are?"

"Yes."

"Are you back together now?"

"Not officially, no. But I will be. We will

be. Very soon. That's what I want, and I think that's what she wants."

"John, you said that two years ago. If you were going to get back together, you would have been back together by now. She doesn't want you back. She doesn't. It's time you face reality. She doesn't want you."

I had had enough. "Listen, I'm sorry about Chase, I really am, but I have to go now. Good-bye. Good-bye."

"Don't say good-bye to me!" She actually yelled this, but I hung up anyway.

I resumed my packing but went about it now much more slowly, a sense of foreboding settling in. The call, Rita's desperate and insistent tone, her sadness, everything, rattled me. (Note: adding to my concern was the fact that I had watched the movie *Fatal Attraction* not two weeks before, and worried a boiled rabbit, or more likely, a boiled Stinky Bear, was in my future.) I considered calling her back with hopes of calming her, maybe promise a visit when I returned, but decided against it. Such a response would just encourage her, and Rita was not someone you encouraged any more than necessary.

My ex-mistress was persistent, had no quit in her. She worked out every day for exactly ninety minutes, rain or shine. Elliptical, treadmill, StairMaster, then maybe some tennis; she pushed herself with a vengeance like few women her age. She also had a temper. Once, when I had been detained at school and failed to show up for one of our afternoon sessions, she called and gave me a bloody earful. Another time I saw her fling a tennis ball at a competitor after a disputed line call. The throw had been the talk of the locker room.

My involvement with such a volatile woman was stupid on all levels, her sudden reemergence in my life more than a little worrisome. I feared I had not heard the last from her.

By the time I returned to the lobby, everyone, including Red Bear, was waiting impatiently.

"That was quick," I said to the girls.

"Not like we had to post bond or anything," Mindy said, flipping the bear at me.

"Thank you." I caught Red Bear against my chest and examined her furry head to furry foot. "Where was she?"

"In the Dumpster," Mindy said. "Where she belongs."

I held her out at arm's distance. "That's disgusting."

"She wasn't in the Dumpster," Karen said. "She was on top of it, on the lid."

I sniffed Red Bear, relieved. "Oh, well, that's good. You were lucky."

"Can we go now?" Mary asked. She was holding a large cup of coffee, her big sweet smile gone, replaced by a look of mild irritation. "What kept you?"

"I'm sorry. I had to pack. My room was a mess. Sorry."

"I'll drive," Karen said.

"No, I will," Mindy said.

I turned my attention back to the girls. "I'm driving. You both sit in the back with Ethan. I think you need to spend some quality time with him. Catch up with him. It's your penance."

"God," Karen said.

"God can't help you," I said, taking Ethan's hand. "No one can."

After I pulled over to switch places with Mindy, who threatened to throw herself out of the speeding van because Ethan kept pinching her; and after I switched places with Karen, who threatened to throw Ethan out of the speeding van because he kept pinching her; and after I started singing, *Cracker Barrel, Cracker Barrel, Cracker all the way!* to the tune of "Jingle Bells" in

Grandpa Bear's Morgan Freeman voice; and after Mindy offered me twenty dollars to please stop with the fucking singing; and after I took the twenty dollars and stopped fucking singing but then launched into a loud episode of *Hard of Hearing,* Red Bear's new reality TV show (Red Bear, shouting: "Speak up!" Grandpa Bear, shouting: "Shut up?" Red Bear: "Speak up!" Grandpa: "Shut up?"); and after Mindy offered me another ten dollars to stop the Bear thing and I said you'll have to do better than that; and after Karen upped it to fifty dollars and I accepted but then refused because I wouldn't take a personal check, we stopped at a Buffalo Wild Wings because Mindy said she would rather chew her own arm off than step foot in the Cracker Barrel that was located right next door.

"I pray that Grandpa Bear has a heart attack," Mindy said.

"That's not funny," I said, suddenly thinking of dear dead Chase.

Mary, who had been mostly quiet through the afternoon's ordeal said, "I think you did a great job, John. Thank you for stepping into the breach. You put on quite a show."

I handed Ethan his Etch A Sketch and eyed Mary with suspicion. When she wanted to, she could be as sarcastic as the little one.

"Really? Seriously?"

"Yes. No one else was helping. Thank you. I don't know how you kept that up for so long."

I looked over at my sullen, greasy-faced daughters and felt my chest swell. "Well, thank you. I appreciate being appreciated. Thank you."

"Ethan loved it. Didn't you, buddy? Wasn't Dad funny?"

Ethan drained his water, said nothing.

"I admit, I enjoyed today's episodes," I said. "Especially *Hard of Hearing*. While it's entertaining on a certain base level, it's also important. It deals with the challenges of hearing-impaired teddy bears, a group that doesn't get enough attention."

Mary cupped a hand behind her ear. "Whaaat?" she asked.

"I said —" then caught myself. Mary, my sweet-sweetie, had actually made a joke. I pointed at her, winked. "Well played."

The girls ignored us. Over the top of her menu, I thought I saw Mary studying me. Her eyes were alive, and I wondered if she were smiling.

I cupped my hand behind my ear. "Whaaat?" I asked.

After we finished eating, I asked the waitress

if she could recommend a place nearby for dessert. Despite the effort required to host the Bear marathon, I was in a good mood, raring to go. It was early, Ethan was still ensconced in his Etch A Sketch, Mary still had bemused/happy eyes, and the girls were still too hungover to speak, so I didn't necessarily want the evening to end.

"Dessert." The waitress pondered my question. She reminded me of one of my students: young, pale, purple hair, clueless. "We have dessert here," she said.

"I'm sure you do, but is there anything more local? We're from out of town, and we're looking to explore."

"Explore Mason?"

"Is that where we are? Yes."

"I don't know. Mason isn't very big," she said. "I guess there's a Baskin-Robbins by the Exxon station. Actually, it's part of the Exxon station."

"Is there anything else? Something that's maybe not part of a gas station?"

"I don't know. Nate's, I guess."

"Nate's. What's that?" I asked.

"An ice cream store. They sing when they serve you. It's kind of weird. Little kids like it. I don't know if it's still open, though."

"Wow, perfect. A weird singing ice cream place," I said. "That's exactly what we're looking for. We were just saying that. How far is it?"

"Ten, fifteen minutes." She placed the check facedown on our table and walked away.

"Nate's, a singing ice cream place," I said. "Sounds too good to pass up. I think we should all go. Have some quality family time, explore the region, make some memories."

"Sorry, but I'll pass," Karen said. "I've had enough family time today."

"Don't confuse quantity family time with quality family time," I said. "Too many people make that mistake."

"I'm not going either," Mindy said. "*Naked and Afraid* is on tonight."

"I'm starting to get disappointed."

"Maybe the waitress will go with you," Mindy said. "She seems like fun."

"I'd be happy to accompany you," said Mary.

I tried to swallow my surprise and delight. "Really? Well, thank you, Miss Ex-Wife. Ethan and I would enjoy your company."

"Ethan can stay back with us," Karen said. "We'll take him swimming."

"Swimming!" Ethan finally looked up from the Etch A Sketch.

"We will?" Mindy asked.

"Yes," Karen said. "We will."

"Swimming!"

Mindy's eyes darted around the table. "Right, swimming, yeah, sure."

"Okay," I said, wondering what Mary thought of this arrangement. "You up for some singing and ice cream?"

"Sure." She reached for her red bag. "I'm always up for ice cream."

Even though it had been a while, years possibly, since Mary and I had been alone together in a car, the drive over to Nate's felt very familiar. She sat crossed-legged, looking out her window, while I drove slowly with the radio on low. It was a fine evening, warm and windy, and memories of past drives, past summer evenings together, before the girls, before Ethan, before everything, filled me.

"Nice. Outside," I said.

"Beautiful."

"So, how do you think Karen's doing?"

"She's still in the day-by-day phase. In the long run, though, this is a good thing. I never liked him."

"Neither did I. That jaw of his."

"There were worse things than that about him."

"You're right — there's a whole list. She

can do better than that. She'll meet some-one else."

"She will."

"And I'm looking forward to punching whoever it is."

She surprised me with a small laugh. "I have news for you. You aren't very good at that."

I held my fist up. "Say hello to my little friend!"

"God. Please."

I stopped at an intersection, glanced down at directions the waitress with the purple hair had given me, and made a left onto a dimly lit street. "Glad they seem to be get-ting along again, Mindy and Karen."

"Yes, it is. It is."

"Hope it lasts."

"I think it will." She lowered her window and hung her arm out on the side of the van. I wasn't sure, but I thought I heard her softly humming along to the radio.

"Anyone else call? The cousins?"

"They're calling. But I don't want to talk. They just want to gossip, want the Roger–Karen lowdown. I don't have time for that. I just want to focus on what we're doing now. Get there."

"Does anyone else know where we're go-ing?"

"Just the Sals."

We were now in Mason, a few deserted blocks of dreary-looking storefronts, half of which looked unoccupied. The streetlights hadn't come on yet, and in the twilight, the empty town looked like it was vanishing.

"Ethan had a pretty good day today, for the most part," I said.

"Thanks mostly to you. I should have helped out more. But once you got going, I didn't want to interrupt."

"I haven't really focused on this, dropping him off. I don't think it's really hit me, what we're doing, totally hit me. I don't have time to think. When you're with him, you can't think. You know how it is. And when you have a free minute, you're too fried to think. This whole trip is a blur."

I guess I meant this as an invitation to talk about Ocean View — we were in the shadow of New England, getting close — but Mary didn't respond. She just raised her window and pointed. "There it is," she said.

From the outside, Nate's looked as wacky as advertised. Tucked away at the very end of town, its bright lights illuminated the emptiness of the street, rather than welcomed visitors. The cluttered storefront window tried too hard, offering a carnival of salutations (COME ON IN! IT'S DREAMY AND CREAMY INSIDE! GET IT WHILE IT'S COLD! HOME OF THE WORLD'S BEST BANANA SPLIT), as well as a large crudely painted rainbow on top of which sat a squirrel clutching an acorn. A caption beneath the squirrel read: HE'S NUTS FOR NATE'S!

"Interesting," Mary said. We put our faces up to the window. Other than a life-size stuffed polar bear standing on its hind legs, the place, like Mason, looked deserted.

"I don't hear any singing," she said.

"Maybe they hum between customers."

"You still want to go in?" she asked.

"It's the home of the world's best banana split," I said, opening the door. "We really have no choice."

When we stepped inside, we were immediately greeted by the sweet smell of ice cream and a steady hum of freezers. Standing behind the counter, ramrod straight, were an older man and woman. Thin, stern-faced, and wearing spectacles, if you substituted a pitchfork for an ice cream scooper, they were a double for the figures in the famous Grant Wood painting. They did not look like singers.

I smiled, nodded. "So, is this the singing ice cream place?"

The man looked past me with a one thousand-yard stare. "We're under new management," he said, his voice plain, direct. "Nate is no longer around."

"Oh, so not even one song?"

The woman glared at me then disappeared into a back room.

This left us alone with the man, and I suspected he was uncomfortable. He cleared this throat and shifted his gaze just off to my right. I took a tiny step over, hoping to get into his line of vision, but his eyes kept sliding over.

"So, the singing stopped with Nate?"

"Nate was a fool," the man said.

"I'll have to take your word on that."

"Do you want ice cream?"

I tried one more smile. "We came for the music, but I guess we'll stay for the ice cream."

A shadow flickered across his face.

"Let's see here," I said.

Mary, who was not easily intimidated, seemed unnerved by the man. She stepped partially behind me. "I think I'll have one scoop of mint chocolate chip in a cup," she said.

The man remained rigid, bracing for my choice. I took my time, partly because I couldn't decide between a banana split and the hot fudge sundae, and partly because I had decided that this man needed to be annoyed.

I tapped my chin. "Let's see now."

"We close in ten minutes."

"Wow, that's pretty early."

"That's when we close."

"Wow. Okay, well, this is going to be tough. There are so many good choices, so many flavorful options. Wish I could try them all. Yes, I do. Hey, what would you recommend?"

His chest rose, fell. "What she had."

"Interesting." I tapped my chin a few more times. "But I think I'll have the world's best banana split. I'm going to see if it's better than the one I had in Singapore back in eighty-five. Up until now, that one has been the best." I winked.

The man's chest rose and fell again. "With or without nuts?"

Another chin tap. "Let's see, let's see, with nuts."

More chest. "Nuts are twenty cents extra."

More chin. "Fine. And I think I would like . . . extra whipped cream."

Chest. "That's another twenty cents."

Chin. "Really?" At this point, I had to work hard to suppress a smile. This guy was just too much. "Really? Twenty cents?"

"Yes."

"Seems like a lot." I feigned deep thought, then snapped my fingers. "Go for it." I admit, I was putting on a show for Mary, trying to get her to laugh.

The man jerked the glass freezer open and went to work while we sat down at a wobbly plastic table near the dead bear.

I took in the ambiance and concluded that Nate's was officially the anti-Cracker Barrel; other than the polar bear and the crazy greetings on the windows, relics, I suspected, from the Nate era, it was as cheerful as the Calvinist church.

"Charming place," I whispered.

"Very," Mary whispered back.

The man placed our ice cream on the countertop and said, "Ten dollars," which I thought was expensive.

I was reaching for my wallet when Mary asked, "Why don't we bring something back for the girls and Ethan?"

"Oh yeah, sure. Yeah, good idea." With great pleasure I asked, "Can you make three more world-famous splits? To go?"

He sighed, glanced down at a bulging, black watch, the kind that offers the time in Moscow, Honolulu, Heaven, and Hell, and asked between clenched teeth, "Extra nuts, extra whipped cream?"

"Why not? I just got paid today."

The man yanked the freezer open again, and I retrieved our treats and sat back down. I wished Mindy were there. She would have an absolute field day with this guy.

"Unbelievable," Mary whispered as I handed her the cup.

I was in the middle of swallowing a large spoonful of the extra whipped cream when I realized I had left my wallet back at the hotel. I patted my pockets to confirm, but I knew it wasn't there. I now remembered putting it on the desk when I was changing Ethan into his bathing suit.

"Hey," I whispered to Mary. "I left my wallet at the hotel."

Mary stopped eating. "What?"

"I forgot it there. Can you pay?"

"I don't have my purse. I left it in my room."

"Do you have any money?"

"No. Do you?"

"No."

"Nothing?"

"No."

"You sure?"

"Yes."

I looked at my half-eaten banana split with extra nuts and extra whipped cream. Mary looked at her half-eaten cup of mint chocolate chip. Then we both looked at the Calvinist laboring past closing time on those banana splits.

"Shit," Mary whispered.

We sat in silence, our ice cream melting, the hum of the freezers swallowing us. I glanced at the door then at the dead polar bear. If there had been a clock on the wall, we surely would have heard it ticking.

"Tell him to stop making them," Mary whispered.

The man finished the second banana split, wiped his forehead with his forearm like a coal miner, then started in on the third.

"You tell him," I said. "Tell him we have a special-needs son. Work that in."

"Fine." Mary stood and approached the counter but at the last second veered off to the left and pulled a napkin from a metal dispenser. She quickly sat back down.

"You tell him. This was your idea."

"Let's call the girls."

"We have the car."

I nodded, considered my dissolving banana split, then carefully raised my eyes and watched as the man violently shook a can of whipped cream. He stopped, frowned, shook it hard again, then went into the back room.

"Run." I had not planned on saying this, but I did.

"What?"

I grabbed Mary's elbow. "Run, the van is right out front. Come on, come on. Let's go. Run. We'll send him a check."

Mary, eyes wide, pointed wordlessly to a sign by the door that read NO CHECKS.

"We'll send him cash. Come on, let's get out of here. He probably killed Nate. Has him stuffed in a freezer. Come on." I half dragged her to the door.

As soon as we were outside, Mary yelled, "Oh my God! He's coming!"

"Holy shit!" I ran around the van, got in. Mary stood frozen by her door, uncertain, a former officer of the court having a crisis of conscious. Either that, or she was going to pull a Patty Hearst and claim I was kidnapping her. After staring into the shop for what seemed like forever, she dropped her cup onto the curb and jumped in.

"Hit it!" she yelled.

I pressed the gas, and we roared off like Bonnie and Clyde. In the rearview mirror, I saw the Calvinist start to run.

"He's chasing us!" I yelled. "He's actually running after us! He's nuts!"

"We're nuts!"

"Nuts are ten cents extra!"

"Nuts are twenty cents extra!"

Mary covered her face. She was laughing uncontrollably and stamping her feet. "Drive! Drive! Drive!"

We were still laughing when we pulled into the parking lot of the Courtyard. Mary, exhilarated, kept summarizing our grand caper, her voice and face animated and alive in a way I hadn't seen in years.

"I can't believe we did that! What if he finds us?" She kept looking over her shoulder.

"He's not going to find us."

"We have to send him some money."

"Fine, I'll send him a check."

"No checks!" Mary said.

"Right, no checks."

When she laughed again, I reached for her hand, and she let me hold it.

"We have a good story to tell the girls," I said.

"Always an adventure with you." I wasn't expecting what she said next. "When I married you, I thought, this guy will make me laugh. He'll keep things interesting."

"Well, I've certainly kept things interesting."

"I remember your saying our lives together would be an adventure."

"I said that?"

"On our honeymoon."

"Hilton Head." I squeezed her hand.

"We should have had more fun. Should have done more things. Tried to do things. We just gave up. It's not his fault. It was our fault," she said. "We should have tried harder. We had lives too. But it was hard. It was hard."

"It won't be that hard now. We're going to have time. We can have our adventures, still have them. Everything's going to be okay. We're going to have a happy ending, you'll see. We all will."

"You and your happy endings."

"There's nothing wrong with happy endings." I leaned over and kissed her on the cheek, but before things could go any further, she let go of my hand and unlocked her door.

"What's wrong? What are you doing?"

"Nothing's wrong. I'm going. It's time to go."

"Go? Come on, it's still early. We can go somewhere else. Get coffee. Or we can stay right here. Or, maybe, we can go to my room. Look for my wallet."

"I don't think that's a good idea."

"Why?"

"Because it isn't. Things are complicated

enough. We don't need to add to them."

"Add to . . ." I sat back. "Can I ask you something? It's been more than two years. How long is my penance? I'm willing to wait as long as it takes, but I would like to know what I'm up against."

"Good night, John."

"Mary."

"I'll see you at breakfast."

"Fine. Fine. Good night then. Fine."

She opened the door and walked away, her arms pumping. It wasn't until she disappeared into the hotel that I conceded she wasn't coming back.

"Mary, Mary, sweet contrary."

Later, staring up at yet another hotel ceiling, sleep as far away as Maine, I berated myself for the way the evening had ended. It had been a good night, a fun night, and I ruined things by rushing. I should have let it be, allowed things to take a natural course. Mary was right. This was not the time or place. Things were complicated enough. Ethan, this trip, were all about him. We needed to stay focused. Everything else would have to wait.

I shut the lights, tried to get comfortable, closed my eyes. I then sat up, grabbed my phone, and, of course, called Mary.

Before she even had a chance to speak, I blurted out, "I love you, you know that? I love you and I always will."

Silence, then Mindy. "Thanks, Dad. Good to know."

I froze. "Shit! God damn it, shit!"

"Sorry, but I'm having a little trouble following this conversation."

"What? No!" I sat up higher, thinking fast. "I just wanted you to know that, okay? I wanted to, you know, tell you that."

"Sure you did."

"I did. I did. All of you. I love all of you. This trip has made me realize that, appreciate that." I was rambling now but couldn't stop. "Is Ethan there, is he there?"

"He's sleeping."

"Already? Okay then, all right. Well, tell him that too, in case he wakes up. Tell him I love him too."

"Hold on, let me grab a pen. Okay, Loves. You. Too. Got it!" she said. "I'll make sure he gets this first thing. Hey, while you're at it, you want me to tell Karen? She's right here."

"I'm going."

"So how was that singing ice cream place? Have a good time? Live up to the hype?"

"It was fine."

"Hey, you want Mom's number?"

"I have your mother's number."

"Need help dialing it?"

"Good night."

"Loves. You. Too."

"Good night."

I turned off the phone and tossed it onto the other bed. I could only imagine the conversation the girls were about to have. It was then that I caught sight of Stinky Bear by the window, button eyes amused.

"Shut. Up. Idiot," I said.

12

The next day, after Karen got up early and went for a run, showered, then headed back out again to gas up and wash the van; and after she stopped at a Walmart and bought a bag of oranges and water bottles for everyone and a new digital watch complete with peeping buttons and flashing lights for Ethan; and after I asked Mindy what she had accomplished that morning, and she shrugged and mumbled, "Brushed my teeth"; and after I spent a half hour sitting in the rear seat with Ethan, studying the back of Mary's head in the front seat, trying to read her always hard-to-read mind; and after I decided to text always-hard-to-read Mary a short, generic, but playful message: *Hi, Baby! It's. Nice. Outside!;* and after Karen, who was driving, glanced down into her lap at her phone and said, "Dad, did you just text me?"; and after I jumped in my seat and said, what? no! yes! then whispered shit under my breath while staring stupidly at my phone, we decided to stop at a Burger King for an early lunch where life, in the form of an increasingly persistent Rita, decided to once again intrude.

Ethan, who had been fiddling with my phone, eagerly answered the call while I sat, helpless, my mouth jammed full of fries, calculating the odds that it was someone other than who it was.

"Hello?" Ethan asked. "How. Are. You?" He had obviously never met Rita, so at this point in the conversation, there was no indication that he was talking to the woman who had once begged me to spank her while having sex.

"Who is it?" Mary asked.

I reached over and causally yanked the phone away from Ethan.

"Me. Phone!" He made a grab for it, so I jumped up from the table. "Hello? I'm sorry, who is this? Oh yes, Sal. Hi."

As feared, it was Rita. "John?"

"Let me talk to Sally when you're done," Mary said.

I covered the phone. "It's Sal . . . Valentine, teachers union."

"How many Sals do you know?" Mindy asked.

"Hey, Sal," I headed for the door. "Calling about the fall meeting?"

"Hello? John? Are you there? Hello?"

It wasn't until I was safely outside, that I risked addressing her. "Listen, you can't call me anymore on this trip, okay? No more, please. I'm going to block your calls from now on, do you understand?" I glanced back into the Burger King. "I'm serious, okay?"

"Chase died while we were having sex."

"I'm sorry, what?"

"He died right on top of me."

I came to a hard stop, a fake smile frozen on my face. I had anticipated her saying any number of things, but obviously not this. Speechless, I peered into the restaurant, thought I saw Mary peering back, then finally forced a laugh and said, "Well, that is interesting."

"We were talking about getting engaged."

"I'm sorry to hear that. I really am."

"I don't think I can go on. I don't think I can. I can't eat, I can't sleep. I don't think I can do this."

I kept up with the smiling and shook my head, not sure if Mary was watching. "Yes, you can. I'm sure you can. Listen, not a good time. Really not a good time. But I will call you later, I promise."

"Don't hang up. Please John, don't."

"I understand what you're saying, but I really have to go, really do. But I promise I'll call." I threw my head back, forced out yet another laugh, and turned off the phone.

The day went south after that. Ethan, exhausted from another day on the road, became fretful the second we were back in the van. Shoving my worries about Rita aside, I worked to change his mood, furiously running through a number of classic Stinky Bear routines, including my special-occasion, tour de force: Stinky waking up Grandpapa Bear by farting in his ear.

Unlike the day before, however, Ethan wasn't impressed, and continued to whine, yell, and occasionally pinch me. I kept at it for close to an hour, until, mouth dry, head pounding, I finally ran out of steam.

"Do. Now?"

"We have to stop," I said. "Someone else has to take him."

"Eat. I. Starving! Eat. Now!"

"You're not hungry, Ethan. We just ate." I turned away from him and looked out my window at Connecticut or New York or Massachusetts; I had no idea where the hell we were.

"It's my turn," Mary called from the front

seat. "I can take him."

"Thanks. Stop. Pull over."

Mindy, who was driving, mumbled something and kept going.

"Mindy, stop so we can switch, okay?" I yelled.

Mindy glanced back. "I said I don't want to stop on the road. Next exit."

"Do. Now?"

I sat back, rubbed my temples. "Nothing, Ethan. Look at the clouds. It might rain. Or snow. If we're lucky, maybe we'll have an earthquake and it will swallow us all."

"Do! Next?"

"I don't know. Here, here!" I rooted around on the floor, reached into the bag of oranges, and held one out to him. "Do you want this? I can peel —" Before I could finish, he snatched the orange and, with his perfect aim, threw a hard strike at Mindy, hitting her squarely in the back of the head. She jerked forward, and the van veered off the road, toward a steep ditch.

An explosion of chaos followed. Mary tried to take the wheel. Karen covered her head with her arms and cried out, "We're falling!" Ethan became hysterical, grabbing at my neck. When I felt us tipping over, I closed my eyes and braced for impact.

"Hold on!" I yelled.

Miraculously, we didn't tip. Instead we skidded down into the bottom of the ditch, where we rocked back and forth to a stop.

No one made a sound. Both Karen and Mary had their faces buried in their hands. Mindy stared straight ahead, gripping the wheel. Even Ethan was quiet.

Finally Karen asked, "Is everyone okay?"

Mary turned around. "John?"

Heart racing, I glanced down at Ethan, whose head was now in my lap, eyes silent, scared. "We're fine," I said. "No one's hurt. He didn't mean it. Everything's okay."

Mindy apparently didn't see it quite that way. She slammed her fists onto the steering wheel. "I can't take this anymore! I just can't take this anymore! Look what he does to us! Look what he's doing to us! He almost killed us, killed us!" She continued to pound the steering wheel with a ferocity I had never seen from her before.

Mary reached for her. "Mindy! Please!"

"Leave me alone!" she screamed. "Just leave me alone. I can't do this anymore. I'm going home. I'll get a ride. I'll walk. I don't care. But I can't do this anymore. Every minute is crazy, every minute is nuts. Who can live like this? Who? No one can! We don't deserve this; no one does. I could never have friends over. We never went anywhere. We couldn't talk in our own home. *Talk!* Our whole lives we've been held hostage — our whole lives! It never changes and it never stops!"

She started to cry, and this ignited Ethan, who began to cry as well.

"Mindy, you're upsetting him!" I yelled.

"Upsetting him? *Upsetting him!* Are you fucking kidding me?" With that, she jumped out of the van and climbed up a nearby embankment by the side of the highway.

I tried to calm Ethan. "Someone has to get her. I can't. I'm stuck back here."

Mary lowered her window. "Mindy, get back in. Come on, get back in. Please. Don't do this."

I watched Mindy sit down on the top of the hill and put her head between her knees. I could tell she was still crying by the way her shoulders were shaking.

"Oh, baby." Mary opened the door and was about to get out, when Karen stopped her.

"Mom, don't. Wait in here," she said. "Just wait in here."

"What?'

"Wait in here. I'll get her." Karen jumped out of the van and quickly made her way up the hill to Mindy, who was really sobbing now.

"Are you okay?" Mary asked me.

I sat in the backseat, Ethan's head cradled in my lap, and watched as Karen put her arms around her sister and drew her close, their shoulders both shaking together. "We're fine," I said. "We're fine."

The sun broke through a cliff of low-hanging clouds just as it was setting. Ethan stopped dribbling to stare and point.

"Sun!" he said.

I nodded. "Yes. Sun. It's setting. It's going away for the night."

He stood still for a moment and watched the city skyline turn pink before returning to the task at hand. "Go, Illini!" he cried as he launched another shot.

We were performing another reprise of the Illinois–Arizona game, this time in a small, hilly excuse of a park just south of Boston. We had been there for close to an hour, killing time, my less-than-enthusiastic play-by-play filling the quiet evening. I was tired and defeated, and unlike my Illini, I had no comeback in me that night.

After the near accident and Mindy's breakdown, we drove for a while in stressed silence. Once we found a roadside Courtyard, we went our separate ways; the women to their respective rooms, and Ethan and I to the pool, then a walk, then dinner. Throughout the afternoon, I repeatedly tried to call Mindy, but she hadn't picked up.

I flipped Ethan the ball and watched him dribble toward the basket then awkwardly pull up and bank a shot from a few feet away. I cheered then checked the time. It was close to seven thirty, and I knew the sometimes dicey transition, from basketball to bed, would have to begin soon.

"One more basket!" I yelled.

"Ten!"

"Okay, ten more. But hurry. It's getting dark outside."

"Mom!"

"Mom?" I turned and saw Mary approaching, making her way down an incline by the swings. She was wearing one of Mindy's black hoodies, and her arms were crossed in front of her as she walked, a pensive pose. Ethan ran over.

"Hello! Hello! Hello!"

"Hi, baby." She hugged him hard.

"How did you find us?"

She shrugged. "I went for a walk, heard him yelling."

"Oh yeah. He's very into it tonight."

Ethan returned to the court and resumed his shooting.

"He's good at it," she said.

"Thank Kyle Baker for that."

"Thank you for that," she said. "You spent a lot more time with him than Kyle did."

It was nice of her to acknowledge that, so I shot her a smile, but she didn't smile back. She just watched Ethan play through worried and tired eyes. "So, how's Mindy? I tried to call," I said.

"Karen was with her when I left. They went to get pizza together."

"That's nice, that's good. At least they're together. Did you eat?"

She shook her head, waved at Ethan.

"Is Mindy going home?"

"She's not going anywhere."

"Never seen her that way."

"She's always been wound too tight," Mary said. "That's why she is who she is."

"Karen okay?"

"She's fine." Ethan was chattering away incomprehensively, trying, I think, to imitate my excited commentary. Mary kept her eyes on him. "John," she said. "I think we need to get to Maine, to the home, as soon as we can. Tomorrow. I think it's time we get there."

I turned cold. "They're not expecting us until Wednesday."

"I think it's time we get there. This is

wearing on us. The Sals are already there."

I didn't think I heard her right. "What do you mean, the Sals? What are they doing there?"

"I asked them to come."

"What? Why?"

"I want my sister there. I want her there."

I paused. "Oh. Sure. Okay."

"We can make it tomorrow," she said.

"Tomorrow. Okay. Tomorrow. We won't stop. I'll call the hotel, get our rooms early."

"Karen already did that."

"Oh, okay." We were both watching Ethan now. In the growing shadows, he was setting up for a free throw, positioning his feet while he bounced the ball, his face a mixture of concentration and delight. He had no idea what was happening, no clue what the next day would bring.

He sensed our eyes on him, stopped dribbling, and looked back. Then he pointed up at the sky.

"Sun. Gone!"

I didn't turn. I just kept watching him.

"Yes, the sun is gone," I heard Mary say.

Later that night, after I gave Ethan his bath and his meds and dropped him off Mary's room, I called Rita. I owed her this.

I admit, I was relieved when I got her

voice mail. I had made a sincere effort, and this would have to do.

"Hi, it's John . . . ," I began. "I'm calling to say I'm sorry about Chase and what happened. I really am. It's very hard to talk on this trip, but I want you to know that I feel bad for you. I really do. That must have been terrible. What happened to you and to him. Terrible. I didn't know him well, but apparently you did. The whole experience sounds terrible. I can't imagine how tough that was. I know you'll get through it though. I know you will. It's going to be very hard to talk on this trip, but maybe I'll call later when I get back. I'm not sure when that will be though. So, anyway, anyway, good night, Rita. And please take care. Take care."

I hung up, stared at the ceiling, then called her again.

"Hi, it's still me, John. I also want to say that I know things are hard right now, but they won't always be hard. You'll adapt, you'll survive, even though right now you don't think that's possible, you will. You, you take one step after another, one step. You just stare straight ahead. You'll feel bad for a while, hopeless, then one day you won't feel as bad, one day you'll catch yourself not thinking about it as much, and the next day, you'll think about it a little less. Then one day you'll wake up, and it won't be the first thing on your mind, and then you'll . . . and then you'll have *adjusted,* things will be in a different order, the pain will still be there, it will always be there, but you will have adjusted, and you'll stop being angry all the time, you'll stop crying, because there're other things you have to do. Things get better and you go on, you go on." I caught myself, stopped. "I'm rambling here. So I better go. Good-bye."

Another breath, more ceiling, another call. "I don't know why things happen. No one does. I'm pretty sure there's a plan, though. I hope there's a plan but, man, I don't know, I don't know, I mean, I don't know anything. I don't have answers other than, I guess, you can't quit, you can't ever quit. You have to play it out. You have to." I thought I might be finished, but I guess I wasn't even close. "I'm taking Ethan to this place tomorrow, this home, but I'm not sure I can leave him now. I love him so much, so much. I love him more than anything. It's so hard though, it's so hard. I don't know if this is the right thing, it's so far. It's in Maine. But I think I have to. I'm going nuts. I drink too much, the Bears . . . I can't imagine leaving him, I can't." I caught myself. "I'm sorry. I didn't mean to turn this into a thing about myself. I'm sorry for you. You were a good friend. Just don't give up. Please don't give up. We can't. We can't." I stopped and tried to calm myself but couldn't. "I'm sorry, but I have to go now, I just . . . I have to go, so good-bye, Rita, I'm sorry, I'm sorry, but good-bye, good-bye."

I put the phone down, closed my eyes. I was crying now, crying so hard that I was scaring myself.

The next morning, Mindy was Mindy again. Phone in one hand, Starbucks in the other, Bud Light cap on at a jaunty angle.

I helped load her luggage into the back. "How's your head?"

"I obviously have amnesia, or I wouldn't be getting back into this van."

Since I had volunteered for early Ethan duty, I climbed into the rear and arranged my tools of the trade: the Bears, photo album, Etch A Sketch, and digital watch to help me get through my shift.

The plan was to make a beeline to Maine and, if possible, get to Camden by late afternoon. I was dubious, thought we were being too ambitious, but we got off to a good start: Ethan was quiet, the traffic light, and the weather nice.

We stopped for lunch in Hampton, New Hampshire, just off the interstate. It was in a corner booth at a crowded Roy Rogers, just as Ethan was beginning to fidget, that Mary did something that shocked us all. After years of living with him, eating with him, sleeping with him, after years of navigating the sometime tumultuous waters of a long relationship, she performed her very own Stinky Bear routine.

"Hey there, Ethan, what are you eating?" She held Stinky up on the table and wiggled him from side to side. Ethan looked at her, then desperately at me, his face tight and worried. For the first time in his life, he looked embarrassed.

"What's wrong, cat got your tongue, little mister?" Mary, apparently under the impression that Stinky was a ventriloquist doll, was trying hard not to move her lips when she spoke. Plus, her voice was high, squeaky, and, in my opinion, sounded absolutely nothing like Stinky Bear.

"You sure were good this morning at breakfast and in the van. Yes, sirree Bob, you were. Quite a pleasant young man."

Though I may never have loved Mary more than in that exact moment, and though I was thrilled to see my sweet-

sweetie trying to have fun again, I simply could not abide this abomination. "He would never say something like that," I said.

Mary stopped wiggling Stinky Bear. "Say again, mister?"

"I'm sorry. But if you're going to do Stinky Bear, *do* Stinky Bear." I was, of course, kidding, but . . . I kind of wasn't.

"Hey, Mr. Nichols, why don't you finish your yummy roast-beef sandwich and let me handle this?"

"First off, he would never use a word like *yummy,* never. And he would never call me Mr. Nichols. He calls me Daddy-o."

"Okay, Daddy-o."

"Hey, Mom, you're kind of weirding us out," Karen said.

"Well, I'm sorry," Mary said, her lips stretched and straining.

"Maybe you should try Elvis," Mindy said.

Mary was not discouraged. "So, sonny boy . . ."

"Sonny boy?" I asked.

"Ethan, what are you eating for —"

Before Mary could finish, Ethan snatched Stinky and solemnly presented him to me.

"Sorry," I said. Everyone, including Mary, laughed as I assumed the Stinky Bear reins. "Thanks, girl, for trying," he said. "While we appreciate the effort, you better leave

Stinky to professionals like Daddy-o. You could hurt yourself."

"Point taken, Stinky Bear," Mary said.

"By the way," Stinky said. "You look pretty nice today. I like it when you wear your hair down."

"Thank you, Stinky." Mary bit into her sandwich.

"Yeah, you sure look good to me."

"Hey, Stinky, you got the hots for Mom?" Karen asked.

I nodded Stinky's head. "Always have," he said. "And always will."

The brief ride through New Hampshire was one of the most pleasant of the trip. It was a beautiful summer day, the sky blue, endless; the road, sun-drenched and open. Karen drove at a good easy pace as we made our way over hills. Most important, Ethan had slipped back into a deep and wondrous Quiet Zone, drawing in the backseat while Mary dozed next to him. Every so often I would hear his watch beeping, which continually fascinated and delighted him.

While I sponged up the scenery, Mindy and Karen fell into an odd conversation, odd because it didn't include questions of where we were eating or staying that night.

"All I'm saying is that we have too many

states," Mindy said. "It's a waste. We should condense them."

Karen agreed. "Yeah. We probably don't need North and South Dakota. Both of them."

"Exactly. Look at where we are, New England, all these, little, tiny, mini-states. I mean, does Rhode Island really need a governor? Rhode Island? That's like being governor of my patio."

"You have a patio?"

"Yeah, I'm in a walk-up now."

Karen was about to respond, when her phone went off. She glanced down. "Shit."

"Banana Dick? Mr. Chiquita?"

"Mr. Chiquita."

"Fuck him."

"I did that for five years, and it wasn't any fun."

"Hey," I said. "In case you've forgotten, your father is sitting back here. Your *father.*"

Karen's phone kept ringing. "Damn him!" She lowered her window and held it outside, about to drop it.

"Do it, girl!" Mindy said.

"No, stop, stop!" I yelled. "Those things are expensive. Come on. Just don't answer it."

Karen brought her hand back in and raised her window.

"Do it!" Mindy said. "Cut the cord! It's the only connection you still have with him. He can't find you without that phone. Cut the cord! You're a Free Girl Now. Tom Petty. Do it, girl!"

Karen lowered her window. "I like that song."

"Karen Elaine Nichols! Do not throw that phone out! Do you hear me? Do not! It's expensive, and you'll hit another car." I reached forward and tried to grab the phone, which, by now, had stopped buzzing. "Just give it to me. Give it to me."

"Give it here," Mindy said. "I'll throw it out."

Karen dangled the phone out the window, considering. Then with a backward flick of her wrist, she dropped it.

"Free Girl Now," she said.

"Karen!" Over my shoulder I caught a glimpse of the phone breaking into pieces on the highway. "I can't believe you just did that! What if a car were coming?"

"No cars were coming," Karen said.

"Wow!" Ethan cried from the far backseat. He was slapping my headrest, delighted. "Wow! Wow! Wow! Outside! All. Gone!"

Mindy and Karen exchanged high fives.

"What happened?" It was Mary from the back. She had pulled her earphones out and was struggling to sit up. "What's going on?"

"Nothing. Go back to sleep," I said. "You just missed some irresponsible and dangerous stupidity, that's all. Nothing out of the ordinary."

"It's so cramped back here. I can't move. We have to get rid of some of these things."

"Hey, Ethan, come up with me," I said. "Come on, we'll look at the pictures. Come on, let's give Mom some more room."

Ethan happily scooted up to the middle, where I buckled him. I was just beginning to search for the photo album when my phone went off. I froze. Rita, it could be no one else.

"Is that your phone?" Mary asked.

"I don't know. I don't think so." I was still frozen, afraid to move, breathe. I had no idea where my phone was.

I heard Mary moving around behind me. "I think it's here somewhere. I hear it. Ethan had it."

"He did?" I was trying hard not to appear frantic. "Forget it. It's no one, probably just Sal." I turned around and, along with Mary, began to look for the thing, clawing at the bags in the backseat, tossing them aside.

"Got it," she said.

What happened next was nothing less than divine intervention. Looking back on it, I'd like to think Ethan knew exactly what he was doing, that he, with one amazingly well-timed gesture, decided to thank me for a lifetime of baths, basketball, and Stinky Bear. I would remember that moment for a long time: how he grabbed the still ringing phone from Mary, how he looked me dead in the eye before doing what he did. How I did absolutely nothing to stop him.

Mary yelled. "He's opening the window! John, get it!"

I finally made a token effort to grab Ethan's wrist but had no intention of stopping him. He finished lowering his window and threw the phone out. I saw it bounce once on the road before disappearing.

I felt the van slow. "Should I stop?" Karen yelled.

"Forget it. Keep going. It's gone." I exhaled, tried to regroup. "See what you guys caused? Monkey see, monkey do. He was just imitating his smart, older sisters. It's not his fault." I was trying to act angry, but my voice sounded sing-songy.

"I can't believe he did that!" Mary said. "Ethan, that was bad! Very bad! And John, you just sat there! You could have grabbed it. You just sat there."

It took everything I had not to kiss Ethan. "It's the girls' fault. Monkey see, monkey do," I repeated. "They were acting like idiots."

"What are you talking about?" Mary asked.

"The girls were acting like idiots. Karen threw her phone out while you were asleep because Roger kept calling."

"She did what?"

"Idiot," Ethan said.

"Right, Ethan, right."

"Karen. Idiot!"

"Yes, she is," I said.

"Mindy. Idiot!"

"Absolutely. It runs in the family."

"Dad. Idiot!"

"Hey, I wouldn't go that far."

We were laughing when I saw the sign on the side of the road: WELCOME TO MAINE: THE WAY LIFE SHOULD BE.

"Look," Mindy said, pointing. "We're here."

"Finally," Karen said. "Maine."

We all stared at the sign as we passed. No one said another word.

13

Sal was leaning against a black Escalade, blowing streams of smoke through his nostrils in the parking lot of the Ridgewood Inn. He was wearing a Boston Red Sox cap and an enormous Sox T-shirt that still fit him tight across the chest. He smiled, flicked the cigarette away, and pushed off from the SUV.

"How's my favorite family?" he said as we piled out of the van. He swallowed me in a sugary Old Spice hug.

While we were still in heavy embrace, I heard both Mindy and Karen mumble, "Hey, Uncle Sal," then saw them scurry past, toward the inn's wide wooden porch, dragging their luggage.

Sal released me. "That's all I get? Hi. Bye? That's it?"

"It's been a long afternoon," I said.

Ethan, red-faced from crying, emerged from the back of the van with an exhausted

Mary. The last three hours had been among the hardest of the entire trip. It had taken everything we had not to stop. When he saw his beloved uncle, though, he exploded with delight, running frantically toward him, skinny arms waving. He leaped into Sal's arms.

"Sal!"

"There he is, Mr. Big!" Sal said, tussling Ethan's hair and smiling. "Now, that's more like it!"

"Hi, Sal," Mary said. "Where's Sally?"

Sal let Ethan go and gave Mary a hug. "Yeah, she's in her room taking a nap. How you holding up? Gotta be tough, this whole thing."

"We survived," she said. "Thank you for coming,"

"Yeah, we flew into Boston and drove up. Made a little detour, drove by Fenway, first time, if you believe. And I got to say, I wasn't all that impressed. From what I saw, Wrigley is better. Wrigley has got more class, more something, history. All they got is the wall there. Here, give me that." He took Mary's bag from her.

"Your back," she said.

"Forget the back. Here. Come on, give it to me."

Ethan ran ahead, up the porch steps, and

Mary hurried after him while Sal and I, saddled with bags, slowly followed. I was exhausted, my head crowded, and I needed to be alone for a while. I was in no mood for anyone, particularly Sal.

"How was the drive?" he asked.

"Started out great, but the last few hours were total hell."

Sal readjusted the shoulder strap of Mary's bag. "Yeah, me and Sally thought this was crazy. All the way from South Carolina."

"You mean all the way from Wilton, Illinois."

"Yeah, that's right. Jesus. This whole idea is crazy. Everything."

I could have easily ignored this casual comment, but chose not to. During the last horrible hour on the road, between pleas for Ethan to be quiet, I had reconsidered the Sals' sudden presence in Camden, growing increasingly suspicious and angry. What, exactly, were they doing here? When, exactly, did Mary call them?

"What do you mean? What whole idea?"

"You know, the whole thing."

I stopped walking. "What whole thing?"

"Nothing. You know, the whole thing. The home, everything. We'll talk about it later."

"Talk about what later?"

"Nothing. Just want to make sure you're okay with everything, that's all. It's a big decision."

My suspicions were being confirmed. I sensed one last gang tackle. "Did Mary and the girls put you up to this? Huh? Is that what this whole thing is about? You and Sally all of a sudden being here? Is this some kind of a setup? Some kind of intervention? Some last-ditch effort to try and get me to change my mind? It's not going to work, Sal. So you came a long way for nothing. We decided as a family we're doing this. He's staying here for at least six weeks, probably forever."

Sal stopped at the bottom of the porch steps. "For Christ's sake, relax, John. No one put me up to nothing. I don't know what you're talking about. I just thought maybe you might want to talk, make sure you're okay with everything."

I wouldn't let it go. "What do you mean make sure I'm okay with everything?"

"Forget the whole thing. I make one comment, you go nuts." Sal waved his hand. "Go take a shower, and we'll grab a drink. They got a bar downstairs." He started up the steps.

I didn't move. "I'm not sure why you're here, okay? But I can assure you that there's

410

nothing to talk about. There's nothing to talk about at all."

I made my way up to my room, dropped my bags in the closet, opened the window, and stared over a tree line at the water. I tried to calm myself by focusing on a small cluster of sailboats as they glided into the harbor, but my efforts were for naught: things were quickly closing in. We were finally here. We had come to the end.

My anxiety was building, when Mary called my room. "Should we head up there?"

I closed my eyes.

"Hello? John? Are you there?"

"It's late."

"It's not even three o'clock."

"They're really not expecting us until tomorrow. I'm tired. I don't want to go."

"The girls want to go. And it's been a year since I've been there."

"Nothing's changed. I was just there."

She didn't say anything. I opened my eyes. "Mary?"

"You don't have to come. We'll be back in a couple of hours, and then we can get something to eat. So relax, take a nap. The Sals have Ethan for a while."

"I want to be with him."

"The Sals have him. They're gone. Sal wanted to show him some boats or something."

The mention of Sal cleared my head. "I think we need to get something straight. I'm in no mood to debate anything with you or . . . or your Tony Soprano brother-in-law, okay? This is hard enough."

"What are you talking about?"

"You know what I'm talking about. I now know why you really wanted them here. Some last-ditch effort, some muscle to persuade me. What, he's going to threaten me? Break my legs? I'm not scared of Sal."

"Take a nap. It's been a long day."

"I'm not going to take any shit from him or anyone else. Okay? This is difficult enough."

"Stop yelling."

"I'm not yelling."

"We're going to the home," Mary said. "We'll see you in a while."

"Fine! Do whatever you want!" I slammed the phone down and took deep breaths.

Sal picked a lobster place on the water that Mary and I had been to the year before. Though I remember the food being good, I had no appetite. I alternated between looking out at the darkening ocean and staring at Ethan, who was innocently spooning lobster bisque. The girls, though subdued, seemed strangely relaxed, chatting away about a reality TV show. No one was talking about Ocean View, a fact that confused and irked me. Didn't they know what was happening the day after tomorrow? Didn't they know?

Throughout the evening I had repeatedly asked about their impressions of the home and received only brief but positive responses. Whenever I pressed the issue, the subject was changed. I tried once more to engage them.

"So, you all liked it? Ocean View?"

"Well, I've been there before," Mary said.

"Yeah, we told you, we thought it was nice," Karen said.

"Yeah," Mindy said. "Real nice."

"So, that's it?"

"What else do you want us to say?" Karen asked. "It's really nice."

"So, that's it, huh, that's it? Nothing else? That's it?" I threw my napkin down and went to the men's room, where I splashed water on my face and then gave myself a good look in the eye. On my way back to the table, I detoured to the deck. There was a harbor full of weathered colorful lobster boats, all gently bobbing in the twilight.

Behind them, where the harbor opened up, a wall of fog was rolling in. None of this changed my mood. I was impervious to the charms and beauty of Camden. It was now nothing more than the place I was supposed to leave my son.

I returned to our table. Ethan was smiling while Sal whispered something in his ear. The women were chatting away. It was then that I realized the terrible truth: no one was going to talk me out of anything. We were going through with this. We were really leaving him, leaving Ethan. I found it hard to breathe, felt things closing in again. I closed my eyes.

"John? What's wrong? John?" I heard Mary ask.

I jumped up and rushed out of the restaurant, weaving between tables, bumping into chairs, cries of "Where. Dad. Be?" chasing me, a question, a plea.

Later, after fielding concerned calls from Mindy, Karen, Mary, and even Sally; and after I refused Sal's offer to go for a walk and smoke one of the Cuban cigars he had "got" from "some guy"; and after I did about fifty free throws; and after I paced the room, then lay on my bed then paced the room again, I forced myself to open my laptop. Ethan was sleeping with Mary so, for better or for worse, I had the night to myself.

I turned on my computer and found the essay I had started weeks before: "My Hopes for Ethan." Ocean View asked parents to articulate their dreams for their children prior to official admission. I had tried many times to complete the essay.

I want Ethan to be happy. That's what any father wants for his child. To simply be happy. To go through the day being loved, wanted, and watched over. I want Ethan to be in a place that cares for him. A good place, a safe place. A place where he can watch the sun set, see the moon rise. A place he can call home.

That was all I had, so I read it over, made a number of attempts to finish, but got nowhere. So, rather than write, I revised, editing that single paragraph over and over. In the end, all I was left with was: *I want Ethan to be happy.*

I studied that sentence until my eyes burned, and the words became distorted, fat, and blurry. I probed it from many angles before realizing it was not entirely true. To be sure, I wanted Ethan to be happy, but the reality was, the truth was, the person I *really* wanted to be happy was me. The person I *really* wanted to take care of was me. That was why I was doing all of this. That was why we were all here.

I shut the laptop, did some more free throws. Then I stood by the open window for a long time, looking into the darkness, the ocean air filling my room with whispers and sighs.

I had my Ethan-is-talking-normal dream that night. We were, as always, home in Wilton, sitting on the deck, eating cereal as we often did in the morning. I was staring at the finch feeder, watching the tiny red-and-yellow birds flit around the food. Ethan was drinking orange juice.

"The Cubs won last night," he said to me. His voice was a song, high and sweet, heartbreaking.

I watched him eat. I never spoke during these dreams. I just wanted to hear him.

"We should go somewhere today," he said. "Maybe we should go to the park."

I reached out to brush his hair away from his face.

"I'm glad I didn't die that time," he said. "I'm glad I stayed alive."

I woke up with a start, and in my Ambieninduced daze, came to the inevitable and obvious conclusion: I could not go through with this. I could not leave my son in this strange place, so far away from home, so far away from me.

I was calm, bordering on numb, when morning finally arrived. I watched the sun rise over the ocean, the light, unraveling over the water, before making my way down to the lobby for coffee. I figured I'd be the first one there, but found everyone but Ethan standing in a half-circle by the front door.

"What's going on? Where is he?"

"We have to talk," said Karen.

"Is everything okay? Is something wrong?" It was then I noticed that Sally wasn't there either. "Where's Sally? Is she all right?"

"She's with Ethan in the van," Karen said. "Dad, you're not coming."

"What?"

"You're not coming," she said again. "We're going to register him and take the official tour and everything. You're going to stay here with Uncle Sal."

"What are you talking about?"

"Stay here, John," Mary said. "You're not up for this. Just stay here. We'll take care of everything. He's going to be okay."

"Where is he?" I started to push past them, but Sal grabbed me by the wrists. "Just relax, John."

"He's staying, Dad, at least for now," Karen said. "It's for the best. We'll get him registered, then we'll be back. We know you don't want to leave him, we know you can't. So we'll handle it. You'll see him again this afternoon. Everything is going to be fine."

Mindy started to cry, and Karen took her hand and continued. "We saw the home yesterday, and you're right, it's a nice place, it's a beautiful place. They have the gym and the pool, and the attendants seem nice. And the café has lots of pickles. And they have those special bikes he can ride, those big bikes." She stopped and looked away. "He'll be happy there, we think."

"When they get back, I'm going to rent a boat," Sal said. "He'll love it. I'm gonna bring some food on board. A little wine. We'll have dinner on the boat. I got those cigars."

"What are you talking about? Food, boat!" I pried myself away from Sal. "He's not staying, I was wrong. He can't stay. Mary? Mary? Say something! I was wrong. I've been thinking about this. I was wrong. This place is too far away. It's crazy. I don't know what I was thinking. He can't stay here, he can't. It's ridiculous. It's so far!"

Mary couldn't meet my eyes. She looked down, and then she, too, was crying. Karen took her hand too. "Dad," she said. "This whole trip, we saw how hard it is. We barely made it here. Let's stick to the plan."

"We can't leave him! We can't! I'm just going to take him out again."

"Daddy," Karen said. "Please. Just stay here. Please. Please." They all turned and walked away.

I tried to follow, but Sal grabbed me by both wrists, this time much harder. "They don't want you to make a scene up there, John. You got to take it easy on this. You'll get Ethan all excited. We'll take a walk, get some coffee. It's going to be okay. Everything is going to be okay. But you gotta do what I say now. Do what I say, and don't make this hard, because I ain't letting go. I ain't letting go."

Sal took me to a coffee shop in downtown Camden, and pushed me down and into my seat. I was still in shock.

"So." Sal rested his huge bear arms on the table. "How you doing there?"

I glanced out the window. It was sunny out. Nice outside.

Sal raised his cup, tiny, toylike in his bear

hands. "It's not like you haven't left him before, John," he said "Those two weeks at that camp up in Wisconsin. That special-needs place. He loved that place. You told me yourself, he didn't want to come back. This place is just like that camp, but a lot nicer. I went up there before you got here. Ate lunch in the dining room. They let me eat there. Got good food, an indoor pool. They come into town every day. Shop, eat. They integrate with the community pretty well. The nuns, they told me that. Some of them even have jobs." He took a sip of his coffee.

"Ethan is never going to have a job."

"So? That's some big tragedy? Who wants a fucking job?" He smiled, drank more of his coffee. "Mary said you gonna take a trip or something. Drive around the country, maybe head out West. You ever been to Vegas? I can put you up there. The Mirage. I'm comped there. One of my clients. Won't cost you nothing but room tax. Place is okay, ain't the Wynn, but it's okay. Nothing wrong with the Mirage."

"I'm not going there."

"What are you going to do?"

"I don't know." I looked out the window again. The streets were crowded with people in shorts and wide-brimmed hats. A day in

Camden, Maine, a day in paradise for them. I closed my eyes. I hated this town.

"I'm not leaving him," I said.

"Hey, you'll visit."

"I should be up there now."

"You don't need to be nowhere right now except sitting in that chair. Let the girls handle it. You done enough. You got everyone this far. Let someone else do some lifting. Besides, you want to break down up there, get everyone upset? Ethan? You're in no condition."

"When did you all plan this?"

"Plan what?"

"This. Everything. My not going up there."

"Oh." He scooted his chair closer to the table. "Well, we've been formulating it for a while, discussing it. Calling one another, putting the, you know, the strategy together. Mary said the trip changed her mind. She knew you could never go through with it though. The girls were starting to come around, and then they saw the place and loved it, so we made the final decision yesterday, decided to give it a shot. It all fell together, the pieces fell together like clockwork. We weren't supposed to talk about it at dinner last night. See, that was another part of the strategy. Karen's idea. They didn't want to upset you, one of your last nights and all. They wanted it to be, you know, all pleasant. A family dinner. The girls, they're concerned about you, the drinking. They worry about you. They love you. They're good girls. They love you. That's got to be nice, huh? Having daughters who love you. Wish they were my daughters."

"I thought you were here to talk me out of it."

"Yeah, well, surprise." He smiled and finished his cup. "Coffee's good."

I closed my eyes, wondering what Ethan was seeing, what he was feeling. What did he think of the pool? His room? The gym? Did he shoot his first basket? Did he know that this was where he might spend the rest of his life? Did he know we were going to leave him?

I opened my eyes, stood. "I should be up there now. I'll be all right."

"Sit."

"Sal."

He pointed at my chair. "You can go tomorrow. Now, sit down now. I promised the girls. Don't make me get dramatic here. We got enough drama going on today."

I slowly sat back down.

"They're just registering him. Paperwork,

a physical, and another tour of the place. Let the girls handle it; it's their turn." He pushed my cup toward me. "Drink. Relax. Afterward we'll go walk around, take in the town, get lunch somewhere. This is a real tourist area. Really nice. We got to explore Camden. They say it's where the mountains meet the sea."

"I'm not exploring Camden."

"You gotta lighten up."

"You think this is easy, sitting here? He's my son."

Sal's face softened at that. He leaned forward with hunched shoulders. "Hey, I know it's tough. I've seen that kid grow up. Been there most of the way. All your kids, the girls. They're like my kids, like it or not. I know there's been times when you haven't liked it. Hell, I know there's times you haven't liked me, but you let me be around, and I appreciate it. That was good of you. And with Sally's health, you, the girls, Ethan, you may be all I got one day."

He stopped and picked up his cup but put it right back down. When he spoke again, his voice was slower and softer, like he was sharing a secret. "Now, you know, I ain't Mr. Perfect, no one ever going to call me a saint. But I done some good things. Especially some of the stuff I did with Ethan.

I'm good around him. Ball games, the parks. Taking him for hot dogs. Took him to the Bears game that time." He pointed at me and smiled. "And you told me not to do it, remember that, you made a big stink, but he was fine. The whole time, didn't make a peep, not a sound, four hours, overtime, taking it all in, big eyes. You drove me nuts, every minute calling, asking how he was doing. We had a great time. Beat Philly. I tell you, I cleaned up that game. Twenty Gs. That spread was all messed up." He paused, shook his head. "I gotta tell you, he makes me do something good, that's all I'm saying. A bad guy doing something good. Plus, I mean, I love him, maybe not as much as you, but I love him. I'm his uncle. He's my nephew, only got one."

I looked Sal in the eyes, my brother-in-law of more than thirty years, a man I took pains to avoid, who at times, I could barely tolerate. Now this. "You're not a bad guy," I managed to say. "Ethan loves you. You're not a bad guy, Sal."

My comment must have caught him off guard. He glanced away, embarrassed, then smiled. "Hey, now, don't go telling no one that. I got a reputation to keep." He patted my hand once, then went to get more coffee.

There are times when you have to rely on other people, sit back and let them help you, be quiet, be appreciative, and stay out of their way. The day we registered Ethan at Ocean View was one of those days, a day that my family came forward, picked me up. I felt helpless, ashamed, but I knew they were right. I didn't want to go up there and wasn't sure I could do it the next day.

I spent the rest of the morning and a good part of the afternoon with Sal, walking the streets of Camden in a daze, trying to think things through. We had lunch somewhere and then ended up on a bench that overlooked the harbor.

"Mind if I smoke?" Sal asked.

"It's fine."

Sal lit up. "How you doing over there?"

"I'm okay."

He shielded his eyes with his hand, scanned the water far below. "They must be Red Sox fans up here. And Patriot fans, since they got no other teams. Must be strange rooting for teams so far away."

I nodded, said nothing. Sal blew smoke.

"Place like this, makes you think, though," he said. "Clears your mind. You think about your life, everything. Mistakes you made. Bad shit you've done. I've done some things, nothing major, but things nonetheless."

"We've all done things," I mumbled.

"What?"

"We all have regrets."

"Oh yeah? What'd you have to regret? What, you stooped that woman? That don't make you a bad person, don't make you evil or nothing. I told Mary, that was a mistake. She should have given you a pass on that. I told her that. You get one pass on that issue, I think. Men are men."

"You never did that."

"Jesus, Sally, she'd cut my balls off."

I leaned forward and rested my elbows on my knees. "I've done other things."

He chuckled. "You? The professor? Yeah, like what? Cheat on your taxes?"

"I could have looked harder for a place closer to home. Maybe they were right; maybe I was trying to find a place as far away as possible. I didn't think it at the time, but that's maybe what I was doing. I was doing this for myself."

"So, that's all you got? That's your big crime? Finding a place that cost, what, a hundred grand for your son? Best place in the country. That's all you got?"

"I've done other things."

"Yeah?"

I continued to look straight ahead, down at the water. "When he was about eight, he almost died."

"Who? Ethan?"

"Yes."

"Yeah, I remember that. He had that thing. That attack, that thing."

"Seizure."

"Yeah. We were all worried."

"I remember waiting in the hospital, wondering if he was going to live. And for a second, a second . . ." I couldn't finish that sentence.

"And for a second, you thought it might be best if he just went, end all the suffering," Sal said.

I opened my eyes, looked at him.

"You were thinking it would maybe easier for him, maybe for everyone."

"Yes." I choked back sudden tears. "How did you know that?"

"Because that's maybe what I would have thought."

"What kind of father thinks that? What kind of man thinks that?"

"You thought that, you didn't wish that. Big difference." Sal squinted out over the harbor, dropped his cigar, stepped on it.

"You know," he said. "You gotta take it easy on yourself. You did everything you could, John, everything you could."

"I should have done more."

"Here." He put his arm around me, and I buried my head in his shoulder, wept like a boy. "Come on. Get ahold of yourself. No one's dying here. Sun's out. We're in fucking Maine. We're going on a boat tonight. I'm bringing lobster on board. Nine-hundred-bucks' worth. Cleaned the ocean out; they got nothing left down there."

I sat back up, sniffled. "I'm not leaving him."

"John."

"No. I'm not."

And that was when I told him my new plan. Looking back on it, I suspect it was my Overall Plan all along.

We met everyone back at the inn late in the day. Mary and Sally looked wiped out, their faces pale and blank, but the girls didn't seem much worse for wear. Mindy was wearing a new blue-and-white Ocean View sweatshirt with a picture of a sailboat.

"Got it from a nun." She shrugged. "She wanted my Bud Light hat."

When Ethan stepped out of the van, he was all smiles, and I hugged him like I had never hugged him before.

"Hi! Dad! How. Are. You?"

"Good. I'm good, Ethan. Did you like Ocean View? Play some hoops up there?"

"Yes!"

Karen handed me a file thick with papers. "You have to sign some things," she said. "They need them tomorrow."

I took the file. "How did it go?"

"Great," Karen said. "He likes it. Likes his room. Seemed like he liked everything. I think it's going to be okay."

I gave her a hug. "Thanks. Thanks for doing that. Thank you." Then I hugged Mindy. "You too. You too." Karen smiled, but Mindy's eyes started to mist. She quickly walked away.

"I'm beat," Sally said. She had her arm around Mary's waist as they walked into the inn. I took Ethan by the hand and followed.

"I got the sailboat!" Sal yelled out behind us. "At six. Sunset cruise. It'll be nice. Don't be late or I'll leave without you."

I thought I would take Ethan swimming, but as soon as we got back to my room, he climbed into bed and pulled the sheet over himself. While this wasn't totally unexpected — midday naps weren't uncommon for him back home — I was still surprised.

"Don't you want to go swimming?"

"Sleep."

"Really? You sure?"

"Sleep."

"Okay." I pulled off his shoes, then sat on the bed and studied his face. When I tried to brush back his hair, he pushed my hand away.

"Leave. Now."

I kissed him on the forehead and then watched him fall asleep, my mind whirling. When I heard his heavy breathing, I walked over to the table by the window and called Mary on the hotel phone.

"I was going to call you," she said.

"So, how was it, really?"

"Fine. Not bad. The girls made all the difference. Two of the aides recognized Mindy, took her picture, so that kind of lightened things up. And thank God for Karen. She handled the papers, asked the right questions, helped the doctor with the checkup. Everything went okay."

"How was he? Do you think he liked it?"

"Well, he was in a good mood. So, that's a good sign. He shot some baskets in the gym and ate a big lunch. So, a solid start. We met his aide, and she seemed nice."

"Tomorrow's going to be hell," I said.

"You don't have to come."

"Of course I'm coming."

"Then we'll get through it."

"Listen" — I glanced back at Ethan, kept my voice low — "I've been thinking about this whole thing again."

"Don't."

"No, listen. I've been thinking that maybe I'm going to stay here in Camden for a while."

"What? Why? You know, you can't see him. No contact for an entire month."

"Well, I think I'm going to stay longer." I paused before revealing my new plan. "I think I'm going to move here, live here. You know, permanently. I mean, I am. I'm going to move here."

She didn't say anything, so I went on. "I'll rent a house or something, a room. Camden is nice."

Mary remained quiet.

"Hello? You there?"

"What about your job? Your place?"

"I'm going to quit. Believe me, they won't care. They'll be relieved. I'll get most of my pension anyway. And I'll sell the condo, so I'll have some cash."

"So you're going to just pick up and move across the country."

"Yes. Yes. I'm not leaving him. He can stay

in the home, and I'll see him when I want. Every day probably. Maybe I can get a job up there. I don't know. Hell, I'll probably end up being a bartender somewhere. But I'm staying and that's it. I'm not leaving him. I'm staying as long as he does."

I had come up with all of this just hours before, but the more I said, the more it made sense and the better I felt.

"Hello? Mary?"

"Want some company?"

I didn't think I heard her right. "What?"

"I said, you want some company?"

I was confused. "What do you mean? Like Sal?"

"Me, John. Me. I was thinking of doing the same thing."

I swallowed. "Are you serious?"

"The house is empty. I'd probably be a little closer to the girls. What's back there for me?"

"You mean, you would stay. With me?"

"Yes."

"Just you and me?"

"Yes."

It was my turn to be quiet. After a moment I said, "That would, well, that would be wonderful."

"I don't want to rent, though," she said. "I'm sure we can find something to buy."

I was still confused. "So, we would stay in the same place, live together?"

"You are so obtuse."

"Sorry, but I'm processing a lot."

"It will be our big adventure. You owe me one."

"What happens if he doesn't like the home, it doesn't work out?"

"He's going to like the home."

I held on to the phone, speechless, afraid I was going to say or do something that would ruin all of this. Finally I just said, "That would be great."

"We're probably getting ahead of ourselves. Let's get through tomorrow. Let's not tell the girls or anyone about us yet. Let's focus on Ethan. Get through tomorrow."

"Sure. Fine. My lips are sealed."

"How is he?" she asked.

"Taking a nap. He went right down."

"That sounds like a good idea. I think I will too. I'll see you in a little bit."

"Okay. On the boat. Hey, one more thing. I love you."

"I know that, John."

Captain Jack was waiting for us at the dock. He was a sprightly man of about seventy with a shock of white hair and a crinkly, sunburned face. His grip was firm, though, when he took my arm and helped me onto his boat.

"Watch your step, young man," he said.

I waited for Ethan to board, then took him by the hand and led him to the front, trying to contain my excitement. I had never been on a boat like this before, a large schooner, so I compartmentalized, pushing all my worries and concerns about the next day aside. I tightened Ethan's orange life preserver and scanned the horizon. It was a magnificent evening: blue sky, bluer water, all encased in a warm breeze.

"Nice out," I said.

It took a while for Sal to load all the food on board — he had bought enough for an Atlantic crossing — and when he finally finished, we pushed off from the dock.

Ethan clutched me as the boat first moved, the sense of motion disconcerting, but exciting. "Wow."

"Wow," I said.

He continued to hold me tight, and I carefully sat down with him and pointed out some islands and other boats. He was, as always, obsessed with the weather.

"Windy."

"Yes, it's windy. But not too bad."

After a few minutes the girls joined us.

Karen, in a pair of white shorts and white deck shoes, looked born for the boat, while Mindy, in standard evil elf attire, looked anything but. She stood over us, holding on tight to the ropes.

"I'm trying to decide when the perfect time to throw up is," she said.

"Probably after we eat," Karen said, sitting down next to me.

"That's what I was thinking."

Karen smiled, pushed her hair out of her eyes. "So, Daddy-o, you got something to tell us? Some good news about you and Mom?"

"What, no, why, what?" I then realized what she was talking about. "Oh."

"Oh," Karen said.

"Your mother cannot keep a secret. No one in this family can."

"Windy!"

"Yeah, it's windy, Ethan," Karen said. "We're glad for you, Dad."

"Yeah," Mindy said. "I was positive you were gay."

"I have been pledged to secrecy," I said.

"Windy!"

I ran my hand through Ethan's hair then smoothed it down. "I don't know how long he'll last on this boat. In about an hour, he might try to throw Captain Jack overboard."

"After an hour with us, Captain Jack might want to throw himself overboard," Mindy said.

"He'll be fine," Karen said. "Uncle Sal bought enough Sprite and pickles to last a month."

Mindy squatted beside us, and we all looked at the ocean in silence, the wind warm in our faces. Once we cleared the harbor, Captain Jack, in an authentic New England accent, offered a brief history of Maine. I was surprised to learn that there were thousands of islands off the coast of the state.

"A lot of islands," I said.

"Maybe you and Mom will live on one," Mindy said. "It will be fun to visit an island."

I glanced over my shoulder and saw Mary and the Sals busying themselves organizing the food. Sal was holding up a large lobster, examining it. "I'll mention that to your mother," I said. "The girls want an island."

"I better go back there and help," Karen said, rising. Mindy followed, working her way unsteadily down the ropes.

"Where. Mom. Be?"

"She's helping get dinner ready."

"Where. Pickles. Be?"

"They're coming."

"Where. Sprite. Be?"

"It's coming."

I feared things were on the verge of deteriorating into Question Mode, but Ethan put his face up to the sky. "Windy!"

"Yes. You like the boat?"

"More."

"We'll be on it for a while. All of us."

I pulled him close, thrilled with the look of happiness on his face. The next day we would take him to Ocean View; lay Stinky, Grandpa Bear, and Red Bear on his bed by the window; shoot some baskets in the gym; have lunch in the café; and then all of us would hold one another and weep unabashedly in a sunlit foyer while an aide named Tammy took Ethan by the hand and led him down a hallway. He wouldn't look over his shoulder when he left, and for that not-so-small miracle, I would always be grateful.

Afterward we would slowly make our way back to the inn, where Mary and I would begin our second chapter while waiting for a month to pass. We would get through that month though, as we always did, day by day, minute by minute, taking the next step together, waiting for Ethan.

But all that was ahead of us as I sat cross-legged on the bow of the boat, moving out toward open sea. Behind me, through the wind, I smelled Sal's cigar, heard Mindy's voice and then Karen's and Mary's laughs, and at that moment everything was fine. The boat caught a large wave and dipped, and when it did, Ethan raised his arms up to the evening sky.

"It's. Nice. Outside!" he cried.

"No," I said, reaching for him. "It's beautiful outside. It's beautiful."

ACKNOWLEDGMENTS

Appreciation and a big thank you to a number of people including: my longtime publisher, St. Martin's, for sticking with me all these years, especially my wonderfully supportive editor, Nichole Argyres, who always makes my books better; and her team, particularly Laura Chasen, who helps keep things moving forward; my agent, Joe Veltre, for his on-target counsel and help on a wide range of issues; Gordon Mennenga, and Tammy Greenwood, for wading through messy early drafts of this book and offering their insight; Stinky Bear, Red Bear, and Grandpa Bear, for their uncompromising friendship over the past twenty years; the people of Elim Christian School who love and support Andrew every day; the folks at JSH&A, especially my partners Jonni, Cheryl, and Deanna, for creating a perfect work/life balance so I can write in the morning; my sons John and Mikey, the best big brothers Andrew could have.

And, of course, Anne, who makes every-day a very good day.

ABOUT THE AUTHOR

Jim Kokoris's work has appeared in the *Chicago Tribune Sunday Magazine, USA Weekend, Chicago Sun-Times,* and *Reader's Digest.* He is the author of the novels *The Rich Part of Life,* which has been published in fifteen languages and for which he won a Friends of American Writers Award for Best First Novel, and the critically acclaimed *Sister North.* A graduate of the University of Illinois, Jim lives in the Chicago area.